EARTHA'S NAME

A NOVEL

j.a.kirby

Without the sheer enthusiasm of Phil Kirby and the blazing red pen of Luke Gray …
this work would never be complete.
I thank them.
j.a.kirby

ONE

EARTHA BORNE

... was the name on the marriage certificate. 1870. The girl studied the papers on the table, smoothing them with her wind-chapped hands. Carefully, folding one, she moved it aside and opened the next as lamplight flickered along the log walls. She had spent hours studying the documents during the last several days. The document said Willis W. and Eartha M. Borne. The names of the land title matched. What was it like to have a name? She could not remember one but had been called a variety of things. She placed the papers in the leather satchel and returned them to the chest that rested at the foot of the bed. Three days earlier, she had found the bodies of a man and woman thawing in the bottom of a partially finished well. Tons of snow had raged down the ravine, shoving them into an icy grave. A pile of splinters and iron marked their final resting place.

An avalanche had buried them early last winter and the couple had silently waited for the thaw. The girl sat by the hole many times since.. for hours.. thinking and watching.. waiting. Waiting for someone to come for them. The cabin was well stocked and organized with dried and preserved food, stored meticulously in tight containers. The wardrobe had a few simple dresses, coats, boots.. every necessity.. every necessity for the first year.

A ledger sat on the shelf and she had studied the writing. They were immigrants and she knew that no one would be coming. Their new life in America had come to an end.

A tin bathtub leaning against the wall had tempted her for days, along with a fragrant bar of soap that lay on a nearby shelf. Late one evening, she pulled the tub onto the covered porch and filled it.. bucket by bucket.. with creek water that she'd patiently heated on the stove. Her filthy and stained clothes were tossed aside and would be burned in the morning. Reverently, she had laid out a robe and underclothing that had been neatly hung in the closet. Luxuriating in the water, she washed hair and body.. always thinking. Leaning back against the tin, she began softly whistling until a slight smile crept across her lips. Gently, she placed her hands across her belly and felt for the life. Yes, it grew inside of her and.. in the end.. it would all be worth it.

Sinking into the frothy water, she thought of the last weeks..

..weaving down steep ravines, slipping on bruising rocks and sharp ice.. crossing the divide with a train of miners and mules.. building camp and cooking as the sun disappeared. Crisscrossing mountains higher than she'd ever imagined. The wind had stung the group as they stood on the Great Divide, peering down into the valley.. every last man, woman and mule regretting the undertaking. At a mud-hell called Frisco, they had

learned of a trail that cut along the Rocky Mountains, eventually leading down into the west valley. The Gore Creek wound through a chilled paradise that smelled of pines, snowmelt and waterfalls. They stopped at a solitary cabin during the early morning and waited expectantly.

-Anybody home?

-Get in there, orphan, and see if anyone's around.

Slowly she pushed the door open. It was not locked or bolted, although the hardware had been installed. The cabin was quiet and tidy, except for a thin layer of dust on the sparse furniture. No life had disturbed the interior rooms for months. Maybe when they came home, she could work out an arrangement with them. Surely. Stepping back to the door, she looked out at the group…

-Nobody's here, Abe. But it looks like they could be coming back.

Abe pulled his pocket watch out, staring at the face as if it worked. It didn't. He peered up at the sky, obviously pondering daylight and distance. This ceremony had been repeated many times during the journey.

-We can't wait. Can't stop. Get back on your mule and let's go. We've got gold to find.

Firmly standing in the doorway, she shook her head.

-I'm not going. This is it for me.

He eyed her through his bushy brows then turned to look at the others.

-What can you do? Looks like she's stayin

He nudged his mule into movement, pulling the one she'd rode for weeks.. never uttering a complaint during the entire ordeal. He hesitated as he peered down the trail. Turning, he led the mule back to the cabin and wrapped the reins around the saddle horn.

-You can keep this mule and tack. God knows you've earned it.

He studied her with respect, then reached into his pocket retrieving what appeared to be a rag.

- Here's some guidance and a little piece of shiny to keep you going for a bit. We'll miss your vittles, but not that stinkin' bag.

The old miner laughed. This girl and her bag had stunk to high heaven since he hired her a month ago. She said her dead sister was in the bag and couldn't be parted with. Sure enough.. when one of the group snuck over in the night and unbuttoned it.. the smell made him jerk back. The bag was, indeed, full of rotted bones and flesh. Over the years, he'd seen crazies come and go. No need to ask why.

-By the way, what's your name, gal? Guess we never were formally introduced.

-I don't know. Never really had one.

As each man rode past the cabin, he tipped his hat. Several mumbled farewells that drifted away into the pines. This forlorn woman had earned their respect on the trip over the Rockies.. even if she did stink. The train wove down the trail leaving loneliness behind. Had she made a mistake? Occasionally, one of the miners would turn to wave at her and she raised her hand in acknowledgement. Panic gripped her and she fought the urge to call after them. The sun disappeared about the same time they did.

When it grew dark, she pulled the bag around the cabin and tucked it against the outside wall. Sliding down to sit next to it, she hugged her knees to her chest. She had hauled it five hundred miles, sneaking her way onto trains, riding shotgun on stages, begging brief rides from any traveler.. whatever it took to get far away from New Orleans. Survival was the first and harshest lesson of her memory.

In the pocket of her skirt she found a piece of dried bread and stuffed it into her mouth. Abe had drawn a crude map depicting what he knew of this part of the Colorado Territory and she studied it. Exhaustion overcame her and she fell asleep next to the dead.

At dawn, she pulled the bag to the pit where the couple lay entwined, partially covered with melting snow, broken branches and dirt. She intended to dump her burden on top and entomb it the same way.. but hesitated. So many dark memories visited her mind. She took off her dress, opened the bag and scooped the disintegrating remains of a small body onto it. After carefully folding the bundle, she found a shovel and followed a winding deer trail behind the cabin. She stopped in a clearing that was warmed by the sun. The snow was almost gone, leaving the earth soft and pliable. Rugged cliffs harbored the spot on two sides and the remainder was bordered by a variety of blue spruce and pine. A good spot. She dug until she was satisfied with the depth and placed the cotton wrapped body inside. After filling in the grave, she covered it with rocks.

-You deserve better than this Jasmine Robideaux and someday I'll make a proper marker for you. No one can hurt you anymore. Rest now, my little friend.

She had found a dark purple crocus fighting its way through the melting snow and placed it on the rocky mound. Spring had barely arrived and this place was already planted with three bodies.

The next morning, she saddled the mule, hoisted the bag, still heavy with its remaining contents, and tied it to the saddle. She'd found a silver hairclip and a ring on the bedroom dresser. Rolling her hair in a loose bun against her nape, she secured it with the clip and slipped the gold ring on her left hand. It was tight and she knew it would take some soap to get it off, but she admired the ivy design of the band.

Lionshead was, according to Abe's map, the only town for thirty miles in any direction. The hand-drawn map placed it to the south of where Gore Creek joined the Eagle River, about three miles west of the cabin. Down the valley.. left on the road about three more miles.. and she might just run into Lionshead. Not much to go on. Approximately six miles altogether.

Abe's map was good enough. After wading the Eagle, she tied the mule to an aspen and sat, resting on the bag. Lionshead, according to the ragged directions, should be just a few miles south on the road. Leaning back against the tree, she hopefully watched the road in both directions. It would not advance her situation if she rode into town on an old mule. She waited.. patiently watching the sun change angle until a traveler appeared on the north road.. a two-horse carriage with a single passenger. She shaded her eyes and stood to smile at the stranger.

-Could you possibly give me a ride into Lionshead?

Dust-devils danced with the breeze as the man looked her over. She was a fine specimen, he acknowledged.. well made with dark auburn hair, pale skin, a few freckles and very green eyes. The mouth was what captivated him. He noticed a slight scar framing the left side of delicate lips and white teeth. The mark only added interest to her features. Someone had smacked her and she probably deserved it.

-What are you doing out here?

He looked around warily as if waiting for someone else to appear. When he was satisfied that it wasn't going to be a robbery, he looked back, taking a moment to study her.

-You alone?

-I know it seems strange but it's such a long story and I'm tuckered out. My mule's lame and I've been waiting hours for someone to come by. I have some business in Lionshead and can tell you all about my troubles on the way. Oh, by the way.. my name is.. Eartha. Eartha Borne.

Raising her skirt just a tiny bit, she flirtatiously curtsied. She laughed with that beautiful mouth and winked.

-Now don't worry. You're safe with me.

She winked again. He was starting to get the picture.

That was all it took. Jon Wilson hopped off his wagon, ran around stubbing his foot on the wheel, stumbled to the ground, jumped up, dusted himself off and helped her into the carriage. He lifted the bag and tossed it in the back. He slapped the reins and clicked his tongue.

-My name is Wilson. Jon Wilson. Whew! There must be a dead deer or something around here. Do you smell that?

-Pleased to meet you. Why yes.. I do smell something.

She curled her nose and laughed.

-Where are you from Mr. Wilson?

-A ways down the valley. The truth is.. I'm from Utah Territory. Heck of a trip. Been days.

-Such a journey can wear you down. Where do you stay at night?

She smiled suggestively and looked in the back of the rig. He had two bags.

-Hotels as often as possible. But I'll camp if necessary.

-This is a nice rig.

-Rented. But I do pay for the best.

He looked over at her and it made her skin crawl. She had been eyed like this before.. too many times.

-What's your business.. or is it improper for me to ask?

A little bragging won't hurt, he thought. Down deep, he knew better but this woman had made him feel careless. His mouth flapped with confession.

-You could say I'm in real estate. It's paying off, too. I transfer land titles that haven't been properly filed. Found some good ones. Folks pay me to do the traveling and filing. They're usually so poor and ignorant.. or maybe foreigners.. that they never quite figure the process out. Poor and dumb. They usually go together. I take my money to the bank in Lionshead. The banker, Claus Jordan, knows how to keep his mouth shut and he isn't picky about tracing the origins.. as long as he gets a cut. You know what I mean? I think you do.

He winked at her and added a leering grin.

-I think you do, little gal. Why there's a spot right here where the rivers meet that I'm about to record.

A large envelope peeked out of his vest and Wilson patted it proudly. He stopped and looked at her sharply. He'd gotten tricked with lust and told too much. A dark look crept over his face and she saw it. He needed a distraction.

-Could you teach me how to drive this carriage?

-What?

-I've always wanted to. And now that I'm all alone, I really should learn. Will you? We could maybe find a side trail where I can practice a little. That is.. if you've got time.

And that's exactly what they did. They spent the morning on a side trail.. two strangers adept at the art of deception. One by choice.. one by desperate circumstance. By noon, Eartha did, indeed, know how to drive a carriage with two fine horses.

As they sat in a sunny spot at the edge of the cliff, Wilson pulled on his boots. The creek raged forty feet below.

-Why aren't these horses branded?

-Just got them. Came from up Montana somewhere. Branded horses are too easy to track. Probably stolen from the native anyway. Who cares? I do business with the traders all the time. They're not exactly churchgoers. Anyway, some of the worst crooks I know are churchgoers. Bible thumpers. I pass through Salt Lake City when I can. It's easy to get lost in the crowd. But I tell you, those Mormons not only thump the bible, they made up another one to suit their ways.

He laughed at his whit.

-You sure ask a lot of questions, Eartha. When we get close to town, you'll need to get out and walk into Lionshead. I don't want anybody seeing us together. I've got a wife or two back in Utah but I think you and I can have an interesting relationship. You're a little rounder under those clothes than I thought you'd be. I'm not saying that's bad. By the way, what's in that bag you've got?! It smells like something died in there.

Wilson heard a click and whirled around to face Eartha who held his Colt 45. She didn't hesitate to pull the trigger. After stripping his body for the second time that morning, she tucked his papers into the bodice of her dress and laboriously pulled him to the edge of the cliff. With a push of her boot, she shoved the body down to the raging water. Nobody would ever find him jammed under the debris and rock. Even if they did, he would be unrecognizable. A bit of blood had lightly splattered her jacket and she peeled it off, tucking it behind the seat. With a click of her tongue, she lightly slapped the reins.

Eartha Borne was going to town.

TWO

AT THE EDGE

… of town, she stopped at a horse trough to splash water on her face and sunburned neck. The last few weeks had taken a toll but she was determined not to slow down. After all.. suffering was one thing she knew all about.

She pulled in front of the Bank of Lionshead, stepped down and wearily jerked the bag out. Eartha steadied herself as the dust settled. The bank's doors were propped open and customers turned to stare at her. Whispers hid behind hands as she pulled her burden into the cool interior. Not a person stepped forward to help her. Another stranger in town and this one.. a ragged looking woman dragging a filthy bag. And the smell that followed her! Apparently, the gold and silver rush was bringing in some riffraff. Of course, anyone new in town would be considered riffraff.

A middle-aged man sitting at the desk in the corner measured her coldly. What is it with women these days? They think they can prance around anywhere without a chaperone? He cleared his throat with authority.

-Can I help you?

He took an exaggerated look behind her as he winked at a customer.

-Is your husband coming along? Perhaps with another bit of luggage?

She looked tiredly at him. She was hot, dusty and the body count was rising.

-No.. he won't be along. I'm here to open an account. Could you get Claus Jordan, please?

-Claus Jordan?! I assure you.. he's busy. What business could *you* possibly have with him?

The man looked around at the others with a smirk on his face. Jason Ping was the name on the desk plaque.

-Where is he, Jason?

Clearly irritated, he walked around the desk to get a closer look at the woman. He removed his spectacles and stared at her with bulging mud colored eyes.

-In his office. Do I know you?

-I want to see him.

-I assure you, young lady.. whose name is..

-I haven't mentioned it.

He smirked again at the watchers and Eartha heard a giggle behind her.

-I said he's busy. I can assist you. It' my job.

-I'm sure you can't do this job, Jason. Just something about you.

Another snicker from behind her.. a smothered giggle.

-Now see here! Leave or I'll have you removed.

Eartha sat down on the bag to read him. She was weary. Angry little men could find many ways to hurt someone if they became offended. By this time, one of the tellers had run to a door and knocked on it. When the door opened, the teller disappeared inside to tell the tale and moments later out came..

15

-Claus Jordan, Ma'am. What's going on?

He was tall, well-fed and dressed like his mama did it. His face was round, his eyes twinkled like blue ice and his tiny cherub lips pursed between pink cheeks. He was, indeed, a banker.

-I would like to open an account. Is this an inconvenient time?

She looked at the few people in the lobby. They remained still.

-I suppose that if this bank can't assist me properly, I'll have to find another. My apologies for disturbing you.

He looked her over.. weighing the situation. People were watching. Customers waiting to see how he would handle this dusty, brazen woman.. and he couldn't afford to offend a possible depositor.

-There isn't another bank within forty miles. Save the threat. Come on in and we can discuss what it takes to open an account.

As he opened the door to his office, he sent a burning look at the corner desk.

-Get her bag.

Jason, stood as tall as his five four body could, straightened his bow tie, and dutifully dragged the bag into Claus Jordan's office. His face was red as he started to take a chair.

-That's it. Get out. And check around the building. It smells like something died around here.

The door closed, leaving Eartha and Claus Jordan watching each other like cats in a midnight alley. Eartha heard the clock on the wall and Jordan could see the trickle of sweat running down her temple.

-Now, what can I help you with? Miss.. Mrs?

-My name is Eartha Borne. My husband is dead and I don't plan on discussing the details with you. Mr. Jordan.. Claus.. may I call you that?

His little rosebud mouth smiled amiably.

-In this bag is a lot of money. More than you've ever seen. More than you've ever dreamed about. If you do business on my terms.. you'll reap the rewards.. and you can continue to con this town.

-That does it. Get out.

-If you try and cheat me you won't live to regret it. The money does, indeed, have a dubious past.. if that's what you're wondering. But before you make any life altering decisions.. let's open that bag and count it together. It'll take some time, so you may want to put a "do not disturb" sign on your door. You can pocket 2% to keep your mouth shut concerning me and my finances.

He stood, walked over and roughly grabbed her arm.

-You'd better take a look inside before you throw me out.

Jordan hesitated, looking over at the bag skeptically. What if she was telling the truth? He released her, reached down and untied the fastenings on the bag. Instinctively, he jerked back as the odor hit his nostrils. Despite the stench, he stared into the bag as if hypnotized and slowly reached in to touch stack upon stack of bills.

Legitimate bank notes. Big ones. Yes, there was more money in the bag than he'd ever seen.

-My God, woman! Where'd you get this? What's that smell!

He fell back covering his nose with his sleeve.

-It's the smell of death and money. You need to decide which one you prefer.

He looked up at her in shock. The cherub lips started to form the question that she had anticipated..

-Listen up, Claus. It's going to be difficult not knowing everything.. I understand.. but no questions. None.

He looked at the bag.. and back at her..

-May I call you Eartha?

-No.

She looked around the room with an expert eye.

-Where's your strong room?

-It's out in the bank, of course. The room behind the barred door. You walked past it. Quite impressive. Brought out from St. Louis.

-I mean the real one. The one I'm sure you built under this bank.

Claus Jordan stared at her, realizing she couldn't be bluffed. Striding to the corner of his office, he moved a small table, peeled back the rug and lifted the trap door.

-Come on over here, Mrs. Borne and I'll show you how safe your money really is. You're right.. this was installed before the bank was built over it. Insurance, you know.

He winked at her and Eartha had the urge to thump his rosy little mouth.

Lighting a lamp, he guided her down the stairs. They were wide and sturdy. Jordan lit an additional lamp and Eartha saw windowless brick walls. In the corner of the room stood a six-foot iron safe with an immense five-letter barrel wheel lock. Clearly, the safe could never be removed from the room. Only dynamite could possibly damage the lock. Claus Jordan stood proudly looking at her.

-So the safe upstairs is for *other* folks money. Yours is kept down here. You probably have a modest account on record for a banker of your stature.

-Little lady.. I mean Mrs. Borne.. *this* safe is for special situations. The one upstairs is for everyday transactions.

Eartha found comfort in the knowledge that she was dealing with a first-rate swindler. Now, at least she knew the playing ground. The giant lock was heavy against her hand.

-What's the combination?

Jordan moved over to the safe, pushed her hand away and blocked her view as he started to move wheels.

-No, Claus, I want you to show me how to do this. What's the combo?

He turned, facing her in disbelief.

-You've got to be kidding. I can't give that to you.

They stood looking at each other, as a chair scraped across the floor in the lobby above. Another standoff.

-I'll give you the first installment on the 2% now. After that, you'll get the equivalent amount every nine months.

After that who knows. Things might just start to snowball.

Claus Jordan reluctantly showed her how to operate the lock. She changed the combination and practiced it a few times. He watched her pull out an abundant variety of boxes and satchels from the safe and stack them on the floor.

-What the hell are you doing now? Those things are very valuable and must be kept down here.

She reached into the bag and handed him his first installment. Looking up, she smiled.

-This is *my* safe now.

-What am I supposed to do with my stuff? There are some very valuable items here and cannot be stored just anywhere.

-I don't really care. You're a clever man.. I'm sure you'll think of something.

Eartha resumed piling neatly bound money into the interior of the vault as Claus Jordan stared down at the back of her head. Why couldn't he just whack her and dispose of her later?.. and keep the money? Standing up, she dusted her hands and skirt off.. turned to look at him and read his mind out loud.

-Because there are witnesses up there, Claus. If I don't come out of your office.. well.. tongues will wag.

She turned her back to him and reset the lock.

-That about does it. Now, let's go up to your office and iron out the details of our partnership.

After repositioning the rug and sliding the table back, Eartha picked up a crystal decanter of brandy from the desk. She poured a shot in each of two glasses and handed one to Jordan.

-You look like you could use this. Here's to a long and rewarding relationship. I've got a lot of shopping to do in this town and a considerable amount of hiring. Therefore, when anyone walks into this bank with a note from me for payment.. pay it. Simple.. easy .. no questions asked. Inform your staff, too. Explain it in terms that they can handle. Lionshead is going to grow, Claus. Miners.. stores.. people will come. Maybe even a railroad. I'm sure of it. Here's to a long and lucrative partnership.

He numbly watched as she touched her glass to his. Reaching across the desk, she took a paper, pen and inkwell. She tapped the pen against her teeth thoughtfully and began to write.

-What's this? The combination?

He smiled over at her, hopefully, then looked down at the paper.

-Your signature is very unique, Mrs. Borne. It seems that you are an educated woman. Where did you study?

-In places you just wouldn't believe, Claus. And.. no.. I'm not giving you the combination.

-Well, are you ever going to trust me with it?

-Highly doubtful.

He sat back against his leather chair.

-How can I pay your notes then?

-You just pay them.. and then I reimburse you.. every month.. or whenever I get around to it. Just keep the stack of notes. As you've noticed, my signature would be a bitch to duplicate. And one more thing.. would you mind getting rid of that stinking bag?

THREE

ACROSS THE STREET

... a young man struggled to hang a new sign on the building. Eartha watched as people passed him.. laughing and rolling their eyes. She instinctively knew the quality of Lionshead. It was small and mean. Although it was a simple task, he clearly needed help. Just a bit of kindness.. a bit of time. He was not much more than a kid and a skinny one at that. Every few seconds, he would reach up to keep his spectacles from dropping off his face and the sign would slide down. He yipped with pain as it hit his head. No one stopped. Eartha crossed the street and took one side of the sign, standing on her tip-toes to lift it as high as possible above the door.

-Here, let me help you.

The movement and statement startled him and he jerked back, stumbling down the footstool. He recovered his balance but was clearly humiliated.

-Yes, ma'am, it looks like I've made a mess of things here. I'm a little afraid of heights.. even if there isn't one.

Looking at her, he burst into embarrassed laughter.. spit flying from his mouth. His eyes were big and gray.. and gentle. Eartha took in the freckled nose and blonde hair falling across his forehead. She cocked her head sideways as she looked up and read the sign.

-Lionshead Assay and Land Title Company. Now that sounds like a fine enterprise. Is it your business, Mr. ..

-Hedeman. My name is Albert Hedeman.

He extended his hand proudly. Eartha enthusiastically shook it feeling how thin he was. Hunger. She'd seen it before.. felt it before.

-My name is Mrs. Eartha Borne. But please call me Eartha. It's so nice to meet you.

-Well then, you can call me Albert.

He looked at her shyly and adjusted his spectacles. She executed a dramatic curtsy, causing him to blush again.

-Albert, let's get this sign up before the sun sets.

For the next hour they laughed like kids anchoring the sign "just right", stepping back into the street to admire their work. The same people who had passed earlier started to pay attention. This was the third new business in town, in as many years. Looking over at Albert, Eartha fanned her face with an envelope she had pulled from her jacket.

-Do you have anything to drink in your office, Albert? Water.. lemonade..

She reached over to steady herself on his shoulder.

-I'm a little hot and dizzy.

-Well, ma'am.. I mean Eartha.. sit down on this bench. I can run to The Hotel Ma Campbell and get us some. It's just down the street. Ma Campbell has the best lemonade I ever had. They're big, too! It'd be my honor and.. I sure would be proud to sit out here in the shade and drink lemonade with you.. so people could see I have a friend.

He looked down at her ring finger.

-I apologize if I seem bold. I see that you're married.. but, the truth is, it's just great to talk to someone. Is your husband in Lionshead with you? I sure would like to meet him. If he's anything like you I know I'd really like him. Then I'd have two friends.

He looked down at his shoes and shyly laughed at his joke. She laughed too and gently touched his shoulder.

-My husband's dead. Killed in an avalanche. But I know he would have liked you, too.

-I'm so sorry, Eartha.

Albert bolted to Ma Campbell's and raced back with tall drinks, barely spilling a drop on the dusty main street. They sat for another hour in the shade of the afternoon making small talk and sipping on the generous beverages. They talked and laughed about silly things that two lonely, hard luck kids would share. Eventually, Eartha absent-mindedly opened the packet she had been fanning herself with. She slapped her forehead lightly with the papers and stared at Albert in amazement.

-Why, I honestly can't believe this coincidence! I think I'm supposed to record this property title, Albert. Isn't that what you do here? Could you look these over and tell me what you think?

He took the papers from her hands and glanced through them.

-These don't look like they've been filled out or recorded properly.. if at all.

-Well then.. I need your services. What an absolute miracle that I ran into you today! Let's go into your office and I'll be a proper client. A paying one, too.

-I could hardly accept payment from you.

-I insist.

Albert Hedeman studied his books and maps with Eartha looking over his shoulder.

-This place up the Gore looks good. Around three hundred and fifty acres.. maybe more. But this other one that joins it.. confluence of the Gore and Eagle Rivers.. a thousand acres doesn't seem quite right. That's a lot of land and there's no name on it. Recording is haphazard out in this territory, but I think I can get a start for you.

-My name should be on it. Right? My husband died before he could get it filed properly.

Flopping despondently into a chair, Eartha looked up at Albert with tears filling her eyes. She reached over to gather up the papers, hands shaking.

-Never mind. It's probably a mess. I'll go home and put it back with my husband's things.

Albert Hedeman tapped a pen on his teeth. His mouth opened and then closed.. then he stood with both hands on the desk. Eartha could almost feel his confidence growing.

-Listen, Eartha. You're my first customer and only friend. I'll be honest with you. I don't know what I'm doing here, but I can't go back to Ohio. Lionshead is my only chance. These papers can be doctored up, but it'll have to be a secret between us and no one else.

She stood.. also planting both hands on the desk. Her face was inches from Alberts as she vowed..

-It's a deal! You'll never regret it. I'll do everything I can to send you business. I'll help get you organized around here. There's business coming to this town and you'll profit from it. More prospectors are passing through every day and they'll stake claims up in those mountains. Ranchers and farmers, too. All kinds of folks.

She leaned a little closer and smiled.

-It sounds crazy. But maybe even a railroad someday.

-No offense, but that does sound a little farfetched.. This is just a little mudhole in the territory.

-You should start recording everything for people. Land.. creek and river locations. Births, deaths and marriages. Anything someone needs a record of. You keep a copy and they keep a copy. Charge your fee. Most people feel more secure when there's an actual record of their lives and property. Be a witness to every transaction of the living or the dead.

Albert sat down, leaned back in his chair looked at her with loyalty and admiration. Eartha reached over, took his pen from his hand and wrote on a piece of paper. She pushed it back to him.

-You take this across the street and ask for Claus Jordan. Tell him you want that put in your account. You do have a bank account, right? Well, get one. This is for your professional services today, Albert. Good honest business.

He looked down at the figure on the paper and stood with a look of shock.

-Eartha this is way too much. Way too much.

She looked over his starving frame.

-It's also a retainer. You've rescued me and I want to do business with you. You're truly an honest man. In fact, I'm proud to know you.

She lifted Albert's limp hand from his side and shook it enthusiastically. Looking down at the paper, Albert thought he might go to Hotel Ma Campbell and order a steak dinner. He felt good about life for the first time in a long time.

-We should put a name on your place, Eartha. What do you think?

She eased back into the chair in contemplation. They tossed many names into consideration.. all sounding pretentious or just stupid. And then it came..

-Big Spruce. There's an old tree out there that has stood some hard times. Name it Big Spruce.

Albert took great care as he wrote the name on his map and records.

FOUR

BERTAND'S MERCANTILE

…was on the north corner of town and was a bustling place. For the first time in her young life, Eartha drifted past goods piled on tables and shelves.. touching and smelling.. without a handler by her side. After blissfully inspecting every corner of the store, she moved to the long counter and picked up a clipboard with an attached pencil.

-Exuse me, miss, that belongs to the store. Can I help you with something?

A thin ferret-like woman stood with her arms crossed on her bony chest. Her pursed lips wrinkled below tiny, black and greedy eyes. A greasy bun had been misplaced on her head so tightly that the skin appeared to have been stretched.

-You can. I've got a lot to do and it's getting late. Start writing this order down and be accurate.

Yes.. perhaps the wrong approach but Eartha could tell by looking at the witch that it wouldn't matter.

-Well, I have never. Bertrand get over here! I think we have a situation.

Bertrand Snibe excused himself from a customer and lumbered slowly over to "the situation". He looked at Eartha and then at his wife.. baffled.

-What, Wilma? *What?*

-This woman is rude and I won't wait on her. In fact, we shouldn't sell her anything. That's what. She tossed this notebook at me and told me to get writing. That's what. It's rude, Bertrand. People from New York wouldn't act this way.

Her nose twitched like a rat's and she looked back at Bertrand defiantly as her left eye twitched.

-Listen, Wilma.. I'm not going back to New York. Not today.. not ever. Now see if you can help Jacobs over there with some coffee and I'll handle this order.

Wilma crossed the floor like a sidewinder glaring back at Eartha. Jacobs looked over at Bertrand with "thanks for nothing" on his face.

-I apologize for my wife, ma'am. The West has been a little hard on her. What can I get for you?

-I do have a long list and a sore hand. I've been digging and planting quite a bit lately. Your name is?

-Snibe. Bertrand Snibe. Proprietor.

-Well, Mr. Snibe, I'd greatly appreciate your writing down my list as we go through the store. -There are a few things that you may have to order.

They walked around for the better part of an hour, Eartha pointing and Bertrand writing. As the list grew, he became wary. She selected a hat and tried it on.

-Ma'am, that's a man's hat. And, pardon me, but can you pay for all this? I don't extend credit unless I know you. And I don't.

-I know what kind of hat it is. And, yes, I can pay.

-How?

-With a note on the Bank of Lionshead.

-That won't work.

-Why don't you or.. Wilma.. walk the block to find out. It'll just take a moment. Ask for Mr. Claus Jordan.. himself. Believe me, Bertrand. You'll be better off for it.

A jar of multi-colored suckers stood on a table nearby and Eartha reached in, took one and popped it in her mouth. She raised her brows and looked at him as she leaned against the display. The ball of candy comically distorted her cheek.

-What's your name then.. if I have to research your bank reliability.

-Eartha Borne.

-Borne.. Borne. It seems like I may have heard that name before.

She didn't bother taking the candy out of her mouth and a bit of sugared drool oozed onto her lip. Raising her sleeve, she quickly wiped it away.

-No relation.

-Did you say Claus Jordan.. the president?

-Mm..hmm.

-Wilma! Get over here. You need to walk down to the bank.

He pulled Wilma aside as he scribbled a note. The woman argued briefly with hands on hips as she glared at Eartha. She spat out a comment about the price of a sucker before scurrying out the door. Ten minutes later, she was back and whispered in Bertrand's ear. He straightened his bow-tie and approached Eartha who was examining an axe.

-My apologies, Mrs. Borne. It's been a bit hectic around here. Miners traveling through.. some riffraff, too. Just can't be too careful. What else can I add to this list?

He looked like a fat cat dipping his tongue in a cream bowl. Eartha walked to the door.

-Who will be picking this order up for you? I won't be able to get it together until tomorrow afternoon.

-Bertrand, we're going to have a long relationship and you'll come to like it and depend on it. I do understand your frustration. Pile and wrap it all up. Delivery tomorrow afternoon will work just fine.

-Delivery? We normally don't. Where?

-Three miles up the Gore.

-Up the Gore? That's a distance to haul all this. There's not much out there. Wild and no decent road to speak of.

-My cabin is out there and we'll be adding to it. Don't worry. I'll make it worth the time and inconvenience. They'll have to unload, too.. and set the tents. The bridge isn't much yet, so it might take some doing. Do you sell rifles and ammunition? Set me up with a nice selection. And I saw a big bear-claw bathtub in that catalog. Could you get me one?

At this point, Bertrand knew better than to react negatively.

-How about a pistol?

-No thanks. Never used one. Make sure there's some seeds in the delivery. Bertrand, this is going to work out well for you. Just one more thing. That fancy pen set over there. Please wrap it with a bow and take it across the street to Albert Hedeman at the Lionshead Assay and Land Title Company.

She scribbled a note, sealed it in an envelope and handed it to him.

-Put this with it, please.

Bertrand Snibe scratched his head as he looked at Eartha's order. The tiny bell on the door tinkled and he looked up. It must have been the wind. He looked around the store and realized that Eartha was gone.

But Wilma stood in a dark corner,
arms folded across her chest.. hate in her eyes.

FIVE

EARTHA RELAXED

... for the first time on blankets and pillows that belonged to her. New ones that didn't smell like someone else. Looking around at the dimly lit interior, she thought of the events of the day.

Bertrand Snibe was as good as his word, especially when he was profiting. He'd sent a dozen capable men and before noon, two large tents had been securely set on the north side of the river. A makeshift plank bridge had been anchored to trees on either side.. one of them.. the Big Spruce. Crossing was precarious and the first few loads were dumped into the water, only to be salvaged downriver. As the day wore on, the workers became adept at negotiating the crossing. Supplies and hardware had been unloaded and strategically placed in heaps around the property, raised on wood crating and covered with tarps.

-Who's gonna live in these tents, lady? You got kin comin'?

-No.. no kin. The tents are temporary until the cabins are built. If you can be trusted and need a job.. let me know. I'll be fair in every way but I expect the same in return.

Working with them throughout the day gave her the opportunity to study each one and listen to interactions.

34

One man stood apart as he worked, not joining the constant banter. He was tall and dark with an oversized black mustache. Some of the crew would look at Eartha sideways when they got a chance and she made a mental note.. who to get rid of at the end of the day. Most of them worked hard and along with their cash, they received credit bonuses at Bertrand's Mercantile.

-I'm sure none of you are thinking that I'm an easy target, so I mention this needlessly. There's no cash kept around here.. only what I just paid you. I do, however, have guns and know how to use them. Someone will be watching my back, so don't get any stupid ideas. You might want to spread that around and save me the grief of planting someone. The good news is.. I'm hiring. I only want honest and reliable workers. If you fit in that category stick around and we'll talk. If you don't, hit the road.

She pointed at the tall dark man.

-I'd like a word with you.

A slight nod was his only reaction. Out of the corner of her eye, Eartha saw two workers elbow each other and knew what they would be saying when she was out of earshot. Standing in the middle of the group, she continued in a quiet voice..

-Tell anyone you know that there's work and opportunity here. It could mean long term security for some. Tell them to show up between nine and four tomorrow.. and the next day. I need some improvements to this cabin and that barn finished. A well dug and water pumped to the cabin. A bridge built just big enough for a buggy to cross but high enough to clear the spring runoff. Two or three more cabins built on this side of the creek and the same on the opposite side. Who's got cattle around here? Chickens.. pigs.. There's paper and pencils. Write down what and who you know. If you can't write.. I'll do it for you. An icehouse will be built and stocked. We might still be able to skid a few ice blocks from up river where the sun never shines. Milk cows. Another barn. As you can see, there's plenty of opportunity for the right folks. If you can do it, you're hired. If you have a family, bring them out. I'm interested in just about everything. A full-time blacksmith. He can build himself a cabin here and a forge. Everything is negotiable. Spread the word. If you all won't mind waiting for a moment..

She motioned for the dark man to follow her to the cabin. He stood in the doorway not moving to enter. His face was serious and he showed no indication of his thoughts.

-How are you with a gun?

He hesitated to reply.

-I am very good.

-*Very good.* I see. Would you be interested in guarding Big Spruce? I can tell you, it would be the most important job of my life.

She loved the humor in that and a slight smile shadowed her lips.

-I am curious about this offer, Mrs. Borne. This seems like a sudden decision on your part since I am a stranger to you.

Eartha pushed a chair toward him but he didn't sit. He stood looking seriously at her. She had learned how to read people.. the hard way. The result was a finely tuned sixth sense. She could trust this one as sure as the sun would set on Big Spruce.

-Here's the deal, Mr. ..

-Tytanos. My name is Theo Tytanos.

-Mr. Tytanos, here's the deal. I need a guard out there tonight, for sure. And after that.. every day and night. A very sharp eye. There's a tent on the other side ready for an occupant. Pretty comfy. If you agree to stand guard tonight, we can discuss all the details. Just make it plain to those men out there that you stand behind me.

He nodded slightly. She stood, picked up a rifle that leaned against the wall and handed it to Tytanos. She also extended her hand and he took it with a quick bow. When they stepped out into the sun, Theo stood firmly behind Eartha with the rifle slung on his shoulder. She pointed two fingers at the men who had smirked and whispered to each other. Tytanos looked at them calmly as he shifted the rifle on his shoulder.

-Don't you two ever set foot on this place again. You'll get paid for your time. Theo Tytanos is now the eyes, ears and enforcer for Big Spruce. And he's a very good shot.

***

As the evening shadow moved across the valley, the last of the buckboards departed. Eartha leaned against a lumpy pile of provisions and watched the flames of the campfire. She was full, warm and safe. And so were the babies inside of her. She knew in her heart that they were twins. Theo stood across the river standing in front of one of the big white tents. The small campfire illuminated his features. He held a fine repeating Winchester that Eartha had taken from an abusive drunk in Denver. It was an unfortunate situation that she did not regret.

She watched as sparks popped and drifted to mix with the stars. It would be difficult to get to her cabin without crossing a bridge at this spot. The water was freezing, deep and swift.. at least a hundred feet above and below the cabin. There were ten acres surrounded by steep mountain and cliff that joined with the river. A natural fortress. As Eartha watched the flames, her thoughts began to focus. Her plans. She would build something good for her children and it would cleanse her soul of the past. A new birth. This place would be everything to them. Big Spruce would be a perfect place on earth. Self-contained. Her children wouldn't need anybody else and they would be safe from the world. She watched the last rays of sun reflect on the mountain range to the east, illuminating it with alpenglow. She stood and walked to the edge of the river, gesturing to Theo. He crossed the planks as if he were accustomed to the challenge.

-Yes?

-Where're you from?

-You hired me out of Lionshead, Mrs. Borne.

-You know what I mean. You're not from this country are you? Italian.. maybe Spanish? Not Mexican.

-Greece. My family comes from an island of Greece. A very small island.

He looked at the river silently, preferring not to talk. A brimmed cap covered his head and he wore his pants tucked into soft boots. An intricate design had been sewn into the tops. When he looked back at her, she saw the fire glitter in his black eyes. They stared at each other soberly, until she burst forth with a laugh. The tension of the day had whittled her to nothing. He laughed in response, still watching her intently. Shifting his stance, he said..

-Why are we laughing?

-Theo.. pull up a stump. Want some coffee? I'm just suffering from mashed nerves. You have a family? Here? If you'll be staying across that river, I'd like to know a little about you.

Hesitantly, he began telling her of his life and journey across the land from New York to the Colorado Territory. As he talked, his eyes watched behind the cabin and moved through the surrounding shadows. Eartha listened, gaining respect and trust for the man. Looking up at the stars, she said..

-So here you are. With a wife, Madlyn, and two little girls.. Alexandria and Ameriki. You are hired, Theo.

-For how long?

-For as long as we trust each other and I have a gut feeling that will be a long time. Move your family out here tomorrow. Pick a spot across the river for your cabin. I think it should be close to the bridge. That way, you can sit on your front porch and look like your guarding even when you're asleep.

He stood.. offended by her tactless comment.

-I have sworn to protect you and this spot. I will build a good life for Madlyn and my daughters. I want to send money back to Greece as a dowry for my sister. This tent is already better than the shack we rent in Lionshead. There is no promise that I will stay here forever. I will stay until you are safe from whatever demons hunt you. Tomorrow, my wife and daughters will meet you. But.. one thing I wonder about Mrs. Borne. Where is your husband buried? Today I did not notice a grave.

-Up on the hill. Not far from here.

-How did he die? If it is not too painful to say.

-Avalanche. He was buried by an avalanche.

Tytanos stood, wordlessly, and then walked to the river. Just before he started the treacherous passage, he looked back and smiled. He knew. He knew it was a lie.

The next morning, as Eartha stood braiding her hair, the Tytanos family arrived. She watched as the procession worked its way across the boards and stood in front of the porch. Theo stood proudly with an arm around his wife Madlyn. Eartha walked down the few steps to stand before them.

-This is my wife.. Madlyn.

With grace and manners, the beautiful woman stepped forward and put her hand out. Eartha took it.

-Welcome, Madlyn.

The girls peeked around their parents shyly. Theo reached back and pulled the oldest gently in front.

-This is my daughter Alexandria. We call her Lexy. It sounds more American.

He looked proudly at Eartha and winked at Lexy who, in turn, giggled.

-Lexy is five.

Snaking an arm behind Madlyn, he pulled the smallest daughter around. She covered her face with her hands, peeking through the fingers at Eartha.

-This is my daughter Ameriki. She thinks that she is invisible if her hands cover her face. We call her Mery. More American sounding. Her years are four.

Theo gently patted the little girl's dark head. Eartha was charmed. She couldn't remember being this close to something so decent. She stepped to Madlyn and put a hand on her arm.

-I want you all to call me Eartha.

The couple looked at each other with obvious disapproval. Theo stepped forward with his cap in hand.

-We are not ready to call you by your first name, Mrs. Borne.

Eartha looked down at the wood floor, thinking of a way to win this.

-Well, that makes it hard on me. I suppose I have to call you, Mr. and Mrs. Tytanos along with the children.. Ms. Alexandria Tytanos and Ms. Ameriki Tytanos. Unnecessarily difficult. Could we possibly start out with first names and if it doesn't work out.. we'll switch to the longer versions? Give me this chance. I have limited control of my pronunciation.

The girls looked up with hope at their parents. Eartha took her last and cheapest shot.

-It's more American.

They agreed. During the next few months all domestic hell broke loose on Big Spruce. The Greeks built their double cabin close to the bridge. It was fine and well furnished. Eartha felt unfamiliar joy watching the little girls excitedly piecing their home together. Part of the irresistible deal was a finely built and furnished bedroom cabin, three acres of their own for a garden and chickens, 10% profit from any crops and livestock sold from Big Spruce and a monthly salary. The entire package was paid by Eartha.

Hard to beat.

SIX

THE WEEKS PASSED

… and Eartha grew large with the babies, preparing for their debut into the world. Except for an occasional trip into Lionshead, she spent her time preparing and watching. Big Spruce began to transform and she felt the dead spots in her heart begin to revive. She trusted Theo and was becoming increasingly fond of his family. Together they planned and built a pond for swimming and fishing. Many afternoons, delighted squeals would drift to her cabin as Lexy and Mery waded in the shallow inlet. A harmless water snake would consistently send them screaming to their cabin. Eartha sat on the steps and daydreamed of the time when her own children would play in the hot afternoon sun.

Livestock was purchased.. ten horses, fifty steers, chickens and a couple of hogs. Gardens were planted and cutthroat trout were appearing in the river-fed pond. Many an evening, they would fry them in a skillet and eat them with their fingers, laughing and talking of the day's events. An honest bridge was built.. sturdy and raised.. not too wide. Life was good at Big Spruce and Eartha Borne planned on keeping it that way.

Late one morning, Madlyn sat on the bridge holding the feet of little Mery as she lay looking down into the river.

The girl dangled a string into the water. A drowned worm bobbed hopelessly on the hook. Glancing up, Mery spied a dusty ball of movement coming up the valley. She recognized her father's figure even at a distance. Occasionally cracking a braided bundle of leather straps against his chaps, he would yell some Greek encouragement at the animals he pushed. When he got closer, the girls ran to him and he pulled them both up to sit on the horse. The flock oozed across the bridge. A few lambs darted out from the noisy group, their tales held high as tiny hooves stomped the dust. Theo dismounted and strode proudly toward Eartha puffing on his clay pipe. He tossed the braided leather on the porch and stood, hands on hips, looking at Eartha. A shadow of defiance briefly drifted across his features as he realized she did not share his enthusiasm. A fuzzy white head and two floppy ears erupted from the bag slung around his shoulders.

-What's going on here, Theo? What are those?

He turned with a disbelieving look and raised his arms as Moses must have when he parted the Red Sea.

-Sheep. These are sheep, Mrs. Eartha.

-I know that. What are they doing here? I don't remember them on the shopping list.

He wrinkled his brow and she could sense a storm coming. Over his shoulder, she saw Madlyn standing on the bridge, hands on hips.. clearly pleased that her man had brought home a flock of sheep. Theo stood firm.

-A place without a flock is no place. I know how to raise them.. herd them.. shear them. It is a good thing for Big Spruce. Think wool, meat and milk. I know how to do it all.

-They'll eat every green thing, Theo.

-No, listen. They roam into the hillsides and will graze up higher. The right dog can move and retrieve them. This is just a small flock.. forty. But as you can see they stick together. No worries. It is a good thing. A continuing resource. You must trust me with this decision.

He stood with legs apart and hands on hips. A furry ball vaulted out of his jacket to plop on the porch. It was a big, white, yelping pup with huge black eyes.

-And this?

With another grand sweep of his arm, Theo announced..

-A Great Pyrenees. The greatest of protectors. The most fantastic breed that walks the earth.

It was clear that Theo Tytanos wanted her to fall on her knees with worship. Instead, the pup waddled over to Eartha and sat whimpering on her foot. She could see the girls staring from the yard with disbelief and pure hope. They stood, holding hands, trying to hear what was said. The pup wet on Eartha's bare foot as she scooted it roughly across the porch.

-Be gone!

Theo looked pleased with the name.

-Yes.. Begone. The perfect name for a great guardian.

He knew the battle was over. The girls were waved to the porch and the pup began the journey of smothering love. Theo kept his eyes on Eartha as he announced..

-His name is Begone and we'll keep him at our cabin. But I tell you now that he will spend most of his time guarding his flock.

As she leaned on the doorjamb, Eartha knew that she'd been outdone. As Theo stepped from the porch, he removed his cap and looked back with a triumphant smile.

-After all, Eartha. Do you not think all is fair in love and war? I love my family and that dog will watch over us all. Especially, when I fall asleep on the porch.

*****

Eartha sat peeling potatoes into a tub between her feet, discussing the progress of Big Spruce with Theo and Madlyn. It was hot and she took a moment to wipe the sweat from her forehead. A few feet away, the girls took turns torturing Begone with love. They smooched his eyes and nose.. whispering secrets in his ears. Eartha thought out loud..

-We need a few more folks out here. Any ideas? They should be poor and desperate. No offense. They can build a cabin across the bridge. You two can help them pick their spots. We can glue this place together with loyalty and build a better future. If you know people that fit the bill, let's recruit them. If it's a couple, they must be married or get that way. You know what I'm talking about. If they are not married.. absolutely no hanky-panky out here. They can go into town for that. Crops.. livestock.. we'll all profit. They'll get an extra bonus, too.. after a couple of years. That way, they'll earn cash of their own to spend in town or save.. or use however they see fit. Theo, I can tell you that we'll need another gun out here. Keep an eye out for a qualified slinger. And a little school. We'll get a good school teacher while we're at it. Let's build a little cabin for her now. Can't have illiterate kids running around. Post in town that I'm looking for a good teacher and will be interviewing in one month. Get it out to that town west of here.. Eagle. There's got to be a good teacher wanting to get out of there. Interviewing in one month at Ma Campbell Hotel. No men need apply.

Gazing out toward the river, she patted her growing belly.

-Madlyn, have you ever helped someone with a birthing?

Madlyn looked in panic at Theo but he did not help with the answer. Looking down reluctantly, she admitted..

-No. I have only had these girls with help from a midwife. I have no skills like that. I would be afraid.

-There's nothing to worry about, Madlyn. I've had a baby before. I just may need some help this time. There's two coming. And in answer to the question in your eyes.. I don't know what happened to the first one.

As her face went pale with remembering, Theo stood and removed his cap.

- Mrs. Eartha, will there be a church?

- No. No church.

SEVEN

EARTHA KNEW

… that her time was only a few months away. The weather was hot and sultry and she found it hard to sleep at night. She would frequently roam to the river in the night and cool herself with the mountain water. The runoff was not as deep as it had been in the early summer but was still swift and could be treacherous. Most of the short-term work was well underway. Theo had found another couple that she thought might fit with Big Spruce.. Angus and Lara McCleod. They had started in Scotland and came out to live with relatives that had built a place down at the confluence of the Eagle River and Gore Creek. In fact, the relatives had started a house on Eartha's land. The land that she hadn't come by honestly.. and so she didn't raise a ruckus over it. Angus and Lara had no children but had told Eartha that they hoped for at least four.

A blacksmith named Benno Kleiman lived in the town stable and kept to himself. Despite his powerful build and skilled hands, he could not bring himself to speak in the presence of others. In agitation, he would throw tools about, which would further alienate him from socializing. Theo had seen his work and relayed that he was a capable metalworker. And so he was in. Benno didn't want a cabin and preferred to live in a one room attachment to the barn.

When Eartha came in to ask him to hitch up the wagon for her, he stood looking at her with disapproval. He pointed at her belly, shaking his head and then staring down at the dirt.

-You don't think it's a good idea, Benno? Me going to town by myself? Do you think that I'll get hurt?

He shook his head in affirmation. Grime covered his face and his eyes looked stubbornly at her.

-I'll be fine now. I won't be gone for long either. Now come on.. I've got a lot of trouble to cause before sunset.

He grinned like a child when he helped her into the carriage but frowned as she crossed the bridge. Eartha Borne had treated him like a human being and he adored her. As the carriage disappeared from site, he went back to pounding his anvil, mumbling a strange language to himself.

Six bumpy miles later Eartha stopped in front of The Evening Star.. the most rundown pile of filthy wood west of Denver. She could have continued into town to the Ma Campbell Hotel.. but just didn't feel like it. She carefully lowered herself from the wagon and walked slowly into the dark interior, holding her hand over her belly and stretching her back.. creating an interesting silhouette against the sunlight pouring through the doorway. The establishment was busy with miners, trappers and drifters.. standing at the bar or sitting at tables. She smelled the familiar fragrance of degradation and perversion, along with rancid bacon grease. Looking up the stairway, she saw a gaunt and soiled woman staring at her. The poor creature didn't have much on. Not even an expression.

The moment froze.. a clink of glass and a laugh from some bastard in the back. A memory ricocheted through her brain.

-Please get me something to drink. With ice. No booze. Water will be fine.

She wiped her forehead with her sleeve knowing full well what the reaction would be. The owner, Kyle Pukeard, snorted.

-Are you kiddin?! We don't serve women in here. Especially one in your apparently used condition. Now I'm not sayin we couldn't put you on sale.. for, let's see.. two for one?

He looked around at the other men grinning. Eartha knew before she entered The Evening Star that it was a snake's den. She just couldn't help herself.

-What about that woman sitting on the steps? It looks like you've got her on something more than whiskey.

-Listen, bitch, you'd better get out while the goin's good.

He started around the bar.

From a back table a voice warned..

-Leave her be.

-Who the hell said that?

Pukeard peered through the dim light toward the voice. A man sat in the corner, his back to the wall. Prior to this moment, he had attracted no attention. Not even the zombie woman on the stairs. His only movement was to remove the straw that was positioned in his front teeth.

-I did and I believe this woman deserves some water. In a glass. With ice. I'll wager you got some back there.

-This isn't a water trough.. it's a damned bar! If she wants water she can git on down the street.

Pukeard stared in disbelief as the stranger trespassed confidently behind the bar. He shoved the tall rack that held, quite possibly, fifty bottles of whiskey. They crashed to the floor, shattering.. splashing the walls and floor with cheap booze and glass.

-Looks like that's about all you got left now. Water.

Rushing at him in rage, Pukeard slipped on the wet floor, hit his head on the counter and fell in an unconscious heap. Patrons rose from their tables and filed out of the bar. No trouble. No booze. No business.

Stepping over the oblivious bartender, the stranger located a dirty glass and wiped it out with his shirt. He dipped the glass into a bucket and offered it to Eartha as he removed his hat.

-Water, Ma'am. Dirty glass. No ice. It's the best I can do under the circumstances.

She took it from his hand and gulped it down, allowing half to spill down her chin into her bodice. She suggestively dabbed her chest with a kerchief, watching his reaction closely. He never lowered his eyes but kept them steadily on hers. She knew he couldn't be twenty yet but was certainly lean and mean. He was of average height with dark hair and hazel eyes, one of which had a noticeable scar beneath it. Overall, he was very nice looking despite the dirt and grime that covered his clothes.

Eartha felt the world begin to spin. With shaking knees, she turned toward the door and stumbled. Crossing the space between them, he took her arm and guided her into the fresh air.

-Listen, lady, who can I get to help you? You're looking pretty pale. Like you've seen a spirit pass by.

Leaning against her carriage, Eartha looked shakily at him.

-Do you want a job?

He snorted out a laugh.

-You're something, aren't you? What possessed you to even step foot in that place? I'm just real curious.

-Stupidity. Old habits. How long have you been in town?

-Got here just now. I'm brand spanking new.

-That's an odd name. Listen, Mr. Brand Spanking New, help me into the carriage and tie your horse to it. You can drive. You know how, don't you? The day's young and we've got a lot to do. My name's Eartha Borne.

She reached over and shook his hand as if they had just met at a social function.

-My name is Coop. Coop Thorson.

He tipped his hat to her and laughed nervously.

-You're crazy, aren't you.

And so.. Eartha picked up a young drifter that knew how to handle himself in a dicey situation. As far as she could tell, his only weapon was a knife tucked in his belt and he didn't have much else. As they drove into town, she explained bits and pieces of the job. They stopped at Bertrand's Mercantile where Coop coveted just about everything he saw except for Bertrand's wife.

They stopped at the bank to pick up cash and make introductions to Claus Jordan.

-Hello, Claus. Just want you to meet my new hand, Coop Thorson. He'll be helping me out at Big Spruce and we'll open an account for him now. I know you'll all treat him with courtesy.

Claus shook hands with Coop but kept his eyes on Eartha as if he thought a spider would leap from her. As they stepped back out onto the boardwalk, Coop took her arm.

-Listen, I don't know what the hell is going on around here but you sure do have an effect on people. And what's with this bank account biz? I don't have one. Never needed one. Cash is king, lady.

-You have an account now with money in it. We'll call it an advance. You'll like it once you get the hang of it. That way, all you do is hand little slips of paper and get what you want. I saw you eyeing the merchandise over at Bertrand's. You haven't had anything new for a long time. Let's go across the street and you can meet Albert.

He was my first friend here in Lionshead. You're my friend now. We are friends, right?

Coop looked at her in fascination. How could she.. in one breath.. be so tough and then so childish?

Albert Hedeman sat at his desk.. head bent over a paper.. studying it with a looking glass. He jumped to his feet, knocking over the chair as he saw Eartha. Dashing around the desk he grasped one of her hands with both of his.

-How are you, Eartha? Looks like you're coming along okay. Feeling alright? Sit down. I haven't seen you for so long.

She answered his questions until he became aware of Coop standing behind her. Albert straightened his vest and extended his hand.

-Albert meet Coop. He'll be out at Big Spruce now. There's so much work to do. I really need him.

Stepping back, Albert looked Coop over from head to toe, took in the worn, dusty clothes and boots. Once again, he tugged on his vest, looking Coop in the eye with a bit of a threat.

-This is a nice woman here. I just want you to know that. You'll play straight with her or answer to me.

Good Lord, Eartha thought. Why does he talk like that? It's going to get him hurt. But Coop had taken no insult. Albert Hedeman couldn't mash a rain-soaked butterfly but he had character and guts.

On the way to Big Spruce, Eartha fervently explained her plans and told Coop about the Tytanos family. As they turned onto the fork where the rivers met, Eartha became quiet as she looked over at the house that was being built. It was going well and looked to be almost complete. She hadn't met these people yet and asked Coop to stop the wagon for a moment. They watched the activity.. a man and woman working like ants. They stopped and waved at the wagon and Eartha waved back.

-You know these folks, Eartha? Do you want to pull in there and talk to them?

-No, but I'm sure I will when the time comes. Here's the deal, Coop, you'll keep your eyes and ears open. I'll expect you to be at the bridge at nightfall with a fire that I can see and that gun we just bought. I've got an extra rifle or two at the cabin and will get you one. You and Theo will share shifts. But one or both of you must always be there after sunset. Do you understand? You can shoot, right? How did you get that scar under your eye?

-Who's Theo? How'd you get that scar by your mouth?

-Okay.. I guess we should keep some secrets. When we get to Big Spruce, you can meet Theo and his family. You'll stay in a tent until we can get your cabin built.

-Cabin? I ain't stayin long enough to build a cabin.

-If you can't commit two years get out now.

Coop jumped from the carriage and looked at her with defiance.

-I've already been jerked around a lot, lady. Won't take any more of that kind of treatment. Won't take it. You treat me fair and I'll do the same with you. That's all I can offer. I could commit to you.. if that's what it takes to

56

get a job.. but don't take it too seriously. If you're not happy with those terms, you can watch the back end of my horse as I leave. Yea, I can shoot.

She studied him, silently, for a long minute. He had an honest and open face. His eyes held no deceit and his laugh came easy. And she trusted him. He stood slapping his hand with the bridle reins.. looking off over her shoulder with obvious indignation.

-Okay, okay. No need to get riled up. I know I'm piling a lot on you right now but I need another good hand out here. The deal continues. It pays big and all you do is watch that bridge. As you can see.. I'm producing and their safety is all I care about. Unless you're an idiot, you'll get bored right away. Ride, rope.. practice shooting. It's all the stuff you wanted to do when you were a little kid. Whatever. Don't bring an overnight woman around unless you've got a ring on her finger. No careless screwing allowed. If you see or hear anything that doesn't seem right.. I want to know. I believe you understand what I mean. I don't care if a cat shits in the pond. If it doesn't seem right.. let me know.

Grinning, he tied his horse and climbed back in, slapping the reins.

-You've got a foul mouth, lady.

-Yes, I do at times. But I only use that kind of language for emphasis.

-You said, their safety. If you don't mind my being bold, how do you know there's more than one?

-Some things you just know, Coop. Some things you just know. And thanks for not asking the obvious.

-What's the obvious?

-Where's your husband?

EIGHT

THE LEAVES TURNED

… crimson and gold, lighting the valley with multi-layers of color. Winds blew colder, turning the same leaves brown and brittle, unable to cling to the branches. It was January and snow fell until it drifted around the cabins and froze the river. Livestock had been butchered and root vegetables were stored in cellars. Dairy cows sheltered in the barn that had been filled with hay. Wool was traded and sold at Bertrand's. Extra hands were hired during the fall for harvest. Big Spruce was profiting. Trout had been pickled or smoked and sealed jars lined walls along with smoked elk and venison. The Scots, Angus and Lara McCleod, had settled into their cabin adding the pleasant addition of fiddle music.

Shortly after arriving in the valley, Eartha had discovered a natural hot spring a quarter-mile up river. It became a soothing respite from the cold and a rock ledge with steps had been designed for easy access. The location was secluded and it was unanimously agreed that bathing nude would be acceptable in most circumstances. However, during those instances, a red flag must be hung fifty feet down the trail to avoid any unseemly blunders.

Time and again, Eartha had warned Madlyn that when she went into labor, she wanted to go to the hot spring and deliver the babies into the warm water. Madlyn had heard rumors about this type of birth but made it clear to Eartha that she had no experience and.. wanted no experience.

-Eartha, why don't you just have them in the security of your home? Not out there like some wolf.

-One will die if they're not both born in the water. I know it.

-You are superstitious! You need a witch or something to help you. Not me.

Nevertheless, deep into the hostile night of January fourteenth, Madlyn and Theo were awakened by a light tap on the door. Eartha stood wrapped in a blanket with a hand on her belly and pain on her face. She doubled over and stepped back into the snow as the water burst from her body and ran down her bare legs, into her boots. Theo held her up, looking fearfully at Madlyn. He knew what Eartha's plan was.

-You cannot make it to the spring. I will take you back to your cabin and we will help you there. Madlyn, go and get Lara McCleod.

-No.. listen to what I say. It's got to be the spring. The warm water will help. I know one will die if I don't do this. Please help me to the spring.

Madlyn had gone for Coop. They carried, pushed and pulled Eartha the quarter mile in the freezing night air.. stumbling and sliding in the snow.. cursing at the absurd misery of the situation. At times, Eartha tried to stand but could only double over in pain, whimper, breathe deeply and take a few steps. She was covered with only a blanket and boots.

At one point, Coop firmly tried to mutiny.

-It's not too late to turn back. In this weather, you'll be delivering two snowballs.. not babies. Listen to me, Eartha. We'll end up burying all three of you out here. We can get you back in time. Don't be so damned stubborn.

The trail seemed to lead into eternity until the pool finally misted in front of them. Eartha handed the blanket to Coop. Her legs were shaking and despite the cold, strands of hair stuck to the sweat on her face. He put his hand under her chin, looking at her with pity.

-Did you want to wear those boots in there?

Miserable hours passed while the men stomped their feet, tucking their hands beneath their armpits for warmth. They shook their heads and watched their breath travel to the skies. Trillions of stars looked down upon this joyful and torturous moment in the life of Eartha Borne. The pain intensified until she didn't think she could bear any more and her last scream reverberated across the valley and against the cliffs. The first was a girl. She wriggled out effortlessly and gasped her first breath with an enthusiastic cry. Madlyn quickly tied off the cord, cut it and wrapped her tightly in a blanket, calling for Theo to take the child. He backed away and stood with Coop, both shielding the child from the winter wind. Snow had started to fall and Eartha felt the tiny flakes melting on her feverish face. She waited.

Nothing happened. No movement.

-Mrs. Eartha, are you so sure there is another baby?

Eartha's breath rushed out of her lungs as she pushed. She focused on the water.

-Yes.. *yes*. He's in there. I've felt two lives all these months. Madlyn, listen. You have to reach in with one hand. You will feel him. If the head is not the first thing, you must turn it around until the head is there. And then gently pull. Gently. I'll push at the same time.

-I can't do that! Don't ask me to do that!

-I will kill you if you don't help me with this. Get Coop over here. He's delivered foals that were in trouble.

She gasped between breaths and her face turned white. Madlyn called to Coop and Eartha looked up at him standing by the pool.

- Help me, Coop. Please.

Coop waded into the water and pulled a baby boy out of Eartha. As he wrapped the infant, he peered at it's tiny moonlit features. Horror spread across his face as he whispered sadly to Eartha..

-He's still. He's stillborn.

Eartha stared with disbelief at his stricken face. With effort she pulled herself out of the water, blood and afterbirth running down her legs and grabbed the baby from his hands. Kneeling in the snow, she cupped the face of the baby in her hand and breathed over its mouth and nose. Nothing. She pulled mucus from his mouth and nose and breathed again. She shook the baby gently then grabbed a handful of snow and rubbed the little face. Madlyn knelt by her.

-Stop! The baby's dead. Don't do this. He is dead.

She tried to take the baby from Eartha but was pushed violently back. Eartha's face had gone wild.

-Come back! You *will* come back.

She breathed into thc little face again and a cry cut through the frozen night. Alive.. he was alive. Eartha held the child to her chest, sobbing as she looked to the heavens.

She knelt, crying endless tears, clutching the child to her.

-Ethan.. Isabelle. They are born. They are named.

NINE

WITH THE TWINS

...came the beginning of a peaceful, prosperous time for Big Spruce and the years passed. The schoolhouse was built and soon a teacher lived in the cabin next to it. Families grew and others arrived. The word had spread that life at Big Spruce was good, secure and reliable. People stopped by, requesting to be taken into the small community. But Eartha was firm. Mathematical balance was her rule of thumb. New people would not be allowed in unless someone or some family left. If a death occurred, only a single would be interviewed. When a child was born within Big Spruce, the acceptable number rose. It was based on Eartha Logic. Therefore, the population of Big Spruce did eventually grow. The formula made sense to her and she defended it against the advice of others. Anyone settling into Big Spruce would be interviewed and vetted by Eartha. The theory appeared to be working. After all, she was the major share-holder.. no matter what.

Ethan and Isabelle became toddlers and recklessly mobile.. suffering minor injuries and illnesses.. nothing that could not be bandaged, stitched or cured. As Eartha watched her precious children play by the porch, she realized that Big Spruce would need a doctor.

Even though an additional citizen would push the "population formula" into imbalance, an exception would be made for a doctor. Eartha asked Benno to hitch up the wagon and called to her children. They had never been in Lionshead and were starting to ask about the possibility. Now was the time.

-Would you like to go to town?!

They'd heard the word "town" enough times to know that it was something they wanted to do.

-Yes! Town!

Holding hands, they jumped up and down with bliss. Eartha and her children, dressed in their best, went to town accompanied by Mame.. the teacher and Coop.. the drifter.

At Hotel Ma Campbell they posted a notice for a doctor. Full-time with all the benefits of Big Spruce. Ma Campbell fussed and inspected the children, winning them over with blue-ribbon lemonade. They paraded to the newspaper office to post an ad for and to have a telegram sent to various communities.

Eartha and her children visited the shops and businesses, chatting with those she had come to know.. somewhat. For years, she had been very elusive about the details of her life. However, it was time that she brought the twins in.

-Hello, Ms. Estes. These are my children, Ethan and Isabelle.

-Hello, Mr. Howard. These are my children, Isabelle and Ethan.

The twins would put their little hands out to shake, "How do, Sir". "How do, Ma'am".

Eartha made certain they were well-dressed and well-mannered. Even so, some people would look over their shoulders with confusion and gossip behind their hands. Why had she waited this long to bring them into town? Why did these children not bear any resemblance to each other?

And it was a fact. Ethan and Isabelle were total opposites. They didn't look as if they could possibly be born from the same woman. Ethan was tall and dark with straight black hair.. like a native. Green eyes like his mother and very quick mentally and physically. He was difficult to fool, even at an early age. Isabelle was blonde and delicate with blue eyes lit with innocence. She accepted every comment as the truth, never suspecting or recognizing deceit. Consequently, her feelings could be hurt quite easily. Eartha had endeavored to protect her children from the outside world and she had done a powerful job.

***

Time ticked as Ethan grew to love planting and nurturing every manner of flowering vine, bush or tree. Eartha sought and ordered many varieties for his vast garden. He delivered countless bouquets to the cabins of Big Spruce, gaining smiles and curtsies from the women and girls. Ethan was stout and strong by the time he was thirteen.. riding, branding, hunting. But his heart belonged to growing flowering plants. When the snows came, he would separate, label and store his seeds, occasionally selling some to the town people.

Isabelle's passion was horses and she eagerly spent most of her days tending them. She would ride the acres of Big Spruce, always with a couple of pups at heel. She loved animals and couldn't bear to see one suffer or be abused in any way. During branding or slaughtering season, she would hide in the woods until it was over. Isabelle gently loved every living creature with a heart as soft as down.

The twins had asked many times about their father. Where was he buried? How did he die? Why'd they come here in the first place? What did he look like? Why did they look so different from each other? Eartha filled in the blanks and eventually, they were satisfied and quit asking. At times, she almost believed the story herself. A pile of rocks in the woods clearing made a temporary marker for her dead "husband", Willis Borne. In truth, he was still buried out by the barn with his wife.

In addition to being twins, Ethan and Isabelle became great (and only) friends, discussing their worlds of flowers and horses. Countless hours passed as they talked of their hopes and dreams. Neither of them could conceive of a life outside of Big Spruce. They loved each other and Eartha above all others.

An afternoon came when Eartha was sitting on her porch admiring the garden in front of her. Ethan had planted right up to the steps and the colors and fragrances were beyond anything she had ever known. Columbines, roses, peonies, daisies, vines with little berries.. her son could grow them all. The area was alive with hummingbirds, bees and butterflies. Truly paradise. Ethan knelt in the dirt pulling out some trespassing weed. A rag was wrapped around his head to divert the sweat. He occasionally looked up at his mother, smiling or making a comment. Isabelle rode up to the cabin with her pups, jumping down to hug Eartha. She walked over to Ethan and listened intently as he praised a plant.. both of them on their knees with heads together.. laughing. They looked up at Eartha just as a ray of sun illuminated their faces.

Eartha's heart skipped a beat with peace and happiness. It had all been worth it. She never thought it possible. If she could just live this moment forever.. she would die happy.

But she didn't plan on dying anytime soon.

As the twins grew older, Eartha secretly started watching for suitable mates for them. Of course, she never mentioned this. They had grown thus far understanding the law of Big Spruce and had never questioned the harmony of it. During their trips to Lionshead, Eartha would make mental notes on possible future pairings. The twins loved going into town to socialize on the expansive veranda of the Ma Campbell Hotel. Sometimes sipping on a complimentary lemonade, they would listen to gossip from a nearby table, grinning at each other in confusion.

One sultry afternoon, Ethan watched as Coop worked with a horse. Saddling it over and over, Coop mumbled to the animal until it became complacent. Dust rose around him in whirls as he wiped his sleeve across his brow.

-Coop, what does bastard mean?

Coop looked over and studied Ethan as he perched on the fence rail.

-Why do you ask?

-Heard it in town. Whats it mean?

-It means a person born out of marriage or maybe.. doesn't know who his dad is.

-I don't really know who my dad was. Am I one of those bastards?

-Your dad is buried up on the hill. Willis Borne. You've seen the spot. He and your mom were married. That's different.

Ethan seemed satisfied with the answer but looked vacantly across the field. Coop thought he felt a cold wind on his neck and pulled at his collar. He looked up at the sunny sky. No chance of a storm.

Coop had remained single over the years and seemed very content. However, he was known to stay overnight in town, now and then, leaving Theo on guard. Questions were never asked and he offered no explanation. He had witnessed enough relationships go south and didn't wish to experience a painful one of his own.

Eartha had never explained the facts of life to her children and hoped that raising livestock would educate them somewhat. She took the easy way out. When the time seemed right, Eartha sent Ethan to Theo since he was a married man. She wove the sorry tale of mating and its consequences to Isabelle who looked stunned and bolted out the door. Later, Eartha tried to revive the conversation with more tact, but Isabelle would not discuss it.

Of course, the twins discussed the situation with each other.. scared and confused..

because they had already done this forbidden and serious thing.

With each other.

TEN

THE REVELATION

… came during that wonderful time of year.. not quite the end of summer.. not quite the beginning of fall. The sun had a different feel and the air a new smell. Autumn was Eartha's favorite time and she hoped that the snow would be late. She had not spent enough time with Isabelle these last couple of weeks and wondered how the girl could be so elusive. At the barn, she made small talk with Benno, watching his powerful arms as he pounded the anvil with the hammer. Eartha was fascinated with his skill in transforming a piece of iron into something useful and, many times, beautiful. One day, she would ask him to make a marker for the grave of little Jasmine Roubideaux that she had buried up in the clearing. At that moment, she turned to look back at the cabin and saw Ethan and Isabelle slide off a horse.

Timing is everything.

Ethan caught Isabelle and hugged her, as Eartha had seen them do many times. She began to turn back to Benno but hesitated, feeling a shadow cross her mind. Turning slowly.. she saw it. A tiny rounding of Isabelle's belly.. so imperceptible. A look between them. Eartha saw it. Saw the way Ethan's kiss lingered on Isabelle's lips.

The grip of hell closed around Eartha's heart. She knew.

Evening crawled past as she went through the motions of living. But it was as if she were in a trance. It was obvious to Ethan and Isabelle that something was terribly wrong. Eartha went to the porch and sat watching.. listening.. waiting for a voice to tell her what to do.. and remained there throughout the stars.. moon.. sunrise. In the pink dawn, she walked over the bridge to the door of the Tytanos cabin. She talked with Theo as the morning light grew and then turned back. Theo stood staring after her. Sadly, he walked to the livery and hitched the mares to the buckboard.

**

The twins were rising early, as always, to get back into their individual beds. Isabelle came tiptoeing into the main room and saw Eartha standing in the dim light in front of the window.
-Isabelle, go tell your brother to gather everything he holds dear. You, too. Pack everything you can carry. Theo is waiting outside in the wagon. You have thirty minutes. You will never come back here. Never. If you do.. I will kill you.

By now, they were both standing in the door shaking.. disbelief on their stricken faces.

-But why?

-Beware of that child in your womb, Isabelle.

The blood drained from her face as Eartha went out and sat on the porch. The twins looked at each other with tears streaming down their cheeks and started to gather things in a daze. Soon after, they came out and Theo helped them pile their bags in the buckboard. He helped Isabelle into the wagon without looking at her face. Ethan stumbled over to Eartha and sank to his knees.

-Please don't make us go. Please. We can undo it. We can undo it.

She would not look at him and went into the cabin, closing the door. As the wagon rumbled up the drive and crossed the bridge, Eartha stumbled to the back garden and crumpled to the dirt. A whimper came from her throat like that of a dying animal. She lay in the wet grass among Ethan's flowers crying every tear that she would ever have. She clawed the damp earth until her nails broke. Clouds crossed the sky toward evening. Thunder and lightning cracked in the air, but she neither heard nor felt it. At dawn the next morning she rose, went into the lonely cabin, bathed, changed and walked to the livery. She sat on the dirt floor watching Benno pound on the metal until it darkened outside. He didn't utter a word.. nor did she.

ELEVEN

THE TRAIN

... took Ethan and Isabelle to Salt Lake City and that's where they settled. The Mormon community happily accepted the young couple and did not pry into their identity. As nature will have it, Isabelle delivered twin boys.. Axel and Jubal. And fifteen months later, another son.. Samuel. They all had the same father, of course.. Ethan.

Axel and Jubal were robust and healthy babies. They were mirror images of each other.. bright red hair.. pale blue eyes and quick minds. Samuel, however, was burdened cruelly by the inner confusion and outward deformity of tangled genes.

The heart and soul of Eartha began a slow journey of healing. Gradually, she began to take interest in Big Spruce and its people. Dark times had come and she spent many days in bed staring at the wall. Theo told Coop that she was dying of a broken heart. Only Theo, Madlyn and Coop knew where the twins had gone. Everyone else was told that they had been sent to college in the East. As the years passed, questions were fewer. But Eartha thought of them every minute of every day. Until the days turned into years.

***

Eartha was hanging laundry when Coop rode up to the cabin. He had spent the night in Lionshead, and had stopped in to look around Bertrand's. He stepped down from his horse, proudly displaying a bolt of cloth.

-How's this look, Eartha? Kinda pretty?

She casually eyed the print. Dark blue with little white flowers. Subdued and proper.

-I think you'll look adorable in that Coop.

-There's a strange thing going on in town, Eartha. Two kids got off the train alone and are asking about Big Spruce.

Eartha stopped hanging clothes for just a second, then looked at Coop shading her eyes from the sun.

- Boys?

-Yep. Two of them. They came in on the train and have been staying at the hotel by themselves. They've got their own money, apparently. Well dressed. They've been asking people what they know about Big Spruce.. and you. It's firing up some gossip in town. Ma Campbell is trying to keep a lid on it but two little redheads. Difficult.

-Alone? How old are they?

-They say they're just about ten. But it's hard to tell. They're such little wise asses. Cute little guys.. freckle faced. They're twins. Crazy, huh? Conductor had instructions to take them to the hotel and paid Ma Campbell to keep an eye on them until they found you.

No return address. Like somebody just shipped em off. Sounds familiar, don't it?.

The comment felt like a punch in the gut but she had it coming. Eartha sat on the steps and Coop knew he was in for a heart to heart. The big pine loomed over them as they watched for a few early stars.

-Coop, do you think they knew what they were doing?

-Ethan and Isabelle? Yep. But, they didn't realize how forbidden it was.

-I waited too long to tell them about sex. Was I wrong?

-Yep.

They sat through the evening discussing issues of Big Spruce.. both thinking about the two kids in town.

The next morning, Eartha went straight into Bertrand's Mercantile. She was roaming around.. taking her time when Wilma Bertrand slithered over to her.

-Well, well, look who's here. Do you know there's a couple of little orphans asking about you? They came in here and bought some candy.. asking a bunch of questions. About Big Spruce and you. They seem awfully wise for their age. Long lost relatives of yours?

She was thankfully interrupted by a scuffle at the door where the twins stood, roughly shoving each other. They stared at Eartha with great interest as if she were an insect under a microscope. After whispering to each other, they stepped forward.

-Excuse us, lady. Are you Eartha? Eartha Borne?

-Yes.

-From Big Spruce?

-Correct.

-Why, we're your grandsons! Axel and Jubal. We've come to stay with you. There's another brother, too.. Samuel. But he'll never get to come. He's not right. Ma has to take care of him all the time or he'll just roam off. She put us on the train to here and told us to ask for you. Here we are. Your kin. We want to go to Big Spruce.

-What about your dad?

-He's dead.

Eartha felt a stab of pain in her chest.

-How?

-We don't know for sure, but ma said he was cleaning his gun and it went off.

She felt the world shift with the old feeling of new grief. Eartha gripped the table and whispered a lost prayer.

-We've got our own money. You can have all of it.

As proof, they pulled money from their pockets and offered it to her.

-Put that back. Do you have anything with you? Clothes?

-Some. But not what we want. All we've got is city clothes. We want to dress like that guy Coop. We talked to him yesterday and knew he'd tell you about us. Help us pick stuff out. Hats. Chaps. Ropes. Guns. We've seen pictures.

They roamed around the store under the sweaty gaze of Wilma who had been eavesdropping. Eartha realized she had to get the twins quieted down and out the door. Two more at Big Spruce. Things would be off-balance now. She had no idea.

-Okay, okay. Stack up what you want but no more chatter right now. And no, you can't have guns. Maybe later.. like another twenty years. Didn't you tell me that's how your father died? Why would you want one?

-Ma said that what happened to pa wasn't anybody's fault. So.. we don't hold guns accountable.

They spent the next hour getting "outfitted" and moved a few little bags out of the hotel. Ma Campbell pulled Eartha into the kitchen.

-Who are they, Eartha? I've tried to get information out of them but they are tight lipped. All they wanted to know was how to find you. They were put on the train in Salt Lake City. They've got plenty of money. What's the story?

The boys were grinning and tussling with each other in the wagon, spilling over with loud excitement. The sight filled Eartha with hope.. something she hadn't felt for a long time. Maybe she was getting another chance. Just one more chance. Later, as they crossed the bridge at Big Spruce, Coop was in the round-pen and the twins tumbled out of the wagon to observe. It was early afternoon and he was guiding a horse through some basic lessons. He stopped and came to the fence to get another look at Axel and Jubal. There was no way to tell them apart. Every feature perfectly mirrored. He took his hat off and looked at Eartha. The twins copied his movement.

-I didn't think you would do it. In *your* mind.. how do you justify two more people? Nobody's left since McLeods came in. The formula is off, lady.

Eartha looked squarely back at him.

-They want to be ranch hands with all the trimmings.. and you're in charge.

-They staying in your cabin?

-Yep. Looks like we'll have to add on.

Coop looked at the boys who were watching his every move. Once again, he pulled his collar up as if he felt a chill. The gesture had become a habit when things didn't feel right. A reaction to his sixth sense. He looked down at the boys and they grinned back at him, pulling their collars up.. mimicking him. They were sure cute, Coop thought.

Cute like wolf pups.

TWELVE

COOP ACCEPTED

... his duty to train the boys in the skills of riding, roping and branding.. every aspect of back breaking ranch work. As time rolled, they became top hands. The three of them spent hours each day together.. Coop assuming the roles of part-time father, brother and friend. Eartha would often ride along. She loved the boys and could see no likeness to their parents. Only her. There was no doubt that they resembled her. Freckles and a wide smile. She studied them, constantly watching for a sign that would reflect the circumstances of their conception. There was no indication that they were inbred. Not in their eyes.. or reasoning.. or actions. They were intelligent and physically sound. Eartha had convinced herself that the bad blood wasn't there.

***

Another school teacher was hired.. Mame Rose. The pursuit of innocent happiness was her main aspiration in life and she spread the rule freely among her few students. Of course, the curriculum also included reading (funny books) writing (scary stories) and numbers (how many worms in a shovel of dirt?). Mame was just plain fun and Big Spruce came to love her. She wasn't a particularly beautiful woman.. light brown hair.. gray eyes.. a gap in her front teeth. It was her spirit that encouraged folks to search beyond everyday life for a moment of laughter.. a little bit of joy. Coop found excuses to improve the schoolhouse. Mame made him biscuits and smothered them in honey. Mame taught him to meditate.. Mame pointed out the difference between pink and fuschia.. Mame learned to fish, only to release the catch out of pity. Mame taught him to giggle until foam drizzled from his mouth. Life was good. Mame Rose was a masterpiece and he loved her. However, things were getting touchy and Coop vowed to do the right thing.

He rode into Lionshead and bought the best ring they had.. a simple gold band. He thought that he would buy her a diamond someday.. one that sparkled like her soul.

***

Eartha dressed up and piled her hair haphazardly on her head. The twins donned their best attire. Black hats.. polished boots.. ties. Completely overdone. Eartha had told them that there would be a special announcement but did not tell them what it would be. They looked so handsome and she was proud of them. Axel and Jubal.. her flesh and blood.

The bell was rung and the engagement announced. Theo and Madlyn with their daughters, Lexy and Mery. Coop and Mame. Benno. Angus and Lara McCleod. The newly hired Doc Briar. Big Spruce had grown. Eartha was ecstatic. There was finally some order in her universe.

-Thank you all for coming. Even though we live around each other every day, we don't take much time to just socialize. Well, we are going to plan a party. A big one. You can invite people from town. I know some of you have friends there. Well, here it is. Coop and Mame are getting married. She looked at Mame with genuine affection.

-I'm so happy. You're like a daughter to me, Mame.

Clapping and laughter.. pats and hugs. It was wonderful news.. a sign of life and love at Big Spruce. Eartha looked at the twins and could clearly see that they were not pleased with the news. They were standing still.. not smiling. A coin that Axel had been tossing fell out of his hand and hit the dirt with a tiny cloud of dust. They were both focusing on Mame as if they were watching an intruder in the den. Eartha tore her eyes from them and continued.

-There's more. Coop and Mame will be the first couple to get married here at Big Spruce. We're building a church. A fine church. And we'll finagle a preacher to live out here. It's the least I can do. Even though the count is off, some rules are made for breaking.

The small gathering voiced their pleasure since many of them had been making the trip into Lionshead to attend religious services. This was the frosting on the cake.

-Start the planning! An engagement party and then the wedding a month later. Coop and Mame, tell me what you would like to do. You know I love you both very much. I feel like I have a real family now.

A little overbearing? Yes. Eartha looked at Mame and saw tears of happiness in her eyes. She looked at the smiling Coop. She looked at the twins.. Axel and Jubal.

They were looking at each other and they weren't smiling.

The months were busy with the building of a simple church.. white with a steeple and bell. It nestled into the woods at the foot of the mountain. Ham was smoked and beef laid up in the ice-houses, chickens plucked, pies and cakes baked. Fiddles were tuned and played. The night of the party came and folks drove out from town. They were curious and pleasantly surprised by the life at Big Spruce. More than a few took Eartha aside and discreetly asked to be put on the "list".

A stranger wearing a starched white collar stood aside, patiently waiting to speak to Eartha. He stepped toward her when she stood alone.

-May I have a moment of your time? I would like to apply for the position of pastor here. The church is adequate and I could build a cabin near it.. as would be expected. I assure you, I am qualified. Quite possibly.. over-qualified.

He looked at her confidently and grinned, obviously entertained by his remarks. A real con.

-I haven't seen you around town, but I don't go in very often. You certainly don't seem like a religious man, despite your costume. Tell me the shortest story possible about your calling and commitment to the gospel.

Eartha could con a con.

-My mission started many years past in the east. I could supply you with a list of parishes, but it is lengthy. There might be a few blank spans in the resume, but nothing serious. However, you don't seem like the type that would get hung up on little details.

Eartha's eyes darkened as she detected a lilt in his voice. There was a southern drawl somewhere in there, despite his attempt to hide it. His skin was tan and weathered. Frost blue eyes regarded her calmly as if he were reading her mind. As if on cue, he smiled a smile that would fool Satan.. but not Eartha.

-Your lying. Pastor.. my ass. You're hiding from the law.. I can smell it on you. You're from the south, too. Where?

He looked at her and laughed as he chewed a bit of straw.

-I can see that we're going to get right to the nitty-gritty. Yep, I'm on the run.. one way or the other. From Baton Rouge. I suppose the law is looking along with a few others. I owe money to some gentlemen down there and thought it best to come discover the West. I heard in town that you might need some spiritual guidance. Well, here I am. I'd say it was a match made in Heaven.

Eartha's eyes focused on a glint of silver beneath the collar and she unwisely reached to touch it. He quickly caught her hand, squeezing just enough to warn her.

-What's that?

She immediately regretted the question and action.

-My, my, but you are curious, aren't you? A noticeable flaw in your personality.. a possible weakness. If you must know.. it's a locket. But don't touch and no.. I'm not showing you what's in it.

-Seems a little sentimental for a man like you. What's in it? A face? A bit of hair? Or did you just steal it off somebody.

-It was my mother's. There's not another one like it.

He had dropped his attitude and lost the charming smile. Eartha sensed that the conversation was nearing an end.

-You're perfect for the job and hired. But understand this.. I'm not a religious woman so don't try any gibberish on me. You're obviously a master of bullshit. What's your name?

-Lud. Lud Cadey.

-Alright, Mr. Cadey.. what I need is another gun guarding me and that bridge. I have a feeling you fit the bill. You're welcome to play preacher to your heart's desire but keeping me alive is what you'll be paid for. This isn't the time or place to iron out the details, so stay in the barn tonight and we'll talk tomorrow. Help yourself to the party.

-What am I guarding you against? If you don't mind.

-I do mind. It's a long story and not one that I care to share with you.

Within the month *Pastor* Cadey built a modest cabin near the church.. also in the pines. Lud endeared himself to his neighbors with a quick wit and sympathetic ear. He also offered good and sensible advice. Big Spruce accepted him and every Sunday the little church was almost full. His sermons were surprisingly authentic and heartfelt.. almost as if he had lived them. A few town people came out to hear him which Eartha did not like. For a man on the run, it didn't seem to bother him too much. He thrived on attention and as time went by, became adept at weaving a good religious experience.

***

Eartha sat at her table going over feed bills when a rap sounded on her door. She opened it to see Mery Tytanos. Her thick black braids rested on her shoulders and her beautiful brown eyes were open wide. She stood shyly in the doorway staring at Eartha.

-Mery! Hello.. come in.

Eartha pulled out another chair.

-I'm not much of a baker, but I do have some root beer in the ice-box. Would you like some?

Mery nodded and smiled timidly, putting one foot inside the door, twisting at the hem of her cotton dress. She had grown into a beautiful, but painfully shy young woman.

Her sister, Lexy had married and moved into town, much to the dismay of Theo and Madlyn.

-Come, sit down and we'll chat. I hardly ever get to see you anymore. Would you rather go out on the porch, where we can watch the river?

They sat listening to and identifying bird chirps for a few moments.. Eartha in her chair and Mery on a stool, sipping on her drink with ladylike manners. Silence. Mery brushed delicately at an imaginary bug on her dress. Eartha knew she had something to say and tried to encourage her.

-I understand that you've been helping Mame at the school.

-Yes, Ma'am. But we need more students. The McCleod girls from down the valley are fun to be around and I love Mame.

-Do you see much of your sister now that she's moved into town.

-Yes.. but I miss her. Her husband didn't want to live out here.

-That's his loss, isn't it?

They laughed together.

-What do you think of the church? And what about that preacher?

That was it. Her eyes darted up to Eartha. She didn't answer.

-I know something is eating at you, Mery. You might as well tell me.

Just a moment of silence followed.

-He scares me.

-Why is that?

-He goes up into the woods and shoots a gun. He's very good. He never misses. What kind of preacher does that? I saw him blast a chipmunk on a stump.. just for practice. He's heartless.

Her eyes filled with tears. Eartha's nerves started to tingle.

-That must have been an accident. I'm sure he feels terrible.

-No. He never misses.

They sat watching the river until Mery saw her mother come out on the porch, waving to her. She rose..

-Now listen, Mery. Don't worry about Cadey. He would never hurt you. Learning how to defend yourself with a gun is sometimes just a job out here. Like riding and roping. Your own father is one of the best shots I've ever seen. It's a skill that's sometimes needed. If he'd killed a snake, would you feel the same?

Mery laughed.

-No, I guess not.

***

Eartha found Lud digging vigorously in his garden.

-Hello there, Eartha. To what do I owe this pleasure?

-Shooting chipmunks, Lud? It makes you look like the psycho that you really are. Talk gets around and then you'll be out of a job.

-You must know it was an accident.

THIRTEEN

THE DAY

… of the wedding, Big Spruce was in high spirits. There was cooking, baking.. lanterns filled and hung. This was the first big occasion that was planned on the place. Lara McCleod baked, built and frosted the wedding cake, carefully storing it in her ice-house. It was a three-tiered amazement.. yellow with blue and pink flowers.

The night was beautiful and Eartha opened her windows to hear the musicians that had been hired from town. Dancing around the cabin, she relished the swish of her dark blue silk dress. She normally wore men's trousers and hat around Big Spruce. It felt good to dress like a woman. She looked at her reflection in a long mirror.. admitting that she still had it. Twirling around to admire herself, she caught the reflection of Lud leaning against the bedroom door.

He was watching her with amusement and something else. It threw her off balance and she grabbed the back of a chair.

-What the hell are you doing in here, Lud?

-Thought you might like an escort to the party.. wedding, that is.

-Are you crazy? Do not confuse a job guarding me as social interaction.

Eartha watched his cold eyes narrow slightly. He took a step toward her and she took one back. Mistake.. now he thinks I'm afraid of him. She walked passed him roughly brushing her arm against his. He let her pass. Eartha turned looking at him, her green eyes glinting with anger.

-Don't you ever come in here again or you're gone. You're only here for an extra gun and to be a fake preacher. I'm starting to think you're not worth it.

-Oh, I'm worth it, Eartha.

He made her sick.

-Mrs. Borne to you.

-Yeah? What *about* that husband of yours? What's the story there? Did ya kill him? Is he really buried under that pile of rocks up on the hill? I don't think so. You're from the south, too.. aren't you.

It was a statement.. not a question. Eartha wanted to lunge across the room, dig her nails into his eyes and rip them out. She had worked hard to hide her southern accent, but he had detected it. At that moment, she hated herself for not kicking him off the place.. but she was afraid to. He was a killer and she needed him. She turned to go out the door and looked back.

-Don't steal anything while I'm gone.

Lud laughed and sat down putting his spurred boot on her table. He struck a match and slowly smoked a cigarette. When he finished, he stamped it out on her floor and strutted out to join the festivities.

Coop and Mame had asked Father O'Riley from town to officiate the ceremony.. no offense to Preacher Cadey..

they did want him to say a few words. Mame had come to know and trust Father O'Riley and.. there was just something about Lud Cadey. Eartha had already informed Lud that there wasn't a snowball's chance for his preaching at this wedding. But Lud got his words in during the ceremony and they were impressive.

-I'm honored to mention the glow of magic in the air tonight. Matrimony is a holy bond between a man and woman that will last for all eternity.. beyond the sun and stars into that heavenly home that we're all headed for. I believe that Big Spruce is patterned after that beautiful place.

What the hell is he doing, Eartha sizzled.. as he wove his speech like a spider, watching the guests.. charming them like a snake. Lud had a way with words and was excelling tonight.

-Oh! I have a gift for the bride.. a keepsake to remember this perfect day in her life.

He pulled a black velvet box from his pocket and handed it to Mame. Her shaking fingers pulled the pink ribbon off and she opened it as Lud smiled sweetly. A locket.. a silver locket. Her hand went to her mouth.. her eyes misted.. along with the eyes of every woman present. Coop smiled and put his arm around her.. shaking Lud's hand.

-Thank you, Mr. Cadey. Thank you. So very thoughtful.

Lud's smile widened as he glanced at Eartha.

-Open it. It's a locket.

They did and found tiny portraits of themselves painted in the metal. Mame was delighted.. Coop was dumfounded.

-How did you do this?

-God is my guidance in all things. It's my gift for you. Coop, I do believe that Mame will be your greatest asset in life.. and you hers.

Eartha wanted to puke. She knew from that moment that no one would be requesting Father O'Riley again. Lud had conned the entire gathering.

The dining and merriment continued as lanterns hung from the pines and in the barn. Fiddle music echoed from the cliffs as the twins had a merry time dancing with town girls. They were certainly behaving well, displaying manners that Eartha had painstakingly instilled in them.

At the end of the evening, Eartha stood on the dance floor that had been built for the occasion and tapped on her goblet with a spoon. The crowd hushed to hear what she would say. Of course, she realized that she would never be able to top Lud.

-Coop and Mame.. I also have a gift for you.

From the back of the livery, Benno led two fine, matched horses harnessed to a beautiful red and black buggy.. polished and gleaming. Eartha stepped down from the platform.

-This is for you. I hope you spend many happy hours in it.

-Oh, Eartha. It's beautiful. You shouldn't have done this. I can't wait to learn how to drive it.

Mame was elated and climbed in before Coop could help her. She ripped her lace wedding gown on a piece of hardware and frowned, but her joy was not easily killed. She giggled and lifted the locket to her lips.. kissing it. Eartha couldn't help but look jealously at Lud who smiled back at her and winked. Mame continued..

-This is the happiest day of my life. Does ripping your wedding gown bring bad luck?

Benno stepped forward and fingered the rough spot on the carriage that had snagged the lace.

- Ya! I can fix this easy. But I cannot fix that lace.

He grinned and everyone laughed goodheartedly at his innocence.

***

The weeks passed and the newlyweds settled into the life they had planned. Coop taught Mame how to drive the carriage and they did, indeed, spend many happy hours in it. Mame had started creating fashionable bonnets and was proud that they were selling well in Bertrand's Mercantile. Life was good. She became skilled at driving the carriage and finally convinced Coop that she could go into town by herself and run errands.. although he never really felt comfortable about it. The horses were well mannered and gentle. She loved going into Lionshead and would frequently pick up things for others that didn't wish to make the trip.. just for an excuse to go. During every trip, she would stop on the narrow bridge that crossed the ravine and listen to the rushing water below. The sound always made her feel at peace and she was ceremonious about taking a few minutes to give thanks for her happiness.

***

Eartha settled in her bed and stretched her toes. She loved this place.. Big Spruce.. despite its heartaches and secrets. She drifted into a nightmare from the past and woke in a sweat. Pulling on a robe, she walked out to the porch. There was a tiny light in the back of the barn and she assumed that Benno was working late. He was such a gentle and good man. She thought she would go down and keep him company for a bit.

But she didn't.

Instead, she walked back inside and poured a drink. Sleep would come easier now. The nightmares did not come as often.. maybe, someday, they would completely stop.

The lantern in the livery glowed dimly as Axel worked on his adjustments. Benno had gone to bed hours before and slept as only the innocent can. Years of pounding iron had left him partially deaf and he was undisturbed as Axel readjusted the wheels of Mame's carriage. When he was satisfied, he extinguished the light and slipped back in darkness to the cabin that he shared with Jubal.

-Where've you been, Axel? It's almost morning. Did you go into Lionshead?

-Nope. Just walking around. Taking stock. This will all be ours someday, you know.

-Axel, you're nuts. Just like our dad. Just like Samuel. What are you talking about?

-Eartha had children but threw them out. We're *it*. We're the next of kin. Did you hear what she said the night of the wedding? She said Mame was like her daughter. That's not right. Our mother is her daughter. That's not right.

Jubal sat up and lit the lantern.

-Don't mess this up for us, Axel. Life is good here. Do not do anything we'll regret.

Axel laughed and stared at the ceiling.. until morning came.

FOURTEEN

WITH THE FIRST RAY

... of sun, Mame danced to the livery and asked Benno to harness the horses. She was headed for Lionshead.

-Alone?

-Yes, Benno.. alone. Don't worry. You know I can handle it. I need more material for bonnets. I'll make you one. What color?

Benno waved to her as she looked back at the giant and she lightly smacked the horses with the reins. He shook his head smiling as he walked into the coolness of the livery, wiping his hands on his leather apron. Once more the comforting pound of the anvil echoed through the morning mist of the mountains.

Mame was living the best time of her life. She loved Coop and couldn't wait to tell him the news tonight. A baby was coming. She wanted to buy something in town to make it special. The road seemed rougher than usual, probably a result of the recent rain. The carriage wobbled briefly causing her to climb down to inspect the wheels. They looked fine. Benno could check them later at Big Spruce.

Stopping on the narrow bridge, Mame closed her eyes.. giving thanks. The water roared beneath her.. the sun warmed her face. It only took a moment.

One moment in time.

A sudden shift of the carriage opened her eyes in alarm. Another jolt and the carriage collapsed violently to the left shattering the wheel spokes. The sudden impact of weight splintered the bridge handrail, as the horses reared back in panic. Mame was flung to the bottom of the ravine, landing in wild rose bushes that lined the rushing water. Her back snapped with agonizing pain as she stared up at the dangling mass.. one horse struggling to regain its footing. The carriage and horse hurtled down the ravine, smashing into Mame's already broken body. The other animal pathetically hobbled along the bridge in pain. Mame died watching the bonnets she had crafted slowly bob down the creek. Her last thought was of the unborn child that Coop would never know.

A man hauling logs found her and shot the broken animal that writhed on the lifeless body. The other horse stood shaking on the bridge, a gash down the length of his chest. There was no doubt that Mame was dead but her fingers moved in the ripple as if they had not noticed.

Lud was sweeping the church steps as the rider from town rode into Big Spruce. He had run his horse into a froth and was clearly exhausted as he stumbled forward.

-Mr. Cadey! Something terrible has happened. Terrible. She's dead. Oh, God. She was in the carriage and was crushed. You've got to hurry. It was Mame. They're down there now trying to pull her out. You got to come now.

Lud ran the short distance between the church and Theo's. Eartha was helping Madlyn do some canning. She stood as Lud strode up the incline but dropped a jar when she saw his face. It was unnaturally white and he stared at the ground, taking big steps. Coop came running over from the livery and they met at the bridge. Lud hadn't taken time to put his boots on.

-There's been an accident. On the Lionshead road.

Coop stared at him in disbelief, his mouth open. Panicking, he looked from one to the other as the hideous thought started to root in his mind.

-Where's Mame? Where's the carriage?

He stepped farther out calling her name. He turned.. staring at them with desperation.

-She didn't take that carriage into town, did she? She didn't tell me.

He started back for the barn but Lud took his arm.. searching for words. Coop jerked away, ran to the barn and bridled a horse. He raced away without another word.

-Eartha, the man said that Mame is dead. No doubt. Madlyn, hurry and get the doc. Tell him to bring some shots of tranquilizer. For horses.. hurry now.

They loaded in the buckboard and jolted out of Big Spruce. At the bridge, Coop had already scrambled down the ravine, falling and tearing at the thorny bushes. Some townsmen tried to hold him back, but he pushed through, falling on his knees. He tried to pull Mame from the carriage. Clawing and screaming like a tortured animal, he pulled at her limp and broken body. Lud jumped from the moving buckboard and shoved Doc's syringes into his pocket. He scrambled to the bottom of the ravine, and pumped the contents of one into Coop's shoulder. Coop looked at him with pain-crazed eyes and slowly sank to the ground.

The hours passed as the recovery of Mame began. Horses and ropes were used to pull the carriage up and a blanket was quickly draped over her body. They took her to Ma Campbell's and laid her in a prepared room. No one could think straight. They had all loved Mame. How could this happen? It was a new carriage. The bridge was strong. What happened? Had something spooked the horses? Had she stopped on the bridge? Why?

***

Axel and Jubal were waiting on Ma Campbell's porch in silence. As the sun set, Eartha walked the mile to the bridge with Lud and Theo in an attempt to clear their heads. As they stood looking down into the ravine, a man that had been moving bits and pieces of the wreckage stopped.. picking at something lodged in the dirt. He kicked at it and then jumped back as if he'd been stung.

-It's a skull! There's somebody else down here! Geez!

Eartha watched with tear-swollen eyes as he gingerly picked up the crumbling skull of Jon Wilson. The crook she had shot years ago.

***

Axel and Jubal sat on the steps of the hotel with hats in hand. There was enough commotion out at the bridge. Axel stood and stretched his arms, looking down at Jubal.

-I'm going to walk around a little, Jubal. I won't be long. Stay here and wait for Eartha.

He walked to the back of the hotel and up the steps into the room where Mame rested. It was empty, except for the body. Candles were placed on a nearby table. Axel walked over to the bed and hesitated for a moment. He pulled the blanket back and looked at Mame's broken face with morbid curiosity. He turned her battered face toward him.. and then he saw it.. twisted and hidden in her hair. The silver locket that Lud Cadey had given her on the wedding day. Axel smiled as he reached down and ripped it violently from her.

He shoved it into his pocket and left the room unnoticed.

FIFTEEN

THE DAYS PASSED

… with grief and confusion as the final arrangements for Mame were planned. She was buried in the clearing above the cabins. Coop couldn't decide about a marker but Benno began laboring each night to make something suitable to mark her grave. He was not a Christian and so couldn't decide what to forge. After endless hours of work, he had created a duplicate pattern of her wedding gown lace.. out of iron.

Coop was crazy with grief. Walking into to the livery stable, he confronted Benno.

-You did it. You were the last one to see her. You should have taken better care of her carriage. It's your fault.

He lunged at the powerful man. Benno picked him up easily and threw him across the ground.

-No.. you are crazy now. I will not have you say that.

Coop sank to his knees and cried tears that landed in the dust, each making a tiny hole in the powder. The big blacksmith put his arms around the sobbing man.

-My friend, this will never make sense. You will never find the answer and so you cry until you can't anymore.

***

Lionshead was in an uproar over Mame and the skull. The sheriff rode out a few times to question everyone about both situations. Finally, Eartha told him to stop coming. It would be impossible to grieve Mame properly with the constant reminder of the skull.

The twins had gotten into the habit of walking out to the hot springs very late at night after everyone else had returned to their cabins. One evening, leaning back to look at the stars, Jubal asked Axel..

-You didn't do something to Mame's carriage.. did you?

Axel looked over at him in the moonlight.

-Are you kiddin me, brother? Are you kiddin me? You know damned well I did and you knew it the night I did it. Loosened her wheel hub. She liked to race that thing just before the bridge at Lionshead. I just didn't plan on the edge of the bridge breaking off. That was a bonus.

-Why, Axel? What was the point? That poor little woman never hurt anybody.

-Revenge. Revenge for mom and dad. Eartha loved Mame. She said like "her own daughter". And I'm not finished. Eartha is next. And then this place will be ours. You feel the same way.. you just can't do the blood work.

But Axel was really thinking.. when I get rid of Eartha.. *and you..* Jubal. This place will be mine.

***

When the next full moon appeared, Axel asked his brother to join him at the hot spring. This was the night. He was going to kill Jubal.

-It's late. No one will bother us, Jubal. My shoulders are aching from working those horses today. Let's go.

-Sounds good. You go ahead, Axel. I'll be right behind you. I want to get this fly tied and try it out in the morning. I won't be long.

Jubal realized that Axel would never stop weaving his distorted web. There would be one "accident" after another if he was not stopped. He opened a chest at the end of his bed, chose an item and headed out for the pool.

Axel lay back looking at the stars, planning how he would handle things once Eartha and Jubal were gone. He hated that bitch and was sick of looking like someone else. No matter how old he and Jubal were, people would comment..

-Aren't they cute? Twins!

-You two look just alike! Can't believe it.

-Oh, let me touch that hair.

Strangers, especially women, would playfully jerk their hats off to rumple the copper hair. It was supposed to be good luck since they were twins. Well, Axel, thought.. that was about to come to an end. He would soon be the only one.

He heard a slight movement behind him.

-Jubal? What took you so long?

No answer. He whirled around in the water just as Jubal brought the claw side of a hammer down on his head. One powerful hit and Axel sunk into the pool, blood bubbling from his wound.

Jubal stood watching the water turn red. It had been a mighty blow and his brother's skull was split. He walked to the river and hurled the hammer into the deepest spot. The moon reflected a glint of silver as the tool sunk in the ripples. Without emotion Jubal stood watching.. making sure that Axel was dead. The water continued to darken as Jubal returned to his horse and rode away from Big Spruce.

Three days later, another body was laid in the ground of the Big Spruce Cemetery. Another bizarre accident had claimed a life. Axel must have slipped on the grass and hit his head on the side of the rock ledge. But where was Jubal? Eartha watched the road hour after hour. Nothing. She traveled to Lionshead, looked around, but asked no questions. What these townspeople didn't know wouldn't hurt her.

Questions ceased as the days and weeks passed. The day came when Eartha had the emotional strength to go into their cabin and tidy up.. to pack a few items away. As she lifted one of the mattresses, she found Mame's silver locket draped in the springs. She went numb as she realized that Coop and Mame's likenesses had been scratched out. Her mind raced. Whose bed had it been hidden under? Axel's or Jubal's? She didn't know which was which.. but she did know that one of them had killed Mame.

Coop had searched pitifully for the locket and eventually believed that it had been carried away by the rushing water. Eartha could never return it to him now with the desecrated images.

The answer to so many mysteries had disappeared with Jubal.

SIXTEEN

THE CHAIR ROCKED

… back and forth.. back and forth.. carrying Eartha with it. She was deeply depressed and wrapped in self-pity. What a mess. What was she doing here? Ruining as many lives as possible? Mame and Axel dead. Jubal gone. She should have known better than to take the twins in. Her eyes focused on a figure crossing the bridge. The familiar form of Angus McCleod twirling his cap while he whistled. He stopped and poked at something on the bridge with his cane. Eartha liked Angus and his wife, Lara. When they came to Big Spruce they said that they hoped for children. But so far, there were none. But they seemed happy with each other. Maybe happier without children. They could certainly rip your heart out.

-Well good day to ya then, Eartha.

-Hello, Angus. What a pleasure to see you today. Come.. sit down. A drink, perhaps?

-Tis only midday.

He eyed her disapprovingly from under bushy white eyebrows.

-Mrs. Eartha, I know you've had nothing but heartache these last few months and I'm sorry to come to you with this. I just do not know what else to do. Axel and Jubal are gone now.. God bless their souls.. both of them.

107

Well.. their cabin now sits empty and it's a good sized one. I could sure add onto it.. at my expense, of course. My brother, Gregory and his wife, Grace, would like to come out here.

-Don't they have a bunch of kids?

-Yes, I'm proud to say four. All girls. Ruby who's five, Opal who's seven, Pearl who's nine, Crystal who's..

-Eleven.

-How did ya know?

-Just a wild guess. Can't do it. It would throw everything here out of alignment.

Eartha stood, hoping that Angus would take the hint. He sat on the steps, looking gloomily at her.

-I know and I wouldn't ask, except.. they're in a bad fix.

She sat back down, realizing escape would not come that easily.

-Well, ma'am, they work hard raising fine crops. Lettuce, cauliflower, carrots.. they even have planted some apple trees that are doing fine. There's nothing they do not grow or cannot grow. Even flowers. Herbs and medicinals. Some town folk are doing business with them now. There's nothing that my brother, Gregory, can't grow and mix. They've built a big ice-house for cool storage.

-It sounds like they're thriving, Angus. I know where they live.. good location.. lots of sun.. right near the river. Near the train tracks. Didn't they just sort of squat on that land?

-Not really, ma'am. There was a man hired to transfer title papers to them some years ago. He said since they were immigrants that it would work out better for them if he handled the paperwork. But he disappeared with their money and the title to the property. Albert Hedeman in town couldn't find no record of who owns it.. but they paid that man. They built a home there anyway and have made a good life for themselves.

Eartha knew exactly where the property was. Right at the fork of the rivers. With Hedeman's assistance.. she had acquired the deed.

-Why do they want to leave it, Angus?

-A couple of months back some riders came out. The Jackso brothers from town. Real trash. Told my brother they had to pay rent and a share of the crops. Cash and crops. They said they worked for the railroad and the railroad owned that land. But then we found out that the Jackso boys go in and sell the crops to the townsfolk at a discounted price. They come out with two big buckboards every week and load up what they want and then ask for $10 per buckboard to haul their crops off. Gregory tried to stand up to them, but they butted him in the head with a rifle. In front of the girls and Grace. If Gregory tries to fight.. well.. he's afraid he will get killed or they'll kick them all off the place. Then one of those brothers looked at Crystal, the oldest, and said something about her almost being old enough to pay rent. Gregory tried to jerk him off the horse but got another whack in the head. He's in a hurtin way now. Mind you, he's no coward.. but he's got a family. There's protection in numbers out here and you do have at least three good guns. At least. The girls are feeling very creepy about the Jacksos, ma'am.

The hair on the back of Eartha's neck rose as a memory oozed into her brain.

-How many are there?

-Five and rotten. Sometimes they stay in that shack down by the river.. just above where the cliffs narrow. They're trying to charge Gregory to pump his own water to the crops. He built that system!

-He can pump water out of the river for his crops?

-Yes, ma'am.. he devised the technique in Scotland. Thinks maybe he can sell it someday.

Eartha sat back looking up and down what she could see of Big Spruce. It was a big job to water crops. Even though the river ran through the valley, they had to haul water or divert it from snowmelt into ditches. When the mountains had snow, the ditches had water.. but when the snow disappeared, so did the water. There had been many a drought year. They raised all the livestock they could, but there were never enough crops.

-Did they complain to the sheriff in town?

-He said it's none of his business.. that it's out of his jurisdiction. Plus, they're related to his wife. I think the Jacksos give him quite a lot for his dinner table to stay out of it. People are hungry for fresh fruits and vegetables and will turn the other way to get them cheap. Most of those townspeople don't like the immigrants and probably get a kick out of this deal. Hardly anyone in town has an ice-house. Lots are too small. Gregory has run out of cash. All he's got is his talent for growing and four wee lasses. Mrs. Eartha..

He lowered his voice.

-One day Grace and the girls were in town and that fella that owns the bar.. Kyle Pukeard.. he came out and told her in front of some folks that when the girls were a few years older, they could work in his bar. Well, Gregory went in right away and cornered Pukeard but it wasn't a fair fight. Gregory got held by the Jacksos while Pukeard punched him. Beat him up bad. I'm afraid he'll be goin back in there and they'll kill him.

-Go get your brother and his family and bring them out. I'd like to talk to him about his pump system anyway, and they'll be safe here tonight. They can still work their crops until we get this figured out. I'll send Theo and the Pyrenees down to guard them during the day and they can stay out here at night. Just temporary.

When Angus left, Eartha walked over to the church to find Lud whittling on soap and smoking a pipe.

-Why Eartha.. how have I earned this visit?

He looked her up and down in that belligerent way that he had perfected and she detested.

-Get Coop and Theo. We have a situation down the road. Why do you waste soap like that when we're surrounded by trees?

They met on Eartha's porch for the better part of two hours discussing "the situation" and possible remedies. The truth was, the McCleods were being bullied by a bunch of two-bit thugs.

The family soon pulled up in the yard.

-Gregory and Grace, come in. The girls can go over to the Tytanos cabin for a bit. This will probably take a while, so you all had better stay out here tonight.

The problem of the Jacksos was cussed and discussed by lamplight. At one point, Lud stood, stretching

-Here's the deal as I see it. Bad guys.. good family.. money to be made. Fear and loathing. Gregory, why haven't you gone in to see who owns that land? If the railroad owns it, you haven't a pot to piss in. But if they don't.. who does?

Eartha looked at Lud wondering who the hell he thought he was, but fearing his train of thought.

-Cadey, I've put everything we've ever had into that place. We paid for that land.. cash. It was stupid to trust him.. we know that now. But there wasn't much choice. That man was hired to go to Lionshead and record it. We had to trust him or lose everything.

-What man?

-His name was Wilson. He disappeared years ago.. so it seems like nobody owns the land now. He bought it from the prior family that lived in that dugout down by the river.. where the Jacksos shack up some nights. I'm an immigrant and don't want to risk my family being sent back to Scotland.. or a workhouse somewhere. We've been there for so many years that I thought the danger was over.

Eartha went to the cupboard and pulled out a bottle along with a few unmatched glasses. She poured herself a shot and drank it, feeling the warmth soothe her aching shoulders. As she did, she glanced over at Lud who watched her with a smirk.

Angus looked at her with disapproval. Lud reached over, poured a drink and slowly sipped as he looked over at her. He narrowed his eyes.. viewing her through slits.

She struggled not to react.

-Tell me about this pump system of yours.

Gregory unrolled a set of drawings and flattened them on the table. Leaning forward with interest, the group studied the designs as Gregory tried to explain. No one seemed to completely understand the mechanics. Eartha tossed a paper back onto the table.

-I don't understand these.. but you do. And it works?

-It does indeed! All you do is build a series of pools that feed each other and increase with depth and pressure. Our place has a natural bottleneck with the canyon. We even have water pumped into the house.

-Could you put some pumps on Big Spruce? Ten or so?

-Sure, I could. But the materials cost. Iron and nails. Do you have a good blacksmith?

-I do and I'll tell you what, Gregory.. you and your family move here until we get this Jackso business straightened out. I'll pay for the materials and some wages if you build the pumps. You can all stay here and

113

teach us about crop production. There's a double cabin about fifty yards over and you can build on it if you need more room. As for that land of yours.. it sounds like we need to build a couple more dams. It'll take some time but next spring when high water comes we'll be ready. In the meantime, let's go reason with the Jacksos.

At dawn, the Jacksos were disturbed by the sound of a buckboard pulling up in front of the shack. They stumbled out, one by one, in filthy long johns, scratching their crotches and shading their hungover eyes from the rising sun.

Eartha sat in the carriage with Coop, holding a shotgun. Lud rode behind, heavily decorated with hardware, including two six-shooters and a rifle.

-Good morning, gentlemen. I'm Mrs. Borne and I have a little business deal to make with you.

-Yeah? What would that be Mrs. Borne?

-We work for the railroad and this is their property. We're hired by the railroad.

Kip Jackso looked around at his brothers, laughing and spit on the wagon wheel. Eartha put her hand up as Lud started around the buckboard, but he ignored it. When the Jacksos focused on his face, they backed up just a little. Lud kept coming.

-How'd you like to suck that back into your mouth?

Eartha felt a tiny sting of affection. She proceeded.

-You don't work for the railroad but I do. Let's start over. I know you're stealing from the family that lives here and abusing them. The railroad doesn't really care but they don't like unpleasant attention. They're planning a project for this property and need hands. Money's to be made, boys. Top dollar. We can use you.

-What for and how much money? The railroad you say? You say you really work for the railroad?

-Yes, Mr. Jackso. The railroad wants to build a series of small dams from this point up.. starting about three miles from here. A sequence of five. Each one a little deeper than the previous one until the last one will hold about thirty feet of water. Built up with pressure and accumulated volume. Don't worry about the little details. Oh, by the way.. how many of you are there?

-Five.

-Well, then it's meant to be. Your lucky number is five. The railroad will supply the manpower. All you need to do is enforce.

-Enforce what?

-The work will not be interrupted and the Scots will come back to raise their crops. Unharmed. No one goes near them. It's the railroad's crop now and they don't want to share it with you.

-You're lying.

-Am I? Why don't you spend a couple of months finding out what I'm telling you now? By that time, we'll have hired somebody smarter and will have started without you.

Eartha flipped a gold piece at the boot of Kip Jackso. He looked down in astonishment, picked it up and grinned at her. The sight of his rotten teeth turned her stomach.

-That's how the railroad pays for this kind of job, Mr. Jackso. In gold. You and your brothers. Now if I were you, I'd keep my mouth shut about this. Money making opportunities don't come along very often.. not in this country. But I can let the powers that be know that you boys are already here and experienced. And they pay for that kind of talent.

Kip licked his lips and scratched his butt as he looked back at his brothers.

-That's a down payment and you'll get the rest when the dams are finished. If you want to whine about the delayed payment.. let me know now.. so I can start looking for a different crew.

-Wait a minute. Aren't you that goofy gal that's got a place up the river?

-Goofy gal? Well, yes.. I suppose you could say that.. but it doesn't mean I can't have a sideline. So, let's have a simple agreement, boys. You ride your horses around and make sure no one hurts the Scots and let them get back to their business. Understand? Don't be talking to them.. don't even look at them. If you want some of their crops, you go in and buy them in town like everybody else. This is railroad policy. Strict. You stay out here in the shack until the dams are built. Policy.

Kip eyed Eartha as he flipped the coin. He'd never seen or felt the coolness of a gold coin and it felt good. He looked quickly around at his dimwitted brothers and spat again on the ground. But this time, not near the wagon.

Gregory McCleod and his family rode back to his farm, the Jackso boys sat on guard at the shack and Eartha hired a crew from Denver to start on the dams.

Benno and Gregory forged pumps and installed them on Big Spruce. Each pond was equipped with a release valve that could move water to the next one below it. By first snow, they had completed the system. They had all jokingly started to refer to Gregory's place as the Scot's

Depot and the name stuck. Unfortunately, the Jackso brothers had a rough winter in the shack by the river and complained continuously. At night, they hovered around their fire like prehistorics, chewing on jerky. Filth covered them but it just wasn't warm enough.

***

As Eartha rode down to survey the situation in the early spring, Kip approached the wagon. She could smell him at ten feet.

-Don't come any closer, Jackso. You stink.

-You would too if you only had a freezing cold river to take a bath in, pretty lady.

-Don't get familiar.

-Okay, okay. When do we get paid? The dams are finished. The damned Scots are safe and rich. Get it? Damned Scots?

She didn't laugh. He shrugged his shoulders and spit some tobacco.

-When do we get paid?

The dams were filling with spring flow and she studied the lowest one. It was full. Water was moving out of the release valve with force. They were armed with water and harnessed power.

-Well, Jackso, it looks like tomorrow will be the big day for you. Pay day. I'll ride out early and see to it personally. You and your brothers will get what you have coming.

-Gold?

-Yes, gold. Maybe a little bonus in silver. As gold and silver as the sun and moon shining on that water.

-That's kinda like a poem, ain't it? You got some learnin, don't ya. Got any more jobs for us? We don't mind if things get rough and we don't mind hurtin.. or even killin folks that get in our way. Kind of like it. Anything that moves or crawls. For a price, we'll do just about anything.

He looked at her slyly.

-Maybe since I got a little money now, you and me can have a drink together sometime, Eartha.

She looked down at him in complete silence for so long that he started to shuffle around and looked down at his boots. There was something in those feline green eyes.

Something that didn't feel quite.. right.

-You and your brothers get a good night's rest because tomorrow you'll be headed for a different position. Stay here one more night. I'm not sure what time I'll be here with your pay.

The Jackso brothers proceeded to celebrate and carry on into the night, passing out one by one.. three staying by the dying fire.. two stumbling into the shack to roll up in dirty blankets. At midnight, the river rose and hands began to open release valves. Fifteen feet of raging water spilled toward the fragile structure and its sleeping occupants. The flood grew in depth and force as it hit the narrow split in the rocks just below the shack. The last thing Kip Jackso saw was the silver of the remaining moon and the gold of the new sunrise. Poetic.

As the moon set, the water ebbed and joined the froth of the tiny canyon. Eartha slopped through the remainder, peering into the cabin. One of the brothers lay face down wedged in the corner. She bent to turn him over when the doorway was darkened by a shadow. As she whirled around, she lost balance and fell in the muck. Lud stood blocking the light.

-It'll look better if you leave him be, Eartha. More like Death arranged them to his liking. You're not that creative. I've seen your cabin.

He laughed and waded closer to her, offering his hand. She refused it, looking around for a weapon. Her fingers

119

closed on a floating stick. Lud moved forward, jerked her up and pushed her against the wall. She could feel his breath on her neck but would not look at him. Lud moved his hand to gently push a string of wet hair from her face.

-Drop the stick. But don't worry, your charms are not that tempting. I could snap your neck and make it look like you drowned here along with the Jacksos. You do fascinate me, but what I really wonder when I look at you is..

Where's the money?

She felt as if an electric shock had run through her and struggled to hit him. He knew. The bastard knew. Lud moved his leg behind her, jerking her off balance. Once again, she fell into water. He backed away, laughed and turned. He stopped in the doorway with his back to her.

-Listen, Eartha. Don't get any ideas about ridding yourself of me. I'm here and there's nothing you can do. Can't go to the law. Better not tell Coop or Theo.. if you care at all about them. And listen, darlin, you couldn't kill me in your best moment. Although I do admit you have a knack for it.

He turned, mounted his horse and rode up the creek without looking back. Eartha stood gasping for breath.. face burning.. looking down at the body of one of the Jacksos. The ego of that bastard! As if she wouldn't shoot him in the back? She gathered her strength, walked out of the shack and looked down the creek. Snagged on a low hanging limb, another body bobbed in the current. Well, she had to admit, cocking her head as she studied the grisly site.. Death could be artistic.

Eartha rode into Lionshead to notify the sheriff, who came out, looked the situation over and declared it a terrible thing that those boys drowned. Patting his round stomach, he looked toward the steep, narrow canyon.

-Another spring flood I guess. Don't ya think, Eartha? Dams kinda got full too fast. Tragic. Musta been quite a shock finding this. Well, don't know about you, but I'm hungry. Hope the wife is fryin something up. Shame. She might take this hard. Related, you know. At least we got two bodies to bury.

His part-time deputy looked at him..

-Aren't we going to search for the other three? To see if they're even alive?

The sheriff looked at him and laughed.

-Down there? Are you kiddin? If any lived.. they can crawl out on their own. Nobody goes down there. Hopefully, they'll get hung up and rot away. Just don't fish downstream of the canyon for a bit.

Eartha rode home alone and dismounted with shaking legs. She limped to the livery, slid behind the door and peered over at the church. The light of a cigarette glowed on the steps. He was sitting there watching her. Keep a cool head, Eartha.. Do not let him see you panic. She lit a lamp, stood straight and unsaddled her horse. Patting his jaw calmly, she fed him a treat. "You're a good horse,

Samson". She turned, walked up to her cabin, shut the door and leaned against it.

What was she going to do now?

SEVENTEEN

TWO WEEKS LATER

... a delivery came to Big Spruce. A large buckboard loaded with cases of wine. Very fine wine. Collect on delivery and addressed to Eartha Borne. Over three thousand dollars. Eartha protested to the driver that there had been a mistake.. maybe one of the bars in town, although she knew they didn't stock anything but rotgut.. or Hotel Ma Campbell?

-No, ma'am. It says right here.. deliver to Eartha Borne.. outside of Lionshead.. at a place known as Big Spruce. That's what that sign over there says. Big Spruce.

-Well, who the hell sent it?

-Let's see.. it's from New Orleans, ma'am! New Orleans! All the way out here. Don't that beat all. Somebody's got some cash. Oh, excuse me. I guess that would be you.

Eartha felt the blood drain to her feet as Lud came bouncing joyfully down the church steps. He placed his hands on his chest and beamed at her.

-Ahhh! The delivery. He hoisted a case down, pulled a board off, gleefully grabbed a bottle and read the label.

-Madeira. *Perfect.*

He pulled a small knife from his boot and expertly twisted the cork from the seal. He sniffed at it.

-Orange peel and tangerine.. with just a hint of dried honey.

As he took a gulp, the red liquid drizzled down his chin. Fine wine dripped to the dust. With the devil in his eye, he extended the bottle toward her. She glared at him as he lifted another case of wine and placed it beside the driver.

-This is for you. A tip.

-Thank you, sir! The missus will sure be tickled with this. I've never really tried wine before, but I'll bet this is a good one! How about payment for this load now? I've got a schedule to keep.

Lud looked at Eartha and she looked back with pure hatred in her eyes. It was from New Orleans. She knew what he was doing.

-You'll have to take a note to the bank in Lionshead. I don't have that kind of money around here.

She looked pointedly at Lud.

-If I have to go back into Lionshead, it'll be extra.

Eartha turned, walked into her cabin and wrote out a banknote for over three thousand dollars. She couldn't play this game with Lud. He knew what he was doing and this was just the beginning. She had to get rid of him. The wine shipment was a threat and there would be more until he bled her dry. When she reappeared, Lud and the driver were unloading the wagon.. Lud joking pleasantly with his hat pushed back on his head. Even when he laughed, he looked lethal.

-Listen, my friend, we can just stack these behind the church. I'm planning a party soon and this will be a real treat for the residents of Big Spruce. The most perfect place on earth.

He grinned at Eartha.

-And, since we're moving it around.. let's put a case up there on the lady's porch. I know how much she likes her wine in the evening. And what about that other item that was ordered? You have a little fancy package to go with this shipment?

-Oh yeah.. dang, it smells good, too! What's in it?

The driver put his nose to the package and took a deep breath, rolling his eyes.

-Just a little something for an exceptional woman. *Exceptional.*

***

That evening, Eartha sat looking at the case of wine that had been placed by her table. Lud had congenially opened the crate and sarcastically bowed before he left. The smaller package rested on her table but she had not touched it. Curiosity was making her finger tips itch. Well, why not? She opened the package expecting a box full of bugs, but found to her delight a dozen French soaps, each wrapped in pink tissue. The good stuff.. creamy and fragrant. She threw it at the wall in total disbelief.. soap clattering on the floor. Plopping down on the chair, she stared at the pillowy packages. That conniving man knew exactly how to get to her. Time ticked. It was late and she felt like hell. Her bones ached and she was chilled from wading around in the water watching the Jackso brothers bob around like apples. What the hell. Lud would never know. She changed into a robe, dropped a bar of soap in the pocket and tied her hair up. She pulled on some boots, grabbed a bottle of wine and headed for the hot springs.

She walked the quarter mile trail in the moonlight breathing in the aroma of the woods. She loved being out in the night.. always had. She felt safe and unseen.. a creature at comfort in the shadowland. When she came to the pool, she dropped her robe and carefully stepped down into the warm water. It was heaven. She pulled the cork from the wine and smelled it. She unwrapped the soap and held it to her nose until her head ached.

Eartha sighed with bliss and immersed her head under the water. She lathered the soap in her hand and began to wash her hair, but stopped suddenly. Had she heard something in the woods? A quiet laugh? She reached for the pistol laying on top of her robe and listened very closely holding her breath. Just a night creature. After being still for several minutes, she relaxed. Nothing. She had the jitters. The air was cold and the water felt like a soft warm blanket wrapped around her.

A half bottle of wine later, the jag took possession. She thought about her life.. cried and talked to herself.. sobbing. Smelled the soap. Felt sorry for herself some more.. cursed Satan and attempted to thank God. But she never felt sincere about it.

Give thanks for what?

Lud knelt in the brush with a clear view of the pool and watched her as she bathed, cried and laughed. She talked to the moon as if it were an intimate and trusted friend. He had not intended to follow her but had the same intention of soaking in the pool. When he realized that Eartha was there, he stepped off and sat within twenty feet of her, planning to eventually reveal himself and make her feel foolish.. or at least scare the hell out of her. He changed his mind as the minutes piled into moonlit confessions. Lud thought he knew all about this woman, but as he watched her and listened.. the doubt grew. He started to regret the job he had been sent to do. He caught the faint fragrance of the soap. The muscles of his thigh became stiff from kneeling so still. He longed to get into the pool and hold her head under the water to get it over with. But then he would know nothing. He was sent out here to find her and the money. One way or the other.. he would finish this.

Eartha rose from the water into the cool night air, wrapping her hair and body with the hooded robe. She carefully stepped into her boots and headed home.

Lud followed her feeling more like a protector than the man that was going to kill her.

EIGHTEEN

LIL DAISY STRANDS

... rode into Lionshead on her mule with a dog running behind. She was weary as she entered the mercantile to ask for guidance. Wilma Snibe looked up from polishing a silver tea set as the doorbell jingled. Greasy strands of hair fell across her eyes as they narrowed. The store had been quiet today and Wilma spent her time thinking of gossip she could spread.. especially about that rotten witch that lived out at Big Spruce.. Eartha Borne. However, Wilma's mind went mercifully blank as she looked at the newcomer. She was a giant in every respect. Tall and wide.. pale blond hair.. nearly colorless eyes that looked back blankly at Wilma. Her hair was intricately braided in a thick design that hung over her shoulder. She was dressed in a dusty cotton dress, a stained cowhide vest and muddy boots that didn't match. She shuffled around fingering the goods with her grimy hands and glanced at Wilma.

-Can I help you? Please do not touch anything unless you plan on buying. In other words, don't touch anything.

The woman stopped and looked dully at Wilma.. who now felt a hint of wariness in the empty store.

- Not here to buy nothin. Just need directions, ma'am. Then I'll git.

However, she did reach over to the candy jar and pull out a penny sucker. After smelling it, she jabbed it into her mouth.. staring at Wilma with empty eyes.

-That'll be a penny.

-What for?

-That sucker you just put in your mouth.

The creature looked at Wilma, pulled the sucker out of her mouth and put it back into the jar.

-Well.. I'll be! You can't just put that sucker back in there.

The woman retrieved the sucker and put it back in her mouth. Wilma looked hopefully around the store to see if anyone was there for backup. Bertrand had gone to the bank.. there was no one. This stranger could send Wilma flying with one slap of her massive hands.

-Okay.. What do you want to know? Directions? To where?

-I want to find a gal that my pa left up somewhere around here. Up on a place called Gore Creek. Pa said she was perty and freckle faced. I wanna find her. Ain't got nowhere else to go. You know somebody like her? Her name's Gal. Pa said she was the toughest gal he ever saw. Said she had reddish hair.. but dark. Like a storm was passin through it.

-On Gore Creek, you say? There's only one settlement up there. Big Spruce. You must be confused. How long ago was it when your pa left her there?

-Years. It was afore I was born. Some years past.

Wilma's mind began to crank. Could she possibly be talking about.. she practically spit the name out..

-*Eartha Borne*!?

-No.. her name was Gal. She had a dead sister with her. She packed her around in a bag and pa said it was a stinkin thing. I weren't born yet when he left her out there. Said she mighta starved if those folks didn't come back to their place. I'm gonna see if she starved or not.

Wilma stared astounded.

-And your name is?

-Lil Daisy. Lil Daisy Strands. My pa's name was Abe.

She wiped her hands on her dress and extended one to Wilma, who didn't touch it. She was stunned over the possible identification of Eartha Borne. Wilma absentmindedly reached over to the sucker jar and pulled a few out, handing them to Lil Daisy who looked back at her in confusion. She shrugged her shoulders and put them in her pocket except for the one that went back into her mouth.

-I got a dog.. and a mule. Want to see em?

Lil Daisy turned and covered the distance to the door in two strides. She whistled as she jerked the door open. A ragged dog trotted in.

-This here's Wouton.

The dog sat, cocking its head to look up at Wilma. He was covered in prickly salt and pepper hair that stood straight out like quills. His ears looked as if they were motheaten. Wouton's nose twitched as a low growl came from his throat. Lil Daisy looked at him with obvious

130

surprise. She jerked the sucker out of her mouth and peered at Wilma with suspicion. Reaching into her pocket, she pulled the extra suckers out and dropped them back into the jar. They were now covered with lint.

-I never seen Wouton growl like that since that crazy coon last spring. Just you. He don't like you. I guess maybe I don't either.

She snapped her fingers and strode out of the store. Wilma scurried after her, watching as Lil Daisy pulled herself up on the massive mule. Wilma couldn't let this opportunity slip through her fingers. Oh, how she could use this. If it was true, she could make a lot of trouble for Eartha Borne. She tried to delay Lil Daisy.

-Wait..wait. Show me how to braid my hair like yours. Where did you learn that? What about directions?

-I'll find her if she's out there. And my name's Lil Daisy Strands, if ya don't mind. Braidin is easy.

Lil Daisy looked at Wilma with something close to pity.

***

The sun was setting warmly on Big Spruce as Benno stood forging a piece of metal in the barn. A hatch of mayflies hovered over the river and Theo thought about a possible trout dinner. He stopped to admire the skill of the huge blacksmith. Begone's grandson, Begone, stretched by his feet, half asleep, twitching sporadically at a fly. The evening was unfolding peacefully.

-You are one of the legendary greats, Benno. You are possibly the best of all metal workers. You have the blood of Thor.. there's no denying.

Benno looked back with a grin and then straightened up quickly, looking past Theo. A giant woman sat on a mule.. not thirty feet away. She had appeared so silently that no one had noticed her. Of course, it could have been the clang of ironwork, but her presence certainly shook both men. Theo was startled.. his eyes searching for the rifle leaning against the wall. He had been hired as watchman. *The* Watchman.. and a woman, a mule and a mutt had taken him completely off guard. Even Begone II was humiliated and charged out toward Wouton. The two slammed into each other in a growling cloud of dust.

-Wouton.. back!

Lil Daisy quickly dismounted, grabbing the dog by leather strings that had been artfully braided around his neck. She moved like a bear.. the white rope of hair swinging with its weight.

Theo grabbed his dog and pulled him back into the barn. Despite her size, the visitor moved with surprising agility and speed.

An uncomfortable moment had settled in with the dust. Eartha walked out onto her porch to see what was causing the racket. Lud appeared with a half-shaved face and a towel in hand.. an unlit cigarette stuck to his lip. Lil Daisy looped a thin rope around the dog's makeshift collar and stood looking at them with childlike innocence. She focused on Eartha walking down the slope toward them. Eartha stopped several feet from her, hands on hips, a dish towel tucked into her waistband. She glanced briefly at Theo, who was looking sheepishly at the great watchdog, Begone. Benno stared at the newcomer with a strangely enchanted look.

-Nice night for a dog fight. Who are you?

-Lil Daisy Strands. This here's my dog, Wouton. He protects me sometimes. Mule is just called Mule. You must be her.

She stepped toward Eartha with a heavy foot.. extending her hand. Eartha bravely took it, half expecting to be flung into the high heavens.

-Well, Lil Daisy Strands. I'm Eartha Borne. I'm not sure what "her" you refer to but come on up to the porch and tell me what you're all about. I've got some stew and biscuits cooking. Hungry?

-Yes, ma'am. Always.

Lil Daisy devoured two plates of stew and biscuits, occasionally tossing a bit to Wouton. Finally satisfied, she wiped her mouth with a sleeve and looked at Eartha in silence.

-What brings you here, Lil Daisy?

-Just wanted to see if you were real.. alive. I heard stories from my pa. Truth is.. I don't have any other place to go.

Eartha's mind froze, but she did not show any emotion. Strands - Strands. *Strands*. Abe Strands. The old miner that she'd traveled over the Rockies with. The only person that knew the truth about her.

-I think you must be confused. I'm Eartha Borne and I came here with my husband, Willis. But years ago, we did come home from hunting and found a girl in our cabin. Maybe that's who your pa was talking about. She stayed for a few days and then left. Headed down the river. Where's your pa now?

-Dead. He died way up north. They all did. Ma, too. Just plain bad luck and a bad winter. I been travelin this way for some time. Pa told me about Gal.. that she was a survivor. It took me a while to learn that word. But he said I could be one, too.

A blank look came into her eyes as she walked out into the yard. Peering up at the clouds, she pulled a pocket watch from her skirt. After studying it for a moment, she looked at Eartha with a sweet smile on her wide face. The timepiece obviously comforted her.

-Can I see that, Lil Daisy?

The woman looked at Eartha with some doubt and then at Wouton. The mutt offered no response.

-I don't trust many with this watch, but Wouton don't seem perturbed. This was my pa's. It guided him through some harsh times.

She handed the watch to Eartha. The second hand didn't move and never had. The crystal face was cracked and for a moment, Eartha considered explaining the difference between a pocket watch and a compass.. but reconsidered. She reverently handed it back to Lil Daisy.

-You look just like pa described. Angel kisses on yer face and red hair with a storm in it.

By this time, Lud had stepped up to the porch and had heard the last comment.

-Now.. isn't that just precious? "Red hair with a storm in it". I love that. Now what were you saying about your pa? I'm Lud.

He bowed to Lil Daisy, took her grimy hand and kissed it lightly. She pulled her hand back and stared at him with shock. The hair on the back of Wouton's neck raised, but he didn't growl.

Eartha held her breath, hoping that Lil Daisy would toss Lud into oblivion. Instead, a flash of delight crossed Lil Daisy's features and she looked blushingly down at her mismatched boots.

-Don't be tryin to treat me like a lady. It's a waste of time. Folks usually stay away from me. Don't know why for sure.. just the way things is.

Lud took a step back.

-I didn't mean to make you jumpy, Lil Daisy. Is that a map?

Like a child, Lil Daisy offered the ragged map. Eartha could see that it was very like the one Abe Strands had given her many years before. Lud reached slowly over, and took the two corners, looking closely at it.

-And that's *it*? That's how you found this place? Why you're a pretty smart little lady, aren't you? Have you talked to anyone else about this?

Lil Daisy looked adoringly at Lud. Eartha dug her nails into her palms. Lil Daisy continued.

-Just that one skinny woman in Lionshead.. in that store with all the perties. Wouton didn't like her and so I don't. She got funny lookin when I told her about Gal and where my pa said she might be found. Her eyes kinda popped big and she whispered.. "Eartha Borne".. just like she'd seen a spirit or some such.

Eartha stood so quickly that she lost her balance and grabbed the back of a chair. Wilma Snibes. Her legs shook and the blood rushed to her brain. Wilma Snibes would undo her. Shit! Would there never be an end to the hunt? How long would it take for Wilma to spread some trouble for her? She reached for Lil Daisy's hand and tried to pull her to her feet.

-Listen, Lil Daisy. There's something I need to take care of, but I'm going to leave you and Wouton for a bit with people that you can trust. Not Lud. I mean it. You can stay here however long you like.. but I'm not Gal. It's just a coincidence that we look alike. She's long gone and it's best if you don't talk about her anymore.

Lil Daisy looked blank again.

-What does co-in-si-dense mean? But, Gal.. I *like* Lud.

Eartha looked at her with frustration and at Lud with evil intent.

-Coincidence means I'm not who you think I am, but let's not spend any more time worrying about it. I'm glad you're here. Now, let's go find Benno. I think you'll like him better than Lud.. and you should.

136

Benno had not taken his eyes from Eartha's cabin since the two women entered it. As they approached the barn he made busy, glancing shyly at them as they entered.

-Benno, as you now know, this is Lil Daisy. She'll be staying for a bit and so I want you to build a temporary room for her here in the barn.. with a door. Makeup something comfortable. I'll be gone for a few hours. Maybe you could take her over and introduce her to the Tytanos family.

He looked panicked, obviously afraid to be left with such a responsibility. But when he looked at Lil Daisy, he drifted into a gentle comatose state. His eyes melted and his head tipped sideways as if he were witnessing a divine miracle. Lil Daisy was looking back. Eartha watched with wonder.

Oh, my Lord.. they're smitten.

NINETEEN

WILMA SNIBE

...was watching dust delicately float amid the last rays of sun that lit the store's interior. The day had been long with very few sales. Bertrand was home with the croup and folks didn't like doing business if he was gone. Well, they could all go to hell. She stood at the top of a ladder listlessly dusting and arranging goods. Her husband, Bertrand, had installed ladder rails, enabling easy access to the highest shelves. Two tall, sturdy ladders were connected to the tracks and Wilma had positioned them side by side. She had draped linens across the steps of one, allowing her to fold and stack them without returning to the floor each time. The jingle of the door bells diverted her attention and she clutched a shelf to keep her balance. She hadn't bothered locking the ladders together and so they slid quite easily. Who would be coming in this late? Well, it didn't matter.. if they didn't want to buy something fast, she would usher them out. No time for a lookie-loo. To her surprise, Eartha Borne peeked around a display of cotton aprons and dresses.

-Good evening, Wilma. Looks like you've got some new dresses in.

Eartha reached up and touched a garment that was hanging from the beam. Wilma was taken off guard. Eartha was never pleasant to her.

-If you're here to buy something, make it fast. We're closed and Bertrand's home sick. I've gotta get home and baby him now after working here all day. But at least I *have* a husband.

She looked at Eartha with a smirk on her lips. Without responding, Eartha walked closer and rested her arm on the unoccupied ladder. It moved slightly and she reached down flipping the lock into place, noticing that the other ladder hadn't been locked either.

-I'm here to return this rope, Wilma.

The woman looked down at her, snorting a laugh. Tiny flecks of spit found their way to Eartha's forehead. She reached up and wiped it away.

-You know I'm not giving you money back for that rope, *Miss* Borne.

-It's brand new. I just bought it here a few days ago.

-I don't care if you bought it three minutes ago. You might be able to fool old Bertrand with your ways, but not me. In fact, I know a few things about you. Like you're not really Eartha Borne. It won't take me long to get to the bottom of things. I'm going to expose you for the fraud that you are and then we'll run you out of town.. "Gal".

Eartha felt the old familiar blood-lust growing in her mind and fought to control it.. just another moment or two.

-Wilma, you'd better take a deep breath and calm down before you say something that you'll regret. Or have you already done that? Let me help make your display a little more interesting. You don't have to refund me for this rope. I'll just leave it with you.

Eartha tossed the rope to the top of the ladder and climbed up until she was level with Wilma.

-I'll just put it back here with the others.

Wilma turned her back on Eartha.

-They don't go there but suit yourself. You're not getting any money back.

Eartha tossed the rope over a beam above the shelves, keeping the looped end in her hand. Wilma turned and looked back at her, comprehension dawning in her eyes. Too late. The rope was around her neck and Eartha pushed the ladder with her foot, causing Wilma to lose her balance. Eartha twisted the rope around her hands and jumped off the ladder, pulling the scrawny woman higher. Wilma clawed at her neck as the rope tightened.. her feet, searching for any foothold, kicking merchandise off the shelves. Eartha put her entire weight on the rope and managed to wrap it around a waist-high horizontal beam that was used for a saddle display. Her hands were burning and she tried to grab a cloth to wrap around them. The rope slackened just for a second and Wilma inched one hand beneath it. Eartha's fingers had gone numb, causing her to completely lose her grip. Wilma dropped to the floor gasping, as Eartha grabbed a rolling pin from a table. She crawled to Wilma, slamming it against the woman's head with all her might. Wilma's head snapped sideways and she crumbled to the floor. Eartha pulled a brightly striped Hudson Bay blanket off a table and mashed it over Wilma's face, leaning into it. The dying woman weakly tried to struggle until her airless lungs collapsed and she became still. Eartha counted to sixty before she removed the blanket from Wilma's face. She was dead. Sliding back, she surveyed the mess as her chest heaved from the exertion. How would she ever be able to get out of this? A table had been kicked over and glass jars rolled across the wooden planks.. others were broken. A dress dangled crookedly from the beam.. one lace sleeve ripped off. There would be no hiding what happened here. She returned to the body, knelt and began to pick up broken glass. Then she remembered what Lud had told her when they killed the Jackso brothers. "Never over-clean the scene."

It took less than thirty minutes to recreate the "suicide". The rope was still around Wilma's neck and with some effort, Eartha re-hung her. It appeared that Wilma changed her mind.. a little late.. and clawed at her neck. Kicked some goods off the shelves. Eartha took the keys from Wilma's belt and locked the front and back doors.. then returned them to Wilma. She replaced the rolling pin and blanket to their original setting. She squeezed through the side window and slid it shut behind her. Wilma was discovered when a midnight stroller noticed the lamps burning unusually late and peeked through the windows. Bertrand was home with the croup and.. by choice.. never came looking for Wilma.

The news turned the village of Lionshead upside down. Wilma Snibe hung herself, but apparently tried to change her mind.

TWENTY

THE HOOKS FROM KANSAS

… were loading their belongings into the wagon parked on a backstreet in Livermore. They would head west and hoped to disappear in the night without any trouble. After having successfully blackmailed several wealthy married men from the east coast to Kansas in the last year, they were always looking over their shoulders.

Ola's mother had died leaving four girls to a heartless father. He was more than eager to get rid of them. Over a period of three years, he sold them all: one to a brothel, one to a boarding house, one to a self-righteous farm family. He had done especially well with the youngest.. Ola. She was a beautiful specimen at thirteen and he traded her to "Reverend Hook" for two thousand dollars and a rifle.

Ola was shoved into the back of Hook's wagon and learned what it was like for a child to become the sick fantasy of an old bastard. Over the next three years, Ola learned the skills of the trade.. how to lure wealthy men into embarrassing positions and extort money from them. Most of Hook's past "daughters" had died or been abandoned on some dusty road with a bag in hand.. worse for the wear. Eventually, many would end up with a self-inflicted head wound or working in an alley.

Hook had perfected his identity as a holy man, and in fact, began to believe that he was called by a distorted higher power. He was convinced that he was fooling men out of their money because they were wicked and the women he used were just paying for Eve's sin. A real self-righteous con. Ola's only experience with the bible was being occasionally hit on the head with it. On their way west, she had witnessed many sermons as Hook stared into the campfire, muttering to himself. He always finished by doing something painful to Ola.

***

A mile or so before they reached Lionshead, the old man pulled the wagon to a stop. He looked Ola over.

-Get back there and pretty yourself up. I want you looking real good. I hear there's a banker in this town named Jordan.. Claus Jordan. He's our target. We're leaving here with most of his money. Now get back there and get busy.

Ola obeyed and began the ceremony of beauty. She brushed her hair and pinned it up, put just a touch of color on her cheeks, lips.. around her eyes.. barely perceptible. She was good at this. She dabbed a bit of fragrance on her shoulders.. one that she had created herself. Over the years, she had learned how to crush flowers and herbs and combine them with oil. They had sold a few bottles in various towns and Ola was inwardly proud that anyone would want to smell like her. Her eyes were big and brown and lined with heavy black lashes. She put on a pink-flowered dress that was a tiny bit low on the bodice. A tiny bit. The black ankle boots that she pulled from a trunk were delicate and high heeled. Her skirt was not quite long enough to cover the lace that peeked out from underneath. She was ready.

Hook's wagon pulled up in front of the Bank of Lionshead and drew immediate attention. He had stolen it from an old gypsy back east and painted over the bright color with brown. But the spirit of the wagon still lived in the intricate carving of the wood. Hook congratulated himself many times for having the skill to steal from a gypsy. He climbed down, adjusted his collar and donned his fine black hat. He pulled out a bag, walked around the wagon and ceremoniously offered his hand to assist Ola. Every man on the street stopped and stared. Those that were not looking ran into the ones that were looking and continued the process.. like dominoes. Ola stood fanning herself, pleased with the attention. If she put on a good show, maybe Hook wouldn't beat her later.

Coop and Lud sat in a buckboard outside the Hotel Ma Campbell. They watched the activity with interest and were soon completely fascinated. Lud handed Coop the reins.

-I've got some business at the bank, Coop. Watch the horses.

-Watch them do what? Nope.. I'm tagging along.

They followed the Hooks into the coolness of the bank along with several other watchers, mostly male. The room became an impromptu social gathering in a matter of minutes. Jason jumped up and scurried into Claus Jordan's office.. breathlessly.. for he had gotten a good look at Ola.

-Mr. Jordan, you'd better get out here. It's getting busy and it looks like we may have some new clients. Looks like a judge or preacher or something.. and a woman. A woman..

-What the hell is the matter with you?

Jason appeared to be strangely agitated. Claus Jordon, now slightly irritated, strode out of his office. His eyes focused on the couple as his greed antennae began to activate. The woman stood with her back turned admiring a painting on the wall. The well-dressed, older gentleman stepped forward, extending his hand. Claus Jordan shook it enthusiastically.

-Welcome! I'm Claus Jordan, President of the Bank of Lionshead.

-I am Reverend Simon Hook of Madison and this is my beloved daughter, Ola.

She turned right on cue, stumbled and fell into the arms of Claus Jordan. He looked down into her face and his little world shook. In one moment, he saw her.. smelled her.. and touched her. Ola. She smiled up at him with those big.. eyes.

-Oh, my, Mr. Jordan. Forgive my clumsiness. It's these new boots that father bought me. I'm not used to the heel yet.

She pulled the edge of her skirt up to show the heel of the boot, but more intriguing.. the hem of the lace petticoat. Lud and Coop, who had been leaning against a wall stepped forward to look, bumping their heads together in the process. The Reverend cleared his throat and continued.

-Sir, my daughter and I have been traveling for months, looking for that right spot to rebuild our lives. A community with good and god-fearing folks. We have sad memories back home. Our beloved wife and mother.. Marta.. passed away suddenly and we couldn't live with the daily grief of our old home. We feel that Lionshead could be the right place for us and will take the next few weeks to decide. I have a small deposit to make with you until the remainder of our finances arrive. We'll be staying at Hotel Ma Campbell until we have decided on whether to build here or not.

Hook strode into Claus Jordan's office as if he owned it.. Ola close at heel. Claus Jordan followed in a trance. When the door shut, the lobby was silent. At last Lud made a low whistle and laughed.

Shortly after, Coop and Lud sat in the Evening Star, downing a shot of whiskey. They glared at Pukeard who glared back as he wiped a shot glass that would never be clean. Coop drummed his fingers on the table..

-I wish there was another bar in this town. I hate that guy. Let's start a bar, Lud. Run him out.

Lud leaned back with a serious face.

-The road to hell, Coop. It'll lead you to a bad place. I don't plan on sticking around that long, anyway.

Coop nodded.

-Me, neither. I thought you liked it at Big Spruce. She built you a church and everything.

-Well, I never intended to stay and Eartha knows that. Don't worry, I won't leave anybody in a lurch. Anyway, looks like there's a new preacher in town. What'd you think about his "daughter"?

-Why'd you say it like that? I've never seen anyone like her. She's as shiny as a new penny.

Lud looked at the young, heartbroken Coop. Mame's death had done its damage. What a truly good and decent person he was. If Lud had ever had a son.. but Coop had all the qualities that Lud didn't.

-Coop, listen up. Some things in this world that are beautiful can also be fatal. Listen, I'm giving you some valuable advice. It doesn't matter if it's a horse, a gun, a snake.. or a woman. Be sure what you're dealing with before you try to touch them. Now, Claus Jordan, for instance. I think it's too late for him. But, it'll be interesting to watch over the next couple of weeks.

Coop looked over at Lud..

-You're not really a preacher are, you, Lud.

It was a statement not a question.

-Nope.

-Does Eartha know?

-Yep.

Coop silently sat back and started shuffling cards.

-I'd still like to burn this bar down with Pukeard in it. Did Eartha ever tell you how he treated her when she came in here? Pregnant with..

-No. What happened?

As Coop told the story of a thirsty and pregnant Eartha asking for a drink of water from Pukeard.. being ridiculed and turned down.. he watched Lud flip a card on the table. The king of hearts. Lud laughed, looking at Coop.

-Well, it sounds like you busted up some of his inventory as retaliation. You're kind of the hero type, Coop.

He jokingly slugged Coop on the shoulder, pushed his chair back and walked over to the bar. Pukeard slithered over to him.

- Another round?

Lud leaned over the bar, grabbed Pukeard's left ear and twisted until it crunched.

-No thanks.

TWENTY - ONE

COOP TOLD

... Eartha about the Hooks. She rode to Hotel Ma Campbell and was greeted by Albert Hedeman and Ma. They sat on the wide porch, sipping on a tall drink, chatting casually. Albert jumped to his feet and pulled a chair out for Eartha, dusting it off with his hanky. She leaned over to kiss his cheek and smiled as he blushed. Ma Campbell reached over and patted Eartha affectionately.

-Howdy, Ms. Eartha! Long time since I've seen you. Too long. Lemonade? Albert, ready for another? We can sit out here and watch the street go by. Lil Daisy is in there keeping an eye on things.

She rolled her eyes but smiled kindly.

-I swear that woman breaks at least one thing every day. But overall, she is trying. She tells me it's her first paying job and she's proud of making her own money.

Ma disappeared into the kitchen and came back with three tall drinks. Eartha took a long draw on hers.

-You do make unusually tasty lemonade, Ma. Just what I needed.. thank you. How're you doing, Albert? How's business?

She reached over affectionately touched his shoulder, bringing on a new wave of blushing.

-It's good, Eartha. I'm always amazed at what folks want recorded and witnessed. A few land titles come in now and then, but I always keep my eye out for any issues. You know.

-Yes and I'll never be able to tell you how much that means to me. You're a good friend and business associate.

He looked down at the hat in his lap with a thoughtful smile. They relaxed on the wide porch, watching guests come and go, exchanging small talk. Ma Campbell's was the only decent hotel and restaurant in Lionshead. Customers could always depend on a good meal, a clean room and a fair price. Eartha and Ma Campbell enjoyed each other's company but understood the boundaries of a hidden past. Ma had never questioned Eartha's acquisition of the property out on Gore Creek and Eartha never asked about Ma's previous life. However, they would do a little gossiping with each other.

-I've heard there's a Reverend and his daughter in town. The girl seems to be causing a flurry of talk. What's your take? Are they staying here?

-Yes, they are and you already knew that. That's why you're sitting here. Pure curiosity.

She narrowed her eyes and looked up at the clouds, squinting as if she saw something interesting. A tiny dust devil played with the wind.

-Here's the deal..

Ma Campbell looked meaningfully at Eartha and Albert. They both leaned closer, eyes and ears open.

-I'm telling you because I know you won't repeat it and it will be interesting to watch it play out. I don't think he's a Reverend and she's not his daughter. There's something just off balance with them. They rented two rooms but he spends a big chunk of the night in hers.

She raised her eyebrows.

-I do believe they're cons.. just haven't figured out who their target is.

They took a moment to look around the table at each other, and feeling a slight buzz from the lemonade, burst into laughter. Albert blushed again and Eartha knew that she would likely have to explain it to him later. Albert had an innocent, sensitive nature and would never be entirely ready for the world. Ma Campbell got up and came back with fresh drinks and a plate of tiny frosted cakes. Glancing down the street, she paused before taking her seat.

-Here they come now. You be the judge.

Reverend Hook and his "precious daughter" were strolling down the boardwalk, arms linked, headed for the hotel. The girl playfully twirled a frothy parasol above her head. She knew she was being watched and made the most of it. After all, one never knew what sucker might be lured in. Eartha inwardly admitted that Ola was a top quality lure. As they ascended the steps, she lifted her peach taffeta skirt, discreetly showing the ever-popular lace petticoat. Eartha knew the cost of such luxury. She had worn similar clothing when called upon and remembered the feel of silk.

Ola curtsied, encouraging the fragrance of lemon and jasmine to drift through the air. It was a unique and delicate fragrance. The Reverend removed his hat and bowed.

Ma Campbell introduced them and he pointedly studied Eartha as if he could view her soul. She had seen this act before. He was trying to intimidate her. Eartha had met many men like him and looked back, patiently awaiting the outcome. His eyes appraised her according to age, financial capability and naivety.

-*Mrs*. Eartha Borne, is it?

-That's right.

-And your husband is..

-Dead.

-I'm sorry to hear that. God does put us through trials. The reason I ask, is that Mr. Jordan of the bank is going to have a little get together for Ola and me. It will be an opportunity to acquaint ourselves with some of the (he cleared his throat) better quality citizens of Lionshead. You see, we may want to settle here. It's really very kind of him. Won't you please attend? Thursday night.. eight.. Claus Jordan's home. Come at seven, if you like. I will be giving a sermon. This occasion will be somewhat formal.

He looked skeptically at Eartha's attire.. boots, pants, shirt, vest and a stained, tattered hat. The style men wear. She looked up at him and pushed her hat back. A ray of sunlight shone through the lattice of the porch and lit her green eyes.

-I'm flattered that anyone would consider me one of the, as you put it.. "better quality folks".

-Oh, I've heard about your enterprise on Gore Creek, Mrs. Borne. Fascinating. I'd like to talk to you more about it. I understand you have a church out there. I might be able to place a blessing on it for you and perhaps give a sermon or two.

-We have a preacher.

-He carries guns, ma'am. That hardly seems proper.

-Reverend, feel free to tell him that. His name is Lud Cadey. If you think you can talk him out of the job, then more power to you. Right now, he's got his spurs dug in pretty deep.

Oh yes, she thought.. spurs, guns, French soap and fine wine. Just about every essential needed to spread "The Word out West".

Eartha stood, nodding to the Reverend and Ola. She hugged Albert who was watching Ola suspiciously. He was clearly not impressed with her charms.

-I look forward to your welcome party. Don't be concerned, Reverend. I have other clothes. I'll bring Mr. Cadey since, I can tell.. you're dying to meet him. I'm not sure we'll make it in time for the sermon. Goodbye, Ma Campbell and thanks for the lemonade. Albert, it's always a pleasure. I guess you two aren't invited.

***

Eartha found Lud standing in the cool interior of the church, studying one of the plain glass windows. He walked backward down the aisle, forming an imaginary frame with his hand for each. He knew she was watching him. The little church was well built and had eight rows of polished pews, a small steeple and simple altar. On Sundays at nine, all seats were usually taken. Several townsfolk came out and most of Big Spruce.. not because they were a religious bunch.. but because Lud loved to entertain and had the gift.

-What're you doing, Lud?

-I'm thinking about stained glass. Santa Fe. Very expensive, you know.

He looked at her innocently. She made the wise decision not to respond the way he expected.

-Lud, something's going on in town and I need you to attend a party with me. Formal.

-A date? Why, I'm so pleased, Eartha.

-Just listen, for once. I'll speak slowly so you can understand.

Instead of a snide return, Lud scratched a match on his boot and brushed past her toward the steps. He pulled a cigarette from a collection in his pocket and lit it, sitting down on the porch. He patted the step and looked up at Eartha.

-Let's talk.

Eartha told him of her suspicions. Lud and Coop had witnessed the couple when they first arrived in town at the bank and had drawn their own conclusions.

155

-What of it, Eartha? You're not turning goody-goody, are you?

-They're swindlers and I know it. Ma Campbell knows it, too. What bothers me most is that horny old Claus Jordan is in control of this town's money. My money.

She didn't mention that Claus Jordan knew a secret or two about her finances. Eartha didn't care what Jordan did if he kept his mouth shut and didn't expose her. Ola would be working for money and information. Information that could destroy Eartha.

-My dear, this calls for a bottle of very expensive French wine, don't you think?

They sat on the church steps as the evening drifted in.. discussing the possibilities. At times, they were silent just enjoying the night air. Benno and Lil Daisy moved about doing chores at the barn. Lil Daisy led Eartha's gelding, Samson, to the blacksmith watching as he effortlessly lifted a hoof and rested it on his thigh. He picked delicately at some dirt that had embedded itself in the frog of Samson's hoof, gently re-assuring the horse.

-There now big guy. No one will hurt you here.

He patted the horse and looked at Lil Daisy.. as if he were also conveying the message to her.

***

About this same time, Reverend Hook was making a deal with Pukeard behind the saloon. They laughed and shook hands.

-By the way, Pukeard.. what happened to your ear?

When Thursday night came, Eartha put considerable effort in her dress and hair. Her gown was dark green, trimmed with cream lace at bodice and hemline. She had indulgently ordered it a few months earlier with the disapproval of the now-deceased Wilma. She was looking forward to the evening, despite the mission that she and Lud had chosen. With some difficulty, she pulled her hair back into a loose clip and rolled it at her neckline. She twirled in front of the mirror and watched as her skirt floated gracefully with the movement. A low whistle came from the door and she startled, dropping the hair pin on the floor. Her unruly hair fell back on her shoulders.

-Lud, damn you! Can't you ever knock!? Do I need to start locking my door?

Her face grew red and he realized he had embarrassed her. He picked up the pin and tried to give it to her, only to have it slapped violently out of his hand.

-You look good, Eartha. Beautiful, in fact. But don't bother locking me out. It wouldn't make any difference. If I want to come in here, I will.

She walked toward the door jerking a shawl off a chair, glaring at him. She begrudgingly did notice how good he looked. Black suit.. white shirt with tie. A gentleman. He usually wore a hat, but tonight his chin length hair was slicked neatly back. He was freshly shaved and smelled like spice. Yep.. she was going to have to get rid of this one, asap.

***

They drove the buggy into town making small talk and had made a truce to enjoy the night despite the company. In fact, they were having fun, laughing about little things that had transpired on Big Spruce and in town. Their sense of humor was equally wicked and Eartha realized what good company Lud could be. The evening was warm for fall, allowing the night birds to pursue a few last insects, creating swirling profiles against the purple sky. On the horizon, tiny stars appeared with glitter. The drive had passed so pleasantly that they regretted arriving at the Jordan mansion.

The party was in full swing at the two-level brick house a mile past town. It was alight with lanterns and candles.. carriages, and buckboards were parked about the yard. Claus Jordan and his plump little wife, Cora, had definitely splurged. Music, dancing, crystal.. food and drinks galore. Ola was a beauty tonight, dressed in baby blue with a bouncy bow in her hair.. dancing, laughing and smelling good. But her eyes always sought Claus Jordan and he was always looking back. Unless, of course, Cora was looking at him. He asked Ola to dance and they did. She asked him to take her out for some air and they went out. Jordan suggested to the girl that she might enjoy seeing his library. She responded with a slight brush of her hand on the front of his trousers. They discreetly disappeared into the quiet secrecy of the other side of the house.

It was a perfectly timed event. Just as Claus Jordan was giving his all between Ola's legs, the library door opened and the Reverend.. along with Pukeard.. walked in and witnessed the situation. Claus struggled to pull his pants up, Ola pushed herself back on the mahogany desk and gathered her lace petticoat between her legs. Reverend Hook leaped forward closing his bony fingers around the neck of Jordan. Pukeard pulled him back.

-You filthy bastard! You've raped my daughter!

The minor tussling turned into major negotiations.

-Jordan, you'll pay for this. I won't kill you because I'm a man of God. Mr. Pukeard, please get the sheriff. He's here. Oh Lord, what if a child is conceived? We've got to leave this place of iniquity, Ola. Oh Ola.. my poor girl.

He took his jacket off and wrapped Ola in it, hugging her to him.

-Wait.. wait, Reverend. Pukeard.. wait. Don't get the sheriff. I'm so sorry. I don't know how this happened. Please listen. Forgive me. What can I do?

No one moved or spoke.

-I've got money. Lots of money. You can settle somewhere else and not worry. If a child comes of this.. I'll send more.

Jordan stumbled toward his safe and unlocked it. He pulled out blocks of bills tied with string and desperately offered them to Hook and Ola. Ola took one with an amused look on her face, but the Reverend walked over, jerked it out of her hand and threw it on the floor. He was going to make this look good. Claus fell on his knees in front of Hook and grabbed at his coat.

-Please, forgive me. Please, don't tell. It will ruin my life. There's more money.. a lot more at the bank. Take this now and then meet me there in the morning. Six.. come at six tomorrow morning. I'll let you in the back door.

The Reverend stepped back and looked scornfully at Jordan.

-I will forgive you. But you must pay for what you did to Ola. You must know that she was a virgin. Untainted. But you are the son of Eve and cannot help yourself. We will be there at six. Come, Ola.

They left Jordan sweating in the library and stepped out into the hall, where Pukeard stood guard. The Reverend handed him a stack of bills and smiled.

-Thanks for being my witness.

- My pleasure.

Pukeard eyed Ola and looked at the Reverend.

-There's no chance of a little bonus is there? Can I have a crack at Ola, too?

-Normally, I'd say yes. But there's no time and, as you know.. it's all about timing.

The party wound down until the last guests were the Hooks. Cora Jordan waved tiredly at them as the Reverend helped Ola into their wagon. Claus Jordan had obviously lost his party mood and stood watching them. Cora looked at her husband wondering if he was coming down with the croup. It had been going around. As the Reverend slapped the reins, he called over..

-See you in the morning, Claus. Don't forget now. Good evening, Mrs. Jordan. You're a wonderful hostess.

Ola sat with a shawl over her head as he drove the carriage away. A short distance down the road, he stopped the carriage.

-Get in the back and put that money in the box. We hit the jackpot this time.

Ola did what she was told and then climbed back onto the seat next to him.

-I'm so tired of this, Simon. Can't we quit now? We've got enough money back there to settle down somewhere and live decent.

She looked at him hopefully in the moonlight. He smiled cruelly.

-Decent? *You*?

He laughed as he backhanded her across the face. Her nose began to bleed and she pulled the shawl up to her face. Tears ran down her swelling cheek.

-Well, Ola honey, I like it. We make good money and, to tell the truth, it kind of turns me on when I see you with another man between your legs. In fact, I think I'll show you something new when we get back to our room. You might not like it, but I will.

He started to think about the possibilities when the horses spooked at something in the road. It was a woman and she was waving her arms for them to stop.

-Reverend Hook! I'm so glad it's you. I've got trouble. My horse seems to have gone lame and I'll need a ride into town.

-Why Mrs. Borne! Is it you?

He stared through the moonlight, trying to peer past her. The carriage was there but the horse wasn't.

-Where's the horse? Where's Cadey? Didn't he accompany you to the party?

-He started walking to get some help. I guess we're just about half way between the Jordan place and town. The horse is tied over there.

At that moment Lud Cadey stepped out of the shadows and effortlessly jerked Hook off the buckboard.

-Get down, Ola and stay here with Eartha. Let's go for a little walk and talk, Reverend.

Eartha put a hand on Ola's shoulders.

-Listen to me now. We have a good horse ready for you. You know how to ride, don't you?

Ola nodded and dabbed at the blood that trickled from her nose.

-Pack only what you really need and take the money. All of it. And his gun. I know he's got one. Put on his clothes and hat. They'll be big, but you can get something else later. We'll take care of the wagon and Hook. Do you have some scissors? Cut that hair off. Try to look like a boy, Ola, until you get to a safe place. There's enough money here.. God knows you've earned it all. And, Ola.. don't go back to this line of work. You'll end hard, if you do.

-What about him? He'll come after me. He'll kill me or worse. All I have is my looks and he'll scar me up. He's done it to women before me. He doesn't like runaways.

A strange sound came from the direction that Lud and Hook had taken.

-I promise you, Ola. You'll never see him again and if you do.. he'll be so worried about crawling away, that it won't matter.

Ola got in the back of the wagon, shoved as much as she could in a bag, got the gun and changed clothes. She found the scissors and jumped down, handing them to Eartha.

-You do it. My hands are shaking too much.

Ola felt liberation with every cut of her hair. She crammed some jerky and apples into the saddle bags as Eartha tied her scant bedroll on the back of the saddle.

-This is going to be tough, but you will survive. Go find yourself a decent life.

Ola rode into the unknown with only the moon as her guide.

***

Lud had pushed Hook ahead of him to a good spot in the trees for a talk.

-Now, Reverend, where shall we start? Well.. okay.. I'll break the ice. I've noticed that you have a few personality flaws. Now, don't be offended, but it sure seems like you enjoy hurting women. Probably little girls, too. I've got a lengthy list of what I don't like about you, but there just isn't enough time. So, let's get down to business.

He punched Hook hard in the stomach. The Reverend doubled over and Lud's knee jerked up shattering his nose. Hook stumbled back into the dry grass holding his nose. It was broken and started to bleed down the front of his suit. The woods were quiet.. except for the sound of horse hooves hitting the dirt as Ola disappeared into the night. Lud put his face close to Hook's.

-Comfy? No need to answer.

Hook started to slide down the trunk but Lud closed his hand around the man's throat.

-I know you're a praying man, Reverend and want to fall on your knees about now. You made that poor girl drop to her knees plenty.. didn't you? Oh well, no need to explain. Those days are over for her.

He ripped a piece of cloth from Hook's shirt and stuffed it into the Reverend's mouth. Lud took a step back, lit a cigarette and took a long drag.. watching the man gag on the blood running down his throat.

-Now, how am I going to get you to promise to leave it at this? No more games.. no more "I'm a Reverend" shit. But mostly, no more Ola. I don't know where she's headed, but I'm relying on you not to follow. Truth is.. I know I should kill you right here and now. You see, that's what I do for a living. I know.. I know. You thought I was a preacher. Well, as you know, God works in mysterious ways. In all fairness, you need some kind of punishment. Not just a sermon. Don't you agree?

Hook tried to move his head.. negative. Lud stuck the burning cigarette on the man's face and left it for a moment. Hook's eyes bulged and he screamed against the gag as he struggled. Lud repeated the burns until the man had the shape of a cross covering his cheek. A mark that would last forever. Tears ran down the Reverends face and snot from his bleeding nose. He jerked at the rope only to feel it tighten around his throat.

-How many times did Ola cry? Wasn't her nose bleeding tonight?

Lud picked up a hefty piece of wood. Gripping it with both hands, he swung it at Hook's knees. The branch didn't break, but some bones did. Another silent scream and Hook slumped to a heap on the ground. Twisting a bit of Hook's thinning hair around his hand, Lud jerked the man's head back.

-Here's the deal. I'm going to help you back to your wagon. Get you set up in it. You're going to start moving as soon as you are able. That means tonight. You've probably got some ointment or something for those burns. Go far, far away, Reverend. Don't think about Ola.. don't think about the money. Just move like your life depends on it. Because it does. Keep your mouth shut about what happened here or I'll hunt you down and finish what I started. Do you completely understand me? Reverend?

Hook's head nodded up and down as the tears leaked from the side of his face. Lud patted him on the back and helped him up on his one good leg.

***

The next morning, at six sharp, Claus Jordan nervously paced back and forth in the bank lobby, constantly peering through the shutters at the street. No one came. He checked the back alley. He watched the clock tick away every minute until seven, the sweat starting to bead on his forehead even though it was a chilly morning. There were sounds of daily life starting on the street. He would open the bank at eight, as usual. The Reverend was going to tell. He'd probably already gone to the sheriff. Jordan slowly opened the front door and peered down the boardwalk to the sheriff's office. Nothing. At exactly eight o'clock, Jason and Mildred arrived and went about the work of opening the bank. The first customer arrived. Eartha.

-Good morning, Jason. I'd like to talk to Mr. Jordan, please.

-Yes, ma'am. Right away.

Jordan walked into the lobby straightening his tie. Without a word, he motioned for Eartha to enter his office. She walked over to his desk, picked up the crystal decanter and poured each of them an early morning drink.

-Sit down, Claus.

TWENTY - TWO

LARA MCCLEOD

... had always dreamt of having children. Holding babies on her hip.. chasing toddlers about.. nursing them through childhood illness.. birthday parties. The good and the bad. She didn't care if they were boys or girls, but in her life vision.. they were always there. A variety of shapes and sizes. Many afternoons passed as she thought of names and envisioned faces. She and Angus had now been married for five years and had not conceived. It was not for lack of trying for they were very healthy and very much in love. She cared for her sister-in-law's four girls as often as she could and was secretly a bit envious of Grace. Gregory and Grace had it all.. a growing business of vegetable production and sales. Gregory had rows of stored seed and dried herbs. He could concoct comforts, teas and cures for everyday ailments. And four beautiful girls. All different as the jewels they were named for.

Grace could feel Lara's pain and often wondered about possible remedies. The two women had privately discussed all known ways to conceive.. time of month, time of the moon.. positions. Lara had tried them all with her beloved Angus. And still no baby.

It was early evening as they sat, feet propped on cushions, sipping on one of Gregory's teas. They had worked all day together at Scots Depot, putting up some late summer vegetables. They sat chatting on the wide porch watching the girls play in the yard below. Grace and Lara had shared many intimacies, but Grace still hesitated voicing her latest epiphany. It was, by far, the most drastic. She glanced at Lara and quietly said..

-I want you to have a baby so much. You've tried everything from religion to witchcraft. I have an idea and I want you to hear me out before you tell me I'm crazy.. or immoral.

She reached over and took Lara's hand in hers.. eyes shining with sisterly love.

-Lay with Gregory. I know you will conceive. I love you and he's very fond of you. Gregory just has a way of planting seeds that grow, Lara. This is no different.

Lara jerked her hand back as if it had been scalded and stared at Grace, who continued.

-Hear me out. Angus doesn't need to know. He wouldn't go for it anyway. But what difference would it make if you got a baby? He would never suspect.. he and Gregory look so much like each other.

By now Lara had jumped to her feet, spilling her tea on the porch.

-My God.. *Grace*!? Do you know what you're saying? It would be a sin. Adultery! We could never do that. How could you even suggest it?

-Wait, Lara. No one needs to know but you, me and Gregory. Never. Please think about this. It would be such a blessing for you and Angus.

Lara slowly sank back to her chair and they sat on the porch in silence. She watched Grace's daughters play in the grass as the sun shared its heat. She could see Gregory striding up from the storehouse. He stopped and bit into a tomato, causing the juice to run down his chin. Lara ran down the steps, mounted her horse and rode past him, barely acknowledging his presence. Gregory entered the house, washed his hands and threw the towel over his shoulder, smiling at his wife.

-Hello, Grace, my adorable.

He playfully grabbed her shoulders and planted a kiss on her mouth. She giggled as she pushed him away, wiping at his chin.

-What was wrong with Lara? She didn't even speak to me.. just rode on past. What's going on?

Grace circled him.. searching his face.. studying him.. thinking of a way to bring up the conversation. He looked at her suspiciously, pulling the towel from his shoulder.

-What? Don't tell me. You're pregnant again?

He looked hopeful. Gregory loved his family and planned on more children. He secretly hoped for a son.. just to shake things up.

-No. But I know someone that wants to be pregnant. Very much so. More than anything in the world.

-I know.. and I've prayed about it, too, Grace. Angus and Lara deserve to have this happiness in their lives. I wish I could perfect a miracle seed to help them.

He laughed.

169

-We'd be millionaires! I know of herbs that can end a life.. but not create one. Doesn't seem right, does it?

She walked over to him and put her arms around his neck, leaning her forehead against his chest. She took a deep breath and started..

-You do have a seed, Gregory.

He pulled back looking at her confused.

-You could give them a baby.

With as much charm as possible, she led her husband upstairs to their bedroom and explained her idea to him as they made love. Afterward, he sat on the edge of the bed with his head in his hands.

-I don't know whether to laugh or cry, Grace. Are you crazy? Did you and Lara talk about this already? Is that why she rode off that way?

-Yes, we talked about it. She's willing. But Gregory, Angus must never know. I don't think he would ever accept this.

Gregory jumped up, grabbed his shirt and angrily buttoned it.

-I can't deceive my brother! What if he found out? Could *you* ever trust me again if I did this thing?

-Yes. Yes, I will always trust and love you. Nothing can come between us. I just want them to be happy and this is a chance. This is the only way. Please, Gregory. Do this for me. Do it for all of us. No one else can. Only you.

That evening they had dinner surrounded by their beloved girls. The night was filled with little joys that come when a young family prepares for bedtime. Baths..

170

stories.. prayers. They tucked their girls under soft quilts and kissed each one goodnight. Grace looked at Gregory over the lamplight. Sometime between sunset and sunrise, he agreed to the plan.

Lara also lay awake most of that night, looking over at her husband in the moonlight. Could she possibly deceive him like this? He had been so good to her. What if it wasn't *his* failure to impregnate her? What if *she* just couldn't conceive? Fifty-fifty odds. If no child came, she would have to live with the knowledge of what she had done.

She stayed away from Scot's Depot for several days. Angus noticed her pre-occupation one evening and pulled her to him.

-What is it? You've been thinking about something for the last few days. And you haven't told me.. I can always tell, ye know.

-Nothing, Angus. Nothing. You know how I am.. always day-dreaming about something or other. I've just been wondering what this winter will bring.

She made up her mind that night and rode down to Scot's Depot early the next afternoon. Mercifully, Gregory was not in the house when she arrived. The older girls, Pearl and Crystal, were busy arranging flowers in the dining room, admiring their creations and commenting on various fragrances. The two youngest were peacefully napping. Grace stood silently in the hallway, waiting for Lara to speak.

-Grace, where's Gregory?

-Down at the warehouse. Have you thought this over?

-Yes. The answer is yes. I'll do it if the two of you are willing.

-We are.

Lara stayed in the house as Grace walked down to get Gregory. She felt the slow creep of panic and nausea. She would leave quickly and forget about this. She started toward the back door where she had tied the horse, but.. stopped. This was her only chance. She wanted a baby. It was now or never.

Gregory and Grace came in the front door. He walked toward Lara with his hat in his hands. She looked at his kind and gentle face and started to cry with humiliation. At that moment, she realized what an outrageous mistake they were making and backed away from Gregory.

-I'm so sorry and ashamed. This is wrong. I can't go through with it.

He reached over and touched her chin gently, then caressed the side of her cheek with his hand.

-No.. no, lassie. We'll get that seed planted and then everything will fall into place. We can do this. Grace and I have prayed about it.. and we know it's the right thing. All will be good when you hold that fine baby in your arms.

She nodded and he bounded upstairs to bathe.. and wait for Lara. He thought to himself as he prepared.. the idea was growing on him. Grace hugged Lara reassuringly.

-You go up now. You know which room is ours. I'll keep an eye on the girls.

Lara ascended the stairs slowly, hesitated, then opened the first door on the right and entered. Gregory lay under the rose-colored quilt with an encouraging smile on his face.

TWENTY - THREE

LARA AND GREGORY

... met three times during the following weeks. True to his word.. Gregory was an expert planter and the day came when Lara knew that she had conceived. When she told Angus, he swore he was the happiest Scot alive.

Angus spread the news at Big Spruce that very day. After best wishes and hugs, he rode off to tell his brother, Gregory. Gregory and Grace who had that wonderful family. Now he would have a child to care for and look after. The world could not be a better place that day for Angus McCleod.

He galloped up the short incline to the house at Scot's Depot and ran up the porch steps, calling out. It was Sunday and no one was working in the fields. Grace and Gregory sat at the kitchen table where they had been sipping tea, deep in conversation. They waited expectantly.

-We've done it. We're going to have a baby! Lara's pregnant.

The couple stared at him and then looked at each other in shock.. then joy. Angus grabbed his brother, hugging him as tears welled in Gregory's eyes. Angus was touched by the depth of his brother's love.

After a few celebratory sips of whiskey, Angus rode back to Big Spruce feeling a warmth and joy in his soul that he had never known. He grabbed Lara in their cabin, hugged her and then placed his ear on her stomach.

-By golly! I do believe that I hear the wee one laughing already. Lara, I'm so happy. And listen to this.. Gregory cried with joy. He's the best brother a man could have.

***

As the months passed, Lara's belly grew and she had never felt such immense joy. She had no regrets or doubts. Angus worked hard, whistled loud and loved his wife with his whole heart. It was happy times at Big Spruce. Livestock and crops were thriving, thanks to Gregory's pump technique. Sales of both were going well, adding to the general fund for the families and operation of Big Spruce.

Finally, the day came when Lara went into labor. Such a long time coming. Her labor was not unusual, but she suffered many hours. And then out he slid.. a fat and healthy baby boy. Angus held the child to his chest and declared..

-We're going to name him Gregory after my brother.

Madlyn, who had assisted with the birth along with Eartha, smiled but stopped at the look on Lara's face.

-No. No, Angus. Not Gregory.

They had agreed not to name the child until it was born, but Angus always had a name in mind.

-Why not? He deserves it. He and Grace have helped us so much through these last months. Why not?

Lara realized that they had not talked about a name for a baby boy. She just assumed, after surveying the odds, that she would have a daughter.

-It would be too confusing. I won't name him Gregory.

-What then? What would you like?

Lara thought. Her father had died when she was a child and she had no brothers. But one name came to mind.

-Duff. Duff McCleod. I've always liked the sound of it.

Angus considered the name and nodded.

-"Duff" it is then, but can Gregory be his middle name, would ye think?

-No. Angus will be his middle name.

Angus thought it to be a strange combination, but he was elated that his son would have his name.

Grace and Gregory soon stood beaming down at Lara holding her new baby boy. Gregory seemed overcome with emotion as he reached down and gathered the tiny child to his chest.

-A boy. Look! It's a boy. Little Duff McCleod.

He commenced rocking and cooing as his wife looked on.

She didn't remember him carrying on like this after the birth of their last daughter.

TWENTY - FOUR

GREGORY COULDN'T RESIST

… visiting Big Spruce many times over the next weeks and months. It seemed quite natural since he was Duff's uncle. A year had passed and it was the toddler's first birthday. The Gregory McCleod family arrived with gifts and food for the ensuing party. The girls bounced out of the buckboard running to grab Duff and took turns spoiling him.

Grace stood back watching the scene. Such excitement over the first year of life. She walked forward and hugged Lara.

-What a fuss over your boy. Especially Gregory. Why you'd think that he'd never celebrated a first birthday.

She watched as Gregory grabbed little Duff and whirled him around. The toddler squealed and kicked the air. Duff was obviously attached to him and his tiny arms encircled his neck. He shakily stood on Gregory's lap and planted a big wet kiss on his face. Everyone laughed as Lara handed Gregory a cloth to wipe the little slobbers off. Angus stood back thoroughly enjoying the moment and again thought what a lucky man he was. Grace stood back in the shadow of a tree, absentmindedly twisting a lock of her hair and was not smiling.

As the evening came to an end, the Gregory McCleods rode off waving and calling until they were out of sight. Eartha walked over to Coop who was stomping ashes around the campfire.

-Would you mind walking me back to my place? We haven't talked for some time and I'd like to do some catching up.

They walked down the short hill and lingered on the bridge to listen to the water.

-How about a little night cap, Coop? We can set out on the porch and study the stars.

-Sounds good. It's been awhile since we've done that.

Coop and Eartha were comfortable in each other's company as if they had grown up together. There was no explaining it and they never tried. There was just a natural trust between them. Coop propped his feet up on the branch railing and looked over at Eartha.

-I thought Mame and I would have a kid someday.

Eartha reached over to brush a fly off his shoulder.

-I know. I miss her, too. But not like you. I know your heart has a scar that will never heal and time won't help. You just get to a point where the pain is bearable. And then, one day, you'll feel a tiny bit of joy over something trivial. A breath of hope.. just a hint of peace. It will feel strange and then a stab of guilt will follow. The "what ifs" can drive you crazy.

-Eartha, I know you've been through something pretty rough. Maybe when we're old and gray you'll tell me about it.. maybe not. I've seen you stand up after some hard knocks. I just miss her so much and I'll always wonder about the accident. Something just didn't add up. I've never figured it out. And her locket.. I've searched down that creek a hundred times. It's not there. Do you think someone could have taken it?

-It's hard to tell. People were all over that place, trying to help. But maybe someone could have found it and kept it. Mame was a strong and good woman. Folks just naturally loved her and so I can't imagine anyone taking that locket on purpose.

They sat in silence for a moment. Eartha could just faintly see the shadow of Lud on his porch and knew he was trying to listen. She moved her chair so that the lamplight would not be on her face.. her back to his cabin.

-There's something else, Eartha. Tonight. Off balance somehow.. I can't really put my finger on it. Everyone seemed to be having a good time except for..

-Grace. I saw it, too.

-Maybe she's sick or pregnant again.

-No. She would have told me.. or Gregory would have announced it. I think her sickness is of the soul. I've never seen her quite like this. But, Coop, there is something I want to say to you. Now, don't take this wrong.

-Mame doesn't want your heart buried up there with her.

***

Down at Scot's Depot another conversation was taking place.

-Grace, can you believe that little guy? I just love him. It's going to be so much fun watching him grow. He'll be a hell of a man, too. I can just tell. Good stock.

With that he nudged and winked at her.

-Don't you ever say that to me again, Gregory. Never bring it up again. What's done is done. Never again. He's Angus's son and don't you ever forget it.

She glared across the lamplight at him and he knew he'd gone too far.

-I'm sorry. That was stupid. You're right.

But as Gregory lay in the dark, he couldn't help but think about the child. He wished that little Duff slept in the next room and sat at the breakfast table every morning. Not up at Big Spruce. Hours later, he stirred and reached over to Grace, starting the movements of sex. She turned toward him as she had so many times over the years and kissed him with welcome. And from his lips came the name.

-Lara.

Grace froze. What had he said? She had to be sure and so leaned over him, kissing his lips. She whispered.

-Yes?

-I love you, Lara.

Grace jumped out of bed fumbling for a match to light the lantern and stared at her husband. He looked at her with sleepy confusion, pulling himself up to lean on his elbow.

-What?! What's wrong?

But he knew what had escaped from his lips. The dream was still fresh. He stared back at her and held his breath, waiting for her words. Grace watched him for a long moment and then pulled her robe tightly around her.

-Nothing. I thought I felt a spider crawling across my arm.

She blew the lamp out, eased back into bed.. leaving her gown on. The remaining hours of the morning passed slowly as they both lay staring toward the ceiling and the cold crept into the room through the open window.

***

As the next month passed, Gregory began to convince himself that what had happened that night between he and Grace.. had not. And as men will try to make sense of the senseless, began to go about his business as usual. He assumed that if the subject was never discussed.. it would just disappear. Days were busy at Scot's Depot.. planting, harvesting and storing. Grace seemed to be coming out of her mood and the girls were always a joy. The visits to Big Spruce had dwindled considerably, causing Eartha to stop by one afternoon. She found Grace sitting on the porch, winding and unwinding a ball of yarn. Grace looked at her and smiled. She looked away and after a moment back at Eartha as if she'd forgotten she was there. No hospitality.. no offer of even a drink of water.

-What brings you here, Eartha?

-It's been a month since we've seen you all. Is everything alright? I don't want to pry but if there is something that has offended you..

Grace stood suddenly letting the yarn roll down the steps.

-Nothing is wrong. I have a headache now. Please excuse me.

Grace walked into the house, leaving Eartha sitting alone.. stunned. After a moment, she walked down the steps and mounted Samson. That look on a woman's face was never a good sign.

The next morning, Gregory stood watching Grace arrange some flowers in a vase. She didn't look at him or speak.

-My darlin' Grace.. let's go into town and pick up some burlap for the warehouse. Gather the girls up and we'll make a day of it. We haven't all been to town in a long time. It'll be fun.

He walked over to put his arms around her, but she moved away.

-You know, Gregory.. you haven't spent much time with the girls this last month. Do take them and I'll stay home. It'll be so good for all of you. Anyway, I've got a headache and could use some peace and quiet. Please do. Bring me something pretty from Bertrand's store though. The girls can help you pick something out.

She moved to him and kissed his lips, looking up into his eyes. He never knew anymore what to expect.

-Well, okay then! Sounds like fun to me. A father and daughters outing.

He stepped back feeling some doubt about the plan but what the hell.. maybe it would help get things back to normal. As he harnessed the buckboard, he felt a longing to see his son. They had not visited Big Spruce in a month. In his heart, he knew that he could not live without seeing Duff. Just then the girls came running to him like colored butterflies in their "going to town" dresses.

-Is it true daddy? Are we going into town to buy mama something pretty? Can we get something, too?

He grabbed two of them, one under each arm and hoisted them into the wagon.

-Today everybody gets something new. Pile in and hold on!

As they drove off, Grace waved from the porch. They would be gone for hours.

She walked to the barn, saddled her horse and rode to Big Spruce.

TWENTY-FIVE

LARA FELT THE CHILL

... of a shadow and turned from the table where she was kneading bread dough. Grace stood in the doorway, twirling a strand of hair in her fingers. She was looking down at Duff who had toddled to her and was hanging on her skirt. He was grinning up at her but she showed no joy as she looked back.

-Hello, Lara.

-Grace! Oh, it's so good to see you.

Grace reached down and picked the child up, kissing his chubby cheek.

-Mmm! He smells so good. Like a cookie. Where's Angus?

Lara hesitated. Something was strange.

-He's out in the field. Not far. Here. Let me take Duff. He'll drool all over you. He's teething.

Grace backed up.. holding the child and shut the door quietly, even though it was a beautiful day.

-Let's have a talk. Just the three of us.

She moved around the room, bouncing Duff on her hip.

-It is a challenge.. taking care of a child isn't it, Lara? So much to do. But the hardest thing of all is to keep them safe. Especially at this age. Well, just like this..

She reached down and picked up a butcher knife from the table.

-Don't you know how fast things can happen?

Grace held the knife in front of the boy and he tried to grab it.

-And that river! Now there's a worry. How fast these little legs could make it to the river. Lara, I just don't think this is a safe place for you to raise little Duffie.

Lara tried to reach for her son.

-What are you doing? Please give him to me.

Grace slowly put the knife down and handed the child to Lara.

-This little arrangement we all have isn't working out too well for me and Gregory. You've got to go and I don't ever want to see you back here. I bought a couple of train tickets. They're open ended. I suggest you use them to find a safer location. You never know when something might come out of those woods and snatch up your precious little son.

She threw an envelope on the table.

-You take that train tomorrow while Angus is out and never look back. Both of you. Otherwise, Duff will have an accident. A bad one. You have come into my marriage and ruined it. If you defy me, I'll tell Angus everything. He'll hate you, he'll hate his brother and Duff will be dead. You'll never be able to prove I did it. Do you understand me?

-But Grace, this whole thing was your idea. We all agreed that we could live with it. What's changed things

185

so drastically? Can't we all sit down and talk again? Work this out? I love Angus and can't just leave him like that.

-You'd better rethink. My husband has fallen in love with you. All he thinks about is you and your brat. Get out. The train leaves tomorrow morning at 10:15. Salt Lake City would be your best bet.

Grace turned and walked out the door shutting it softly as she left. Lara sank to her knees holding the boy tightly until he started to complain. She watched him toddle around the cabin, picking up a toy and sitting down to play with it. Tears streamed down her face as she realized there was no choice. She had to leave a man and a life that she loved. Her heart broke as she walked around touching things that made their home. As darkness filled the cabin that night, she held Angus to her as if it were the end of the world. It was.

At dawn, Angus went hunting. He wanted to provide for his beloved wife and child. When evening came, he returned to a dark and empty cabin. He looked over the river at Eartha's place. Had Lara walked over to visit and not noticed how late it was? He looked at the other cabins, calling her name. She could be in any one of them. He'd go in and start a little fire and maybe even have time to surprise her with dinner. He couldn't wait to kiss her and play with Duff. After he lit the fire, he noticed the note on the table.

Angus, I have left you. The years that we have been married have been a lie and I can't do it anymore. A man came through here selling goods some time ago.. you may not remember him. Duff is his son, not yours. You should have known after all the years without children. I can't live with you anymore. Please don't try to find me as it would just humiliate me and cause further unhappiness. I don't ever want to see you again. I don't love you and never did. I just want out. Lara

The fired burned slowly out as Angus sat in a heap on the floor holding the crumpled note. He stared blankly through the open door of the cabin into the dark.

***

Doc Briar knocked on the door softy, hoping not to wake the baby. It was late morning. He fully expected them to be up and around.. but with a teething child, you never know. Lara had asked him to make a teething gel for Duff. The door creaked open slowly and Doc peered in. He saw Angus sitting in the far corner holding a wad of white paper.. staring at the door but not seeing. Doc walked slowly over to him, bent down and peered into his eyes. He was alive but not aware. Quickly looking around the room, Doc realized there was no Lara and no Duff. He pulled the paper out of Angus's hand and spread it on the table. His shoulders slumped as he read the words.

-Come on, man. Get up, now. Let's go see Eartha.

187

As they walked, he could see reality returning slowly to Angus and the pain with it. Angus hung his head and cried as he plodded mindlessly along. Eartha ran toward them, fearing that Angus had been injured. She helped them to the steps where he sat down and Doc Briar handed her the note. After reading it, she let it float to the floor.

-This is impossible.

She looked at Doc in disbelief and back at Angus. Her eyes were full of questions but Doc motioned her to be silent.

-Angus just needs our help to try and make sense out of things, Eartha.

They gently talked to Angus, getting very few answers and a lot of tears. After some time, Eartha walked down to the river where Theo was working on a pump.

-Theo, hurry and get Gregory. Lara has left and taken Duff. Angus will need his family around him.

He looked back at her.. speechless. He shook his head in sorrow as he hurried toward the barn.

***

Grace saw the rider coming and called to Gregory. She had been expecting a visit and prepared herself.

-It looks like Theo and he's riding fast. I hope nothing is wrong at Big Spruce.

They waited on the porch as Theo approached, hat in hand.

188

-Gregory, you must come. Lara has left Angus and taken the boy. He is in a bad way.

The gathering at Eartha's cabin became sadly silent. No questions had answers and Angus sat quietly looking down at his calloused hands. Lara would never have left him with their child. Something was missing. Theo looked at Grace.

-Ma'am, did Lara seem out of sorts when you visited her yesterday?

-What are you talking about? I wasn't here yesterday.

-But I saw you. I saw you ride off.

-You're crazy, Theo. I wasn't here yesterday. Did anyone else see me?

She looked around at them and they all shook their heads. No. Theo looked dumbfounded and replied..

-Perhaps I am getting old but my vision is very good.

Grace just looked at him and snorted.

-Well, don't you think I'd remember being here? I haven't lost my mind.

Gregory looked at his wife and knew that she had.. indeed.. lost her mind. They had done a terrible thing and it could never be undone. The ride back to Scot's Depot was a tearful barrage of questions from their daughters and there were no answers that would comfort them. Later, Grace sat silently on the porch as Gregory said goodnight to each of his beloved daughters.

-What happened to Duffie, Daddy? Where's Lara? Will we ever see them again? Do you think bad guys took them? Will they come and take us, too?

Gregory tried to comfort them but he had few answers. At the bottom of the stairway, he sat with his head in his hands. He eventually rose and walked out to stand in front of Grace. The evening was beautiful and he gazed out over his green and growing land. Red winged blackbirds shrilled in the willows. Gregory caressed the back of Grace's neck.

-How about I make us some tea, Grace? We can sit out here and talk.. just enjoy the evening. Today was hard for everyone.

-Can you believe what Theo said? He's crazy and should be run off.

Gregory had been in town with the girls most of the day in question. Hours.

-You weren't there then? Even for a few minutes?

-No dammit! I wasn't there. I said that. I..wasn't..there!

-Hey now. Where did you go then? Your saddle was in a different spot when we came back from town. Did you go for a ride?

-No, I didn't. I can put my saddle anywhere I want. It needed some cleaning. I never left this place after you went into town.

He looked at her in the dimming light, then rose and walked into the kitchen to make some tea for both of them. Something special that would make things right.

He took some time about it and came back handing her a cup. She smiled and took it with shaking hands.

-Mmm.. this is good Gregory. Did you put cinnamon in it?

He took a gulp of his and looked over at her. The picture of marital bliss.

-Drink it all up, now. I can make more if this doesn't do the trick.

She did gulp it down and felt the liquid warm her. The moon began to rise as Grace propped her feet on the ottoman.

-I think things will be better now. I mean with Lara and Duff gone. We can get back to our life. Can you believe she just up and ran off like that?! I knew she was a slut when she agreed to lay down with you.

-It was your idea, Grace.

-Well, you didn't seem to have a problem with it. It's over now. They're gone. What did you put in this tea? I'm feeling strange.

-Remember when I told you that there were herbs that could take life away, Grace?

She looked over at him and tried to get up but her legs would not move. She dropped her cup and opened her mouth but nothing came out. Gregory stumbled to her and took her in his arms.. and that's where the oldest girl found them in the morning. Poisoned by a special cup of tea.

Doc Briar did confirm that it looked like they had been poisoned. What a horrible accident. The population of the cemetery on the hill grew by two more.

**

The big house at Scot's Depot was boarded up until matters could be decided. Matters like the McCleod girls that were now orphaned. Angus was their only relative that anyone had ever heard of and he was of no use. They were moved into the double cabin next to Eartha.. the same one that Axel and Jubal had shared. Everyone at Big Spruce cared for them and it was agreed that they would never be sent away.

After the double burial on the hill, Angus went back to spending his time numbly working in the livery and keeping to himself. He would take his dinner with whoever was willing to feed him and his cabin stayed dark. Many nights, he just sat in the dark woods. He paid no attention to the girls.

Lud watched him mindlessly shovel hay and wondered how much longer the man could survive before dying from heartbreak. All life and feeling had departed from him. Yep.. tough times. Wife run off with kid.. brother and sister-in-law poisoned.. although Lud never really liked Grace.. she still didn't deserve a wicked cup of tea. Or did she? He strolled to the livery and stood watching Angus.. sizing him up.. and then stepped forward.

-Hey, Angus.

A blank look and grunt from Angus. Lud knew he was volunteering for a battle.. but someone had to jerk this poor brute out of hell.

-You're a sorry son-of-a-bitch.

Angus raised his eyes not completely comprehending what he heard.

-Huh?

-Do you really think you're the only man that's had a wife run off? And it gets better.. Gregory and Grace killed by an overdose of tea. Are you kidding me?

He braced himself as Angus charged, knocking him against the stall. He felt a rib crack and gasped for breath. But this wasn't his first fight and he raged back. Lud's fist rose and connected with Angus's jaw, knocking him down. Angus knelt in the dirt as blood dripped onto his shirt. He lunged back. Lud sidestepped and hit him from behind with a tool that he'd pulled from the barn shelf. The battle continued until they both knelt in the dirt, gasping, eyes and noses swollen and bleeding. Lud picked up a handful of straw and threw it feebly at Angus. Neither had any fight left.

-Is that all you've got, McCleod?

He chuckled briefly just before a fist hit him hard on the side of the head. He crawled on his knees to Angus and pulled on the other man's shirt.

-Stop feeling sorry for yourself. Get over there and help those little girls. You.. unfortunately.. are all they've got left in this world.

Angus pulled himself to a sitting position and spit dirt from his mouth. Lud reached over and patted him on the back.

-It hurts like hell. I know. But you're going to pull through this, Angus. Now let's go down to the river and wash this mess off. A little cold water on that nose will help the swelling. Those little gals are probably getting hungry about now. Just tell them you fell off the barn.

TWENTY - SIX

EARTHA WATCHED

… Lud… as he washed his clothes behind the church. He was sitting in the sun.. shirtless and barefoot, his pants rolled up, a cigarette stuck on his lip.. singing something out of the corner of his mouth. The muscles in his back moved like snakes under silk and beads of sweat were forming on his forehead. He stretched and squeezed the rag, letting the soapy water run down his back and then swabbed under his arms with it. He laid his head back, looking up at the blue sky.

-You liked that, didn't you.

She jumped back into the shadow of the church and felt the embarrassment rising on her cheeks. He stood and dripped toward her, still rubbing under his armpits with a grin on his face.

-Eartha.. my little kitten.. you know you can't sneak up on a big cat.

He dropped the cloth in the dirt and leaned forward.. one arm on each side of her head. She could smell the soap and the sweat. She glared at him and moved her hand quickly to slap him but failed. He was too fast.

-I see I have caused you some discomfort.

He took a step back and crossed his arms.

-Were you just admiring me or do you want something?

-Lud, you're an ass and someday I'll laugh when you hang. But I want to find Lara and Duff. They belong here and I know she didn't just run off like the note said. You and I know that Grace had something to do with this, but fat chance finding out what really happened. That little secret got buried up on the hill. Didn't you say you used to be a Pinkerton or something? You could find her. Where would you go if you were her?

-Salt Lake.

Eartha plopped down on a bench and looked up at him.

-Why?

-Everybody that runs heads for Salt Lake first. It's easily accessible.. another state.. a decent sized town to hide in. There's only one itchy little problem.

She sat waiting for his answer.. a look of feigned adoration on her face. He looked back at her and laughed.

-The Mormons. They see everyone that gets off that train and where they go. A young woman with a baby would be a sure target for them. Helpless.. in need.. attractive. She would be like honey to bears. They'll scoop her up in no time and marry her off to some old guy that already has three wives. No questions asked.. good breeding stock for the church. But they'll care for her. Don't worry.

-Thanks for your wisdom, but as usual, it sounds like bullshit.

She stood and walked past him to the laundry tub. Picking up a muddy stick, she stirred his laundry with a wicked smile.. then kicked the barrel over. Soapy contents spilled out creating a foamy brown pool mixed with white shirts. Lud slipped in the ooze as he tried to chase her but only reached her door in time to hear the bolt slip into place. He slapped the door.

-When'd you get a lock!?

She answered..

-Don't try to catch the kitten when you're a big *fat* cat.

Silence. He kicked her flower pot as he walked off the porch.. shattering it on the ground.

***

Eartha sat in the passenger car as it lumbered across the desert through Junction toward Utah. It was hot and she dabbed at her face with a hankie. She found it a comfort that she didn't have to hide in the boxcars and deal with the hobos this time. The train was full and her eyes roamed about looking from face to face. All kinds. She should have brought Coop with her, but knew he was busy with his own things.. plus it would do her good to get away for a few days and think about what to do. She had to get the rest of the money.. well.. didn't have to. She *wanted* to.. wanted to drive the last nail in the coffin of JT Pervice and Co. And what about Lud? He knew there was more money but didn't know where it was. She leaned her head back on the seat and thought of all the delightful ways to torture him before he died.

She woke as the train pulled into Salt Lake City. Pulling down her bag, she disembarked and looked around for a Mormon. Any Mormon would do. A group of people stood nearby, hugging someone that had arrived. It had to be them.. plainly dressed with goodness glowing in their eyes. Eartha walked over and lightly touched the arm of a woman.

-Are you a Mormon?

-Why.. yes. Yes, I am. Why do you ask?

-I need some help finding someone that I believe could be here.

The others had overheard and a tall man with a beard looked at her, removing his hat. He put his hand out.

-I'm Brother Buford Oldmon. What can we help you with?

-I'm looking for someone who may have gotten off the train about two months ago. A woman with a little boy. She was alone and would have needed help.

-Let's go into the depot and find a spot to talk.. Mrs ..

-Borne.. Mrs. Eartha Borne.

As they sat in a half-circle around a potbelly stove, Eartha told them everything about Lara's circumstances. Some of the women looked at each other but didn't speak. Eartha could tell that they knew Lara.

After a moment, Buford looked kindly at Eartha.

-We know this woman, but not by the name Lara. One of the families have taken them in. We must ask her first if she wants to speak with you. She may not want to return to Colorado. If not.. we will not let you take her. Come to this same spot tomorrow after the mid-day meal and you may meet with her.

One of the group added..

-There's a fine and safe hotel down one block. The Peery. The food is good and you'll be comfortable.

She put her hand out to touch Eartha's.

-We knew someone would come for her. She is good and her heart is broken. If she has family that loves her.. she belongs with them.

***

The Hotel Peery was a comfortable place. Eartha was shown to her room, overlooking the street below and opened her bag, pulling out a bottle of whiskey. She pulled a chair close to the window, poured some and slowly sipped it in the coolness of the late afternoon air. As she leaned her head wearily against the windowsill, she watched the people passing in the street below. She had forgotten what it was like to study the movement of a city street. Below was a market place.. tents, shops, open bins of produce.. people going about their business. Travelers in colored gowns moved among the more conservative Mormons. Her eyes were caught by the deep red hair of a young man and as she focused on him, her heart moved to her throat. Jubal? It couldn't be. She leapt up, knocking the chair over, ran out into the hall and down the stairs. On the street she stood on tiptoe searching for him. Eartha walked slowly up to his back.. hesitantly tapping his shoulder. He turned and it was.. Jubal.

-Oh my God. Eartha.

He was obviously shaken and stood staring at her. People began to watch, instinctively drawn by the moment. He recovered his breath.

-What.. what are you doing here?

-I came to find someone and found you. I can't believe it's you, Jubal.

She threw her arms around her grandson and pulled him to her. He stepped back and an icy expression covered his face.

-My mother lives here, too. Isabelle. She's been here since you sent her away with Ethan.

-And Samuel?

-He died. He was never healthy.. or right. I understand what happened now, but I still love my mother. The Mormons cared for them after father.. Ethan.. shot himself.

-Do you think she would see me, Jubal?

***

The beautiful Isabelle sat on a bench in the cemetery, holding a bouquet of wildflowers. She was surrounded by headstones, standing near a stone angel.. waiting.. waiting for the mother she hadn't seen for so many years. The mother that had cast them away. Her memory went back to that time.. two babies growing within her.. fear of the future and her forbidden bond with her brother.. Ethan. Her blond curls fell over her shoulder as she bowed to smell the blossoms. She rose and walked to the stone marking Ethan's grave and placed some flowers on it.. putting the rest on the stone of Samuel.. her inherently doomed son.

With Jubal by her side, Eartha walked toward Isabelle. They halted at a distance, observing each other for a moment.. filled with curiosity and pain.. until Isabelle came forward and took her mother's hands. Returning to the bench they stood in silence reading the names on the markers until Isabelle broke the silence.

-We didn't know at the time. We didn't know that what we had done was forbidden. Until it was too late. We didn't realize that our love was wrong.. and then the babies started to grow within me. It was too late.

Her tortured eyes looked up at Eartha.. tears spilling down her pale cheeks.. still searching for forgiveness.

-I shouldn't have sent you away like that. It was my fault. I'd kept you so protected out there. I couldn't face the fact that my perfect world had a flaw.. the human factor.

Eartha covered her face with her hands, thinking back to that horrible moment when she realized what was happening. Isabelle looked at the stone angel and then at her mother.

-You didn't come for us. You never came. Ethan kept saying that you would forgive us. Did you? Did you ever forgive us?

Eartha had no answer but struggled for words. There was no need. Isabelle could read it in her face.

-I'm grateful to have seen you one more time and hope that the rest of your life is happy.. full of things that you believe are worthwhile. I am at peace here and will always stay. Jubal will walk you back.

She rose and wandered slowly through the cemetery like a lost child. Still looking for her mother.

***

Jubal and Eartha sat in her room, indulging in another sip of whiskey, discussing things past and future. He asked about people he'd known. He questioned the tragedy of the McCleods and why Eartha was in Salt Lake. He studied the glass holding it up to the light searching the amber liquid. Looking over at her, he smiled with sincere affection.

-I loved Big Spruce. I have a lot of good memories, Eartha.. some bad.

They sat in silence until Eartha pulled a cloth out of her pocket and unfolded it. Jubal looked down at Mame's silver locket and then at Eartha.

-Is that what I think it is?

-It's Mame's locket.

He continued to study the light in his glass.

-And?

-Which one of you killed her?

Jubal remained silent for several moments, then reluctantly answered with a whisper.

-Axel.

Eartha knew he was telling the truth.

-Why?

-Because he hated Mame. Axel detested anyone and anything good. He told me he was going to kill her. He hated everybody except our mother. He thought that the locket should belong to her. He wanted to kill you, too.. and would have, Eartha. Axel wanted Big Spruce and everything that.. in his mind.. belonged to our parents. Since it's confession time.. you should know something else.

She looked over at him, dreading what she was about to hear.

-I killed Axel.

Eartha didn't respond as she looked out on the street below. He watched her face.. not reading any emotion.

-Do you think Lara McCleod will go back with you?

-I truly hope so. There are a lot of broken hearts back there that she could help. Jubal, I'll be leaving tomorrow afternoon on the train. You could come back if you wanted. No one will know what happened. I don't blame you for Axel.

-No thanks, Eartha. I like it here.

***

The next afternoon, Eartha sat in the depot with her bag. She was not a praying woman and so spent the time hoping. If she could just help one life, maybe it would make up for all the trouble she had caused.. the destruction that had followed her over the years. If she could only help Lara, the McCleod children.. Angus. She thought of the list of people she had wronged.. not to mention those she had killed. Maybe she could talk to the Mormons. They might know the secret. A hand tapped gently on her shoulder and she looked up at Lara holding little Duff on her hip. Eartha rose and took the baby in her arms.

-Oh, Lara. It's good to see you. I have so much to tell you.

-I'm amazed that you found me, but I'm not going back. There's nothing but deceit and heartache there. You have no idea.

-Hear me out. Gregory and Grace are dead. I know about Duff.. you don't even have to tell me. But he looks like both Gregory and Angus. Lara, you can fix this. The girls need you and Angus.. and Duffie. I know they miss him every day.

Lara sat down.. a look of shock and disbelief on her face as Eartha told the tragic tale.

-You must tell Angus that Duff is his son. It will save him. Tell him you wrote the note because Grace had threatened your baby out of jealousy. That's not a lie. You can heal this whole thing, Lara.. by coming back and living the life you should.

They talked into the afternoon.. questioning.. explaining. Lara finally sat back as she looked at Duff.

-We're going home.. to my husband.. to your father.

Duff grinned up at her and then wobbled around the room eventually landing on his diaper-padded butt.

At five they boarded the train. The Mormons, on a hunch, had brought some bags for Lara and Duff along with food. The child slept peacefully, lulled by the consistent rocking of the train. Lara stared out the window until dark. The two women had talked so much at the train station that they had nothing more to say. Eartha relaxed with the rhythm of the train.. thinking about the others she had left in Salt Lake.

One of the scars on her heart began to ache again.

TWENTY - SEVEN

THE COMMOTION

... began early in the morning. Eartha gathered her robe about her, stepping onto the porch. She could see through the early fog that Coop and Theo had stopped two riders at the bridge. It appeared to be a standoff.. guns aimed at guns. She peered through the dim light at the two giant men that sat on mangy horses. They were covered in fur and leather. A generous collection of weapons were strapped to their boots and waists, pistols tucked into belts.. rifles aimed back at Coop and Theo. Hair and whiskers covered their faces, but the piercing eyes were evident. They were mountain men.. fifty years too late. Eartha had heard stories but had never actually seen one. In fact, she thought they had all disappeared years before in the Northwest.

Rough language was passed back and forth.. Coop insisting that they dismount or he would blow their heads off.. the strangers not backing down. The racket had also disturbed Lud who came striding around the church, barefoot and dressed only in his long underwear. He scratched his butt and held a pistol. Eartha ran to stand by his side, instantly hating herself for it. Lud held his gun in the air and yelled through the fog..

-I'm a top-notch shot, boys, so let's not have any misunderstandings. Now don't move a hair on your furry heads. I don't want to write to your mother and tell her what happened.. even though I suspect you were whelped by wolves.

Without further warning, he fanned off two shots into the air, gaining their full attention.

-Now don't get the wrong idea. We don't see many of your kind around here. Thought you were all long gone. You're welcome to a peaceful meal and a camp by the river for the night.

Lud walked gingerly closer, peering with interest at the two.

-Shouldn't you two be frozen up in the wilderness somewhere? A long time ago?

One of the men shifted his massive bulk in the saddle and spat on the ground.

-We hear there's a hot spring around and want to partake of it. I'm Justice Burns and this is my brother.. Vengene. We're not looking for trouble, but our bones are aching. We want some time in the pool and we're willing to trade some fur for it. Got some nice pelts for trade.

Lud looked at Eartha, smiling with amusement, as she nodded her head in agreement. She also wanted a closer look at these two. Lud yelled back..

-Get down from your mounts and take your weapons off. Leave them there. If I get any idea that you mean harm, I'll blow all the fur off your bodies. It'll hurt. Come on over here so we can see you. Coop.. Theo.. get their weapons and keep them.

The trappers slowly touched ground and began producing a variety of weapons. Their fur boots landed surprisingly light on the dirt as they unbuckled guns and removed knives from hidden places. They both squared their shoulders and sauntered within thirty feet of Lud. When they saw Eartha, they removed the mummified animal skulls that had decorated their heads.

-Sorry, ma'am. We know we're not civilized. Folks don't like being around us much and we feel the same way. We'll just do some soaking and camp by the river for a night.. with your approval, of course. We mean no harm. Would you like some nice fox pelts for a little jacket or something?

Justice Burns looked at Eartha and winked. She suspected that he thought it was charming and made no comment. Smiling broadly, he exposed a row of teeth as rough and weathered as the Rockies. White hair escaped haphazardly from his cap and blended with his beard. Vengene stood back a few feet, constantly moving his legs. He was tall and covered with dark hair in contrast to his brother. His black eyes would not meet hers and he studied the ground as if watching a tiny circus.

-Can Vengene have his stick to lean on? He's got bad feet and has trouble if he don't have his stick. Horse or stick. He's got to have one or the other.

Lud looked Vengene over. What could it hurt?

-Go ahead and toss it to him.

208

The moment the stick was in his hands, Vengene stood tall and defiant. It was not clear if he was lame or just emotionally attached to the pole. Eartha spoke..

-Go "partake" of the pool as long as you want. You're welcome, no charge. If you wait a moment, I'll even throw in a bar of French soap. No offense, but you need it. The pool is about a quarter mile up the river. I'm sure you won't have trouble finding the trail. We'll start a hot meal for you.. maybe a touch of whiskey. How does that sound? But by all means.. use that soap.

They both looked at her with obvious appreciation. Carefully backing away, they took the reins from Coop. Lud called after them..

-Take your time, gents. And don't fear that soap.

After they were out of ear shot, he turned to chastise Eartha.

-I must admit, I'm somewhat appalled at your careless hospitality. Did you get a good look at those two, Eartha? They'd just as soon cut your throat as look at you. In fact, there's probably fresh sucker blood on their knives right now. Sometimes, I just don't get you.

***

Fur-covered feet padded across Eartha's porch and there was a quiet tap on the door. Lud and Coop were roasting a leg of lamb behind the cabin, occasionally stirring a pot of beans that bubbled over the fire. It was in the middle of the night, but this was an unusual occasion.

The visitors stooped to enter the door, dwarfing the interior of the cabin. They held their caps in hand and had slicked their hair back, attempting to be as clean and proper as possible. Even after a good soaking with French soap, there was an unpleasant odor about them. Years had passed since they had been inside a civilized home or around a pale woman. They quietly watched Eartha moving about and she could feel their disguised hunger.. and it wasn't just for leg of lamb. She poured them a glass of whiskey, as promised. Justice reached up and roughly grabbed her arm, pulling her down so that he could smell her hair. She tried to pull back as Lud, who had been leaning against the mantel, took a step forward. Justice reluctantly released her.

-My apologies, ma'am. It's just been a long time since we been around something that smells so good. No harm. I'm sorry.

She looked at him warily and then managed a laugh.

-Thanks for the flattery. I could use it around here.

The evening passed with outrageous tales of life and death in the Far North. As the men talked, they fell into the dialect of the old wilderness. Tales of surviving in the Rocky Mountains were rough and humorous.. most difficult to believe. Lud and Coop appeared to relax slightly, even though they kept their guns. Theo and his daughter, Mery, tapped on the door, curious about these unusual visitors. Justice and Vengene pulled tiny carved figures and beaded necklaces out of their fur and offered them to Mery, who backed away with mistrust. Eartha reached over, taking a tiny wooden figure from Vengene's hand.

-Well.. we gotta have tradin goods to go through those mountains. You never know what you'll run into. All kinds of crazies out there. 'Sides.. you been good to us.

Dumping out a variety of articles on the table, Vengene motioned for Mery to take something. She still declined. Justice leaned back and lit a pipe, studying the smoke that curled to the ceiling.

-Yep, I've seen all kinds of savage things.. bear.. wolf.. cougar. But humans beat all for just meanness. I could tell you stories. His eyes became haunted as he stared into the fire. He looked at Eartha and shook his head sadly.

-I see you're a woman of substance. You've got a nice setup here and it didn't come easy. I know yer a righteous woman, so I got to tell you about somethin' we saw. It's quite a stretch out of Lionshead. That bunch of shacks. I guess some call that area Fish Eye.

Eartha glanced at Lud. She could see it in his eyes.. the "righteous woman" part. He would make fun of that later. She had heard a few stories about a bunch of shacks called Fish Eye but had never investigated. Gambling.. prostitution.. those places were all the same. Some of them could be worse than others. She leaned forward and against her better judgement asked him what he knew.

-There's a place there, ma'am.

His eyes clouded as he stared at the wooden floor.

-They've got kids. Kids that don't belong to nobody and they treat em real bad.

He jumped up and hit his head on a beam, tears slowly making their way down his cheeks, his hands transformed into melon-sized fists. He'd obviously had a snout full of whiskey and was about to go haywire. Eartha's mind traveled back to her own first memories. A beginning of pain and humiliation at the hands of adults. Vengene coiled back, looking warily at his brother. Justice grabbed the back of a chair, searching the room with wild eyes.

-I can't stand it. I'm going back in there tonight. They're not doing that anymore to those little cubs.

Justice stumbled out the door with Vengene limping behind him. Lud followed with an amused look on his face, a cigarette hanging from his lip. He reached up to light it when a pole whipped through the air knocking it painfully from his fingers. Vengene stood in the shadows smiling.

-Now we're even.

Justice and Vengene lumbered off into the night. At the bridge, they mounted their horses, yelping into the dark. A sound that was not animal.. not human. They headed downriver and Eartha checked the bolt on her door twice. She went into town the next morning. About half way, she passed a blackened campsite that must have been used by the brothers. It was cold and they were gone.

***

A crowd had gathered at Bertrand's store and she pushed her way inside. Bertrand Snibe marched importantly toward her.

-Wait til you hear this, Eartha. Unbelievable! Fish Eye has been burned down. Every building.. people killed.. their throats slit. Some of them beaten into a bloody pile. A few of them must have ran off into the woods, but there's some kids left behind. Five or six of them. Nobody knows their names or anything about them. The kids say bears attacked! Can you believe it!?

Yes. Eartha could believe it.

-Where are the kids now?

-Some of the church folk have put up a big tent. They're being kept there temporarily until something can be figured out but it can't last long. You know what kind of weather these mountains are going to pull down. Geez. I can't believe it. Nobody even knows where those children came from.

Eartha felt her knees weaken and elbowed past him to catch her breath. She leaned against the building taking in gulps of air. The mountain men. They had done this and she was glad. That scum had it coming. Stepping out, she looked down the street and could see the newly erected tent. She remembered. She remembered what it felt like to be one of those children.

A girl sat alone in the dirt next to one of the tents. She was four or five years old, skinny, dirty and covered only in tattered bits of fabric. The little girl held something in her hand and she was whispering to it. When Eartha came to stand above her, the child hid her hand behind her and looked up with fear. Eartha knelt next to her.

-What's in your hand?

The little girl scooted back, squeezing her hand even tighter around the object, looking at Eartha with defiance. Eartha drew a picture of a simple doll in the dirt.

-Is it a wooden doll?

The girl studied her for a moment and nodded, a tiny tear rolling down her grimy face.

-Did a big bear give it to you?

The little girl nodded and almost smiled.

-Yes. A big white bear! He took us out and told us to hide under the tree. He told us to stay there and then he burned down our house. I think he hurt the man.

-What man?

-The man that owns us. The man that sells us. There was fire and people running around.

The little orphan looked down blankly at the dirt but brought her tiny hand forward and opened it. One of the carved wooden figures lay in her little palm. Eartha gently closed the girl's fingers around it, stood and entered the tent. Other children were there, playing in the dust or taking naps on blankets that had been tossed on the ground. Two women stood to the side in deep conversation. Eartha sized them up in their pristine long dresses.. hair pulled tightly into identical buns. She looked down at her own pants and work shirt.. knowing they would not approve.

-Ladies, what's your plan?

They looked at her with disdain, obviously resenting her interruption.

-As you can see.. we're having a discussion. They'll be sent to a poor house or a fitting institution.. or somewhere as soon as possible. Unless you're a parent.. and that's doubtful.. it's none of your concern. Are you a member of our church? No. I don't think so. Now, if you'll excuse us, we have business to handle.

-I'm Eartha Borne and no.. I'm not a member of your church.

The women stared at each other with obvious surprise.

-You're that woman that lives out on the Gore.

They studied her with renewed interest. She could see it.. smell it. That ferret look social climbers get when they sense money. Eartha turned from their simpering faces and walked away.. not shaking their extended hands.

She had enough money to start a place for these kids. And she knew where she could get a whole lot more. The crowd was still talking as she walked back to the mercantile store. Bertrand walked out on the porch with hands on hips staring at her.

-What are you going to do, Eartha? Something must be done. There's too many weird things happening around this area. There's a killer living among us. Skeletons found in creeks, the Jackso brothers drowning.. Mame's accident.. not to mention Wilma. It did look like suicide but now I'm not so sure. Now this. Did you hear what they did to that man out there in Fish Eye? They practically skinned him.

215

-What the hell do you mean, "What am I gonna do"? I'm not the damned law around here. It sounds like that bastard had a bad end coming. It sounds like everyone out there had it coming.

-Well, nobody in this town knew exactly what was going on.

-Yea, you know what Bertrand? They all say that.

She rode out of town in a dust cloud, leaving a steaming pile of horse manure in front of Bertrand's store.

***

Eartha had plenty of time to think as she rode back to Big Spruce. The sun was setting and she stopped for a moment to watch the cliffs glow with amber. The sight was comforting and she tried to pray. Her soul soared for just a moment, but it didn't last long. It never did. Eartha yearned to do something right, for a change. She nudged her horse and trotted across the bridge determined to do something good. Organizing paper and pen, she began to write.

Ladies, I met you today at the tent that is sheltering the children from Fish Eye. You kindly explained that they would be sent off to an orphanage, poor house or "somewhere". I want that "somewhere" to be the McCleod property called Scot's Depot, where I, along with a trusted staff, can care for them. I will fund this endeavor and keep it running. The property has a fine, large house with many rooms and is in excellent condition. The land produces valuable crops. It now sits empty but will be a stable home for these children.

I feel certain that your fine congregation will enthusiastically donate to this cause, however, we don't really need your help.

I am sending Angus and Lara McCleod to you as my personal representatives. They will have complete authority regarding this matter. Please treat them with courtesy. I truly hope that you don't decline this offer.
My Best Regards, Eartha Borne, Big Spruce

She stepped off the porch folding the paper and headed toward Angus and Lara McCleod's. Lara was tossing feed to the chickens with the help of her nieces and Duff. Eartha reached into the bucket and took a handful, throwing it at the cackling mob.

-How are you, Lara? It's been a while since we've talked. Is everything going well?

Lara looked over at Eartha and tears filled her gentle eyes. She placed the empty bucket on the ground.

-I'm so happy. I feel as if I've been given a second chance. I love my family.. all six of them now. And Angus.. such a good man. We are truly happy. When I realize what could have happened if you didn't come for me..

-Let's not think about it at all, Lara. It's over and you're home now. But, I need some advice and help.

217

She took some time telling the story of the children from Fish Eye and the orphanage that she wanted to create. Lara listened with sorrowful eyes.

-What can we do? What can we do to help them?

-I want to put you and Angus in charge. In fact, I'd like to deed that place over to you. Scot's Depot is the perfect place and it could help so many. I know what a kind heart you have and Angus is a capable man. Bible thumpers can be a self-righteous lot, so don't let them intimidate you. It will be a process. Here's the hard part, Lara.. those kids have been used and abused in ways that you can't even imagine. They think that's what's expected of them. They have never been treated decently and have never played with children that haven't been abused. They deserve a better life. I know it's a lot to ask and your children need to be warned about some behaviors that may emerge. But children can help children in ways that adults cannot. You and Angus could turn Scot's Depot into a refuge.

-Yes! Yes, we accept. I'm sure Angus will agree.

-You'd better make sure. If he's not for it.. I'll understand. Also, I have a bank-note made out to start an account under the name of Scot's Depot. I don't want it named orphanage or home for lost souls.. or anything like that. That place has always been called Scot's Depot. This is all I ask. You and Angus will make every decision. But just think, Lara.. it's already set up for growing all kinds of produce and plants.. and shipping them. It could be a very prosperous place again.. alive with hope.

Lara felt a twinge of fear and doubt. So much had happened at Scot's Depot. Adultery.. deceit.. insanity.. suicide and murder. Scot's Depot alive with hope?

Eartha watched her and read her mind.

-I know what you're thinking. But the truth is.. you and Angus are fine. And so are all of your children. Your suffering will help those poor little kids work through theirs. But, you might have to ride rough-shod over those church bitches. You and Angus will be in control of Scot's Depot and the bank account attached to it. I will be here if you need help, money or bad advice. After you talk to Angus tonight.. if he's in agreement with everything.. I'd like you to go into Lionshead tomorrow and open the account. You, Angus and I as signers. No one else. Start gathering up whatever you need from Bertrand's and deliver my letter to the church ladies. Read it first so you know what to expect from them.. and that is respect, Lara. From here on out, you and Angus own Scot's Depot. Albert Hedeman will draw up the papers.

The women stood and shook hands ceremoniously. Eartha marched back to her cabin, shut the door and weakly leaned against it. She whispered to herself..

-What the hell are you doing now!? Are you crazy? You're gonna need more money.

She would have to return to New Orleans and the thought sickened her. It had been so many years. Would she remember where the money was? Would she have the guts to go back to that place? She walked out on the porch with a bottle and sat down in the rocker, wrapped in a blanket. As she looked up at the darkening sky, Eartha tried to pray. She confided to the stars..

-Listen.. I've asked for signs from you and never got any that I know of. So, I'll do this just for insurance. Maybe you're out there.. maybe you're not. But I'm gonna need some help here.

A voice from the dark answered..

-I'll do whatever I can, darlin'.

It was Lud. Lud standing there.. pants stuffed in boots, shirtless with a towel hanging around his shoulders, hair skillfully tousled. He was obviously entertained by her plea.. as heartless as ever. He simultaneously plopped on the steps and jerked the bottle out of her hand with one move. Leaning his head back on the post, he took a lengthy swig.

-Well, sister, what're you doing out here? Praying? By the way, you're turning into quite a boozer. Not that I care. It's a pleasure to watch you slowly dissipate.

She kicked at him and missed, feeling a sharp stab in her leg.

-Haven't I told you enough times to stay off my porch?

-I know I can help, darlin'.. just ask.

-For starters, don't ever call me darlin' again. But yes. I've got to know. How did you ever find out about the money?

-Eartha, I'm going to be square with you.

His eyes darkened and she realized that he was.. actually.. going to tell her the truth.

-I was hired to find you and the money. All of it. Kill you and bring the money back. Simple assignment, wouldn't you think?

-Why haven't you done it?

-I don't know where *all* the money is. Now it's your turn for the truth. Is it all in the bank?

-Maybe.. maybe not. Why shouldn't I kill *you*?

-Oh, Eartha! I know you're good at that sort of thing. Very good. I've seen your work. But I'm the only one that can protect you from the New Orleans boys.

-I've got Coop and Theo.

-You damned well know they couldn't. They're good guys.. capable.. but they're no match for this and you know it. I've got the cold blood. I figure this puts me in a very good bargaining position. You can't live without me. The Southern boys know I can retrieve their losses. Oh. They also want revenge, Eartha.. almost as much as the money. You were a bad investment. I have to admit, this feels good.. having so much power.

He looked at her in the moonlight and grinned. That maddening, belligerent grin. Eartha stood, teetering slightly and pulled the bottle out of his hand. She turned to go inside but Lud stood quickly and blocked her way with his arm. He lightly touched his nose to hers.

-Can I come in? Just this once?

-Go to hell and get out of my way. You're like a broken record.

He lowered his arms and bowed with a flourish. She slammed the door as he laughed down the steps.

Getting the rest of the money was Eartha's only thought as she lay in bed listening to her heart beat. Her overactive mind prevented any hope of sleep, moving her to slowly open the door and look toward the church. No sign of Lud. No lights.. nothing. She left through the back door, crept into the woods and passed behind his cabin, stopping every few seconds to listen. She ran lightly across the bridge to Coop's cabin and tapped on the door.

-Who's out there?

-It's me.. Eartha.

Coop, wearing a pair of hastily donned trousers, lit a lamp as she entered. Without speaking, he tossed a few pieces of wood on the remaining coals and turned to look at her in the dim light.. silently waiting.

-Coop, I need to tell you some things that.. well.. that you might not want to believe. Maybe some of them will even turn you against me. I wouldn't blame you. You've never questioned me about my life before Big Spruce.. or how I came to this place. You've never asked about my money. I won't tell you everything because I don't believe I could take the look in your eyes. But some pieces you need to know, because I need your help. You may not want to give it after you hear me out.

Coop's expression hadn't changed, but he leaned back in his chair and put his feet on a stool.

-Shoot.

She studied his face.. a face that reflected his strength and integrity. He had a square jaw and a gentle smile. His deep eyes seemed to change color along with his emotions. She remembered, when Mame had been killed, how his eyes turned into black wells of grief. Eartha loved Coop and realized that this moment might be the last that he looked at her with any kind of respect. But she had to tell him.

She trusted him like no other.. and so she began..

TWENTY - EIGHT

THERE IS A PLACE

… in New Orleans, Coop …

"La Longue Nuit"

For decades, countless souls have been bought and sold by a family named Pervice. It was whispered that they had been in the "skin trade" for centuries.. before there even was a New Orleans. France.. Spain.. who really knows? They made millions and millions fulfilling the perversions of their "clients". I was one of their very profitable items. I was born there.. as were others. My crib was a cage where I stayed until they had an order.. and then taken out, cleaned up and costumed to be whatever the occasion called for. Clients sometimes took us off the property to re-sell us.. for days sometimes. If you were returned damaged, they would put you on "the shelf" until bruises healed, bones reset or a disease was treated. I'll spare you the details. Of course, they charged clients extra for unnecessary roughness. My mother was there, too and probably her mother before her. I don't know. I have no memory of her. I don't even know if I ever had a real name.. I've been called so many things. I took the name Eartha Borne from some papers I found in

224

the cabin when I first came into this valley. A couple had been killed by an avalanche and I took their name and property with the help of Albert Hedeman.

I have no idea who or what my father was. On the waterfront, La Longue Nuit was a gambling house and, of course, everyone knew they ran whores. But what the citizens didn't know, or pretended not to know.. was the extreme side of the business.. the real money maker. Children like me were rented out by doctors, lawyers.. priests. You name it.. they crept in from the dark. If they paid enough, they didn't have to bring you back at all. They could keep or kill you. The Pervices didn't care. There was an endless supply of deserted kids on the streets of New Orleans. A few of us were selected for education and manners. That would raise our value. "The gentlemen" liked to think they were getting something special for their money. When I was about thirteen, Fabian Pervice took a liking to me, and after that I was only rented out on rare occasions. There were two of them.. Julienne and Fabian. During the next few years, they began to trust me in their office.. tidying, organizing.. counting. One night, I came across a loaded gun in the drawer of a desk and thought about using it on myself. But what I really wanted was to kill the Pervices and burn that place down.

There was a constant stream of black bags being moved in and out of the office. They usually carried bodies or money. Stacks and stacks of money. Bags of gold and silver coins.. jewelry. One Monday morning.. around 2

225

a.m., I woke up in the office with a drunken Fabian laying on me. I squirmed out from under him and started to sneak back to my room when I saw the bags. Four of them. Full. Very full.

A few days earlier, it had come to my attention that I was most likely pregnant. One month had passed and I knew. My value was going to drop. They had already taken a child from me and I vowed that they would not get another. Even after the perversion that I had survived.. I knew that I was still a human being.

Eartha hesitated, looking away from Coop.

I opened one of the bags and stared down at the neat little stacks that I had tied together countless times. At that moment, I realized that I had a chance. I walked over to the drawer, took out the gun and took a cushion from the sofa. I put it over Fabian's face, shoved the gun in the pillow and blew his brains out. I pulled the trigger four times. No one came.. not a sound of movement in the house.

There was a firewood wagon kept just outside the door. I took a coat off the rack and pulled the bags.. one at a time and loaded them on the cart. It had rained and my bare toes sunk into the mud as I pulled it down the street, jumping at every alley cat that shrieked in the shadows. My heart raced as the wheels bumped along. At any moment, a knife could be drawn across my throat and that would be the end of my escape. The night was dark, but I could see the lights of the church down by the train crossing. I'd been there many times in the hands of Father O'Malley. The churchyard had become a convenient place for the Pervice brothers to bury several victims of La Longue Nuit.

I pulled the wagon along a vine covered path.. to the fresh grave of little Jasmine Robideaux. She had been buried the day before and the dirt was still soft. Jasmine was only four years old when a customer returned her with a broken neck. We dug her grave under the supervision of Father O'Malley. The Pervice brothers figured it was an excellent teaching tool.

As I stood by her unmarked grave, visions of the little girl swirled through my memory. She had only been at La Longue Nuit for a few months, but I became attached to her. She was so little and sweet. The laughter had not been completely stolen from her. However, displaying any human emotion was brutally discouraged.

I knelt and dug my fingers into the soft earth, scooping handfuls out until I felt her little body. She had been wrapped in a bloody sheet and tossed into the shallow hole with no words or tears. I laid her next to the wagon and pulled the bags down, pushing three of them into the empty grave and covering it back over with dirt. I smoothed it with a branch and scattered a few leaves, hoping that any change would not be noticed. It was an older part of the cemetery.. a place that had few visitors. I opened the fourth bag and placed Jasmine on top of the money.. pushing and tucking at her broken body until I could re-tie it. Even though she had been dead for less than a day, the damp New Orleans heat was speeding the decay process. I can't explain why I took her with me. I made a mental map of the location. A stained-glass window depicting the Mother and Child was just above the grave.. on the north side.

It was getting light and I knew the train was going to pull out soon. I'd heard the whistle many times at the house. There was one more thing I had to do. I slid through a side door of the church and went toward Father O'Malley's private room. I listened to his snore for a moment and then quietly pushed the door open. The room was lit with tiny red candles as I tiptoed over to his bed. His eyes flew open and I pulled the trigger, shooting him twice in the face. The blood spattered around the room, a drop hissing on a candle. Bless me father, for I have sinned.

The train tracks ran right past the church.. not more than fifty feet. The depot was less than a block away. I pulled the wagon close to a boxcar and pushed the door open a bit.. I called in to see if there was anyone else inside. It was my lucky night. From the height of the wagon bed, I managed to throw the bag inside and hop in after it. The whistle blew, the train had jerked to a start and I knew I was out of that rotten place. Me.. Jasmine and the money. The next weeks were long and hard. New Orleans to Fort Worth - Fort Worth to Denver. Waiting in alley ways, eating trash and bathing in rain puddles. No one bothered me much, mostly because of the smell

228

that surrounded me. One man made me open the bag to show him what I had, but when he saw the rot-soaked sheet he jumped back and crossed himself. They mostly thought I was crazy. I said it was the body of my dead sister and that I was taking her back to the mountains. Most of them were running from something, too.

In Denver, a group of prospectors took pity on me and offered a mule ride over the Rockies if I cooked for them. One of them was Lil Daisy Strand's father.. Abe. They made a point of being upwind from me. But I did cook for them until they dropped me off here on Gore Creek. Over all, they were a decent bunch.. just looking to discover some hope.

Eartha looked down at her hands with shame.

-Coop, about the time I was at La Longue Nuit.. no one could run from that place. A boy tried. He was eleven. They brought him back and killed him in front of us. We were forced to watch.. then bury him. I've got to go back there and get that money.. and kill Julienne Pervice.. if he's still alive.

***

Her story continued into the night.. telling things that she had never spoken before. As dawn broke.. the cabin became silent. Coop stared into the fire as if he could see the hideous images. Eartha looked down in shame..

regretting the way she had exposed the horrid tale. His silence was painful and she knew he would never look at her again without revulsion.

He finally stood, yawned and stretched his arms above his head. He opened the door and inhaled a deep breath of morning air.. watching the mist as he exhaled.

-Well, Eartha.. I figured it was something along those lines. I just thought it would be a lot worse.

She gasped back a sob and laughed like she was crazy, staring at him. He pulled her up from the chair, put his arms around her and held her head to his chest.

-What did you do with Jasmine's remains?

-She's buried up where Mame and Axel are. I'll mark her spot someday.. some year when an explanation won't be needed. She deserves it. But if I don't get to it.. she's the mound next to the big pine.. twenty feet north of Axel.

Coop ran his fingers through his dark, short hair.

-We'll get through this deal and we'll get your money. Nobody's going to hurt you. I'll make sure of that. By the way, where *are* the Bornes buried?

-Next to the barn. They had been digging a well when the snow slid down on them. I just covered them over and left them in peace.

-That spot where you planted all those peonies?

-Yes.

She looked at him with adoration.. realizing that she was in the presence of the best man she had ever known.

Sometime during that night's confession, an unbreakable bond of trust and loyalty forged between them.

-Coop.. one more thing and then you can get some sleep. Talk to Benno and have him build an iron box. One that can be bolted to the church floor. Have him build it five feet long, four feet high and two and one-half feet wide.. then layer it with hardwood. Lud will love having an altar. But here's the deal.. I want a secret door in that box that is totally hidden.. imperceptible. Have Benno make two iron angels, about six inches high and place them on each side of the altar, facing away from each other. It must be fashioned so that the angels are the mechanism to the latch on the door. But they must be turned at the same time, to face each other, to release the latch. That way, it'll be less likely to be opened by accident. This has got to be our secret, Coop. No one else. Okay.. except for Benno. It'll take some thinking, Coop.. to design this.

He looked at her and laughed.

-Why don't you just put the money in the bank?

-I did that once, but it wouldn't work again. Talk would get out and I'd be found. I know that Julienne Pervice has been hunting me all this time.. or his offspring, by now. They'll find me, sooner or later. More people are coming since Colorado has become a state. A railroad.. mining. Oh, yes. They will find me.

***

She was almost back to her place as the sun touched the bridge.. when Lud came strolling around the church from his cabin. He looked at her disheveled and hollow-eyed appearance.. the hem of her muddied robe.

-Why.. where ya you been, Eartha? You're looking a little ragged around the edges. Got a lover over there somewhere? Let's see.. there's only a handful of possibilities. You're not breaking your own rules now, are you?

He started counting names silently on his fingers. She looked at him with disgust but knew that trying to outwit him was a waste of time.

-Lud, as much as you disturb me with your revolting thoughts.. I do want to do something for this little chapel.

-You haven't been trying to pray again.. have you? Chapel? That's an interesting word. You mean this faux church?

-Yes. I want to dress it up a little. Those stained-glass windows you've been talking about.. maybe a raised pulpit? Maybe even an altar. Some candlesticks and.. angels. What do you think? It would make the church.. and *you*.. look a little more legit. Maybe you could even stop preaching with your gun belt on.

-Don't think so, Eartha. Everything sounds good except that part. Not taking it off. Think of my gun as an extension of me.

Within days, Benno started forging the altar. The stained glass and candle sticks were custom ordered from a craftsman in Santa Fe. The price was sweetened with a bonus if they could be delivered within two months. Difficult and expensive. Lud and Eartha, in a rare moment, agreed that the windows would not depict anything religious.. but instead be designed with natural elements, such as trees.. clouds.. Neither of them were believers but still didn't want to tempt the powers that might be.

TWENTY - NINE

TWO MONTHS LATER

… they received word from Pier Troya in Santa Fe. The windows were ready and he would personally deliver them. It would possibly take another month or more to install them.. a very difficult and delicate process. Would they be able to find accommodation at Big Spruce or would they need to make the trip from Lionshead every day? The altar had also been completed and bolted into the floor of the church. On each end was an iron angel that Benno had spent weeks perfecting during the dark hours of the night.

Pier Troya was coming on the train from Santa Fe to Lionshead with his assistant and the windows. They would be met in town and would be staying in a two-room guest cabin at Big Spruce. Theo, Madlyn and Mery wanted to meet them and would go in early to look around the new shops. The best hand on Big Spruce with a harnessed horse was Theo and Eartha hoped that he could prevent some broken glass. Very expensive broken glass.

The train arrived on time and Theo waited as passengers stepped from the doors. He watched for strangers and there were not many. When a tall grey haired man stepped from the train, Theo guessed that he must be Pier

Troya. By his side a young woman held his hand looking at him and laughing. She was dark and beautiful. Silver earrings framed her high cheek bones and a concho belt encircled her waist. Theo removed his hat and approached the couple.

-Are you Mr. Troya?

-Yes. This is my daughter and assistant, Rebekah. You must be Theo Tytanos? You may call me Pier, please.

The trip back to Big Spruce was long and slow. Even though the windows had been carefully wrapped and padded, Theo overreacted to the common sound of rimmed wheels crunching on hard dirt. He knew that he would have nightmares about this trip. Eartha relied on him and he would not fail. Mery chatted shyly with Rebekah.. relishing a conversation with an interesting young woman her age. She studied Rebekah's blue-black hair wrapped into a chignon at the base of her neck, anchored with a beaded band. She was very exotic with her belted velvet blouse and patterned skirt. She wore shining silver jewelry studded with a blue stone called turquoise. Her eyes were large and oval, fringed with black lashes. Her cheekbones were high and sculpted and her lips curled up when she talked.. as if laughter would accompany every sentence. Mery admired the embossed silver bracelet that she wore. Rebekah searched in her bag for a moment and delighted Mery with the gift of a similar bangle.

The wagon rolled slowly across the bridge, Theo sweating at every creak.. Pier Troya laughing at him.

They stopped in front of the church, where all hands began the careful process of unloading glass by lamplight. Eartha had barbequed some elk, made beans and bread.. popped out a couple of bottles of Lud's wine. Coop and Lud joined and they sat quietly enjoying the simple meal. Pier looked pleasantly surprised.

-Madame Eartha, this is the finest wine. It is fantastic.

Lud proudly chirped up..

-Mr. Troya this wine is named Le Chateau Rouge and is from New Orleans. We're so happy you like it.

He held his glass to the fire and watched the ruby reflection. His eyes narrowed to slits, but Eartha knew he was watching her, with a little smile on his lips. He continued.

-We'll send a case back to Santa Fe with you. A little gift.

Eartha tried not to glare at him, but it was difficult. We? Who the hell are "we"? She would kill him someday and it would feel great. She sat back daydreaming about methods of torture when she was interrupted by Pier..

-Madame Eartha, I thank you for your hospitality tonight for my daughter and myself. We must rest now as we have a lot of work coming. Goodnight and thank you.

He stood and bowed. Rebekah put her hand out to Eartha.

-Thank you so much. We will see you tomorrow. It has been a pleasure.

***

Pier Troya and Rebekah were up early, slowly unpacking and inspecting the glass. They carried each piece carefully and positioned them next to the existing windows. There were seven.. three on each side and one larger behind the pulpit. Coop and Lud arrived quickly to help with this task, under the guidance of Pier. They labored through the next weeks, until the time came to place the window behind the pulpit. Lud and Coop held it, slowly inching it toward the opening as Pier and Rebekah applied mortar and made adjustments. Even though the pieces were made according to precise measurements.. it was still a long and delicate process.

As the sun shone through a window, the colors and light danced on Rebekah's face. Coop watched in fascination and realized how beautiful she was. As he admired her, the glass slipped from his hand. He recovered it and saw the incredulous faces around him. He was embarrassed. Lud stepped toward him and spoke in preacher language..

-My son, don't be angry with yourself. We are all captivated by the beauty of these creations. I, myself, mashed my thumb with a hammer doing the same thing.

He looked at Coop with a knowing smile. Coop almost liked him.. just for an instant.

As the days progressed, Coop became increasingly enchanted with Rebekah, and she with him. They spent a large part of each day looking sideways at each other, attempting shy conversation. During the third week of this behavior, Lud sauntered up to Eartha's porch. He opened the door without knocking and startled Eartha.

237

She was sitting at the table, sipping on coffee and playing solitaire.

-Lud, damn you. What do you want? You'd better start knocking on that door.

-Or *what*? What, Eartha?

She looked so frustrated that he relinquished his attitude slightly.

-I want to show you something.

-Does it have to be now? I'm winning.

-At solitaire? Take a break and come over to the church with me. I promise.. it will interest you.

She could hear sawing and hammering, along with quiet laughter. The sun was setting and the light had, once again, lit the interior with dancing color. Lud put a finger to his lips, motioning Eartha to be quiet. They entered the church and took a seat silently in the back corner. Coop and Rebekah were working on a window as her father stood admiring the angels on the altar. Eartha looked at Lud with a question in her eye. "What?", she silently formed with her lips. He leaned over and whispered in her ear.. "Look at them." And she saw it.. the way they looked at each other.. completely oblivious to anyone else. She recalled that look on two other faces, years ago and the memory pulled at her heart. They spoke shyly and laughed. Rebekah reached over and brushed some sawdust from Coop's hair. Eartha looked at Lud with surprise and he looked back at her with.. *kindness*? They quietly left without being noticed.

-Lud, can we talk for a moment?

-Well, this is certainly a pleasant change. Why not? I don't have anything pressing right now. Unless you want to press.

-Stop it or forget it.

She looked at him waiting.

-Okay, I'm sorry. You just bring out my badder side.

She turned and pulled a bottle out of the wood box.

-Hiding it now? That's a bad sign, Eartha.

She was kneeling and looked up at him. And then she got the giggles, lost her balance and started to fall sideways when he put his hand out. She grabbed it and felt a disturbing sensation. It was warm, gentle and strong. And.. Lud's. With this realization, she pulled back and stood, primly smoothing her skirt.

-That's right. It *is* a bad sign.

She went into the cabin and came out with two glasses. They sipped and gazed at the church.

-Did you see it, Eartha?

-Yep.

-They're in love..or lust.. or something. I think maybe.. love. Coop is capable of that.

-I couldn't stand to see him get hurt again.

-Sorry Eartha, you have no say in this.

They sat silently gazing at the church until the sun disappeared behind the mountain. It started to cool and Eartha looked over at Lud.

-I'm going inside, Lud. It's getting cold out here.

-Thanks for the offer but I won't be able to stay.

Despite herself, Eartha laughed.

***

The next morning, Eartha loaded her pans on a cart and pulled it to the river. She liked to scour the iron with river sand, cleaning and polishing to her liking. But she enjoyed the work.. listening to the river.. trees in the breeze.. the whisper of the mountains. Big Spruce had a heartbeat and breath of its own. The red-winged blackbirds were particularly pleasing to her, as they hopped among the cattails.. trilling.. clinging to the stalk for a ride as it swayed with their weight. She always wondered if they were having fun and the thought made her smile. It was peaceful as she sat back with hands full of cool sand, taking a moment from scrubbing. As she leaned her head back, the rays of sun warmed her freckled cheeks and lit her auburn hair. She was thinking about Coop and Rebekah when a slight sound brought her around. It was Pier Troya.

-Madame, you look so serene that I am sorry to interrupt. However, there is a subject I wish to discuss.

She dropped the sand and wiped her hands on her pants.

-The windows are so beautiful, Pier. Your work is fine. What can I do for you? Anything.

-I will need more time here.

-Of course, that's not a problem. I will be happy to pay you for additional time and work. I know it's difficult. Could you please call me Eartha? Just plain Eartha? No Madame?

-It seems disrespectful. I'll attempt it, if you wish. The job is not the delay. With no offense, we have worked on much larger projects.. even cathedrals. But it was very good for us to get out of Santa Fe for some time.. especially Rebekah. She is part Jicarilla Apache and sometimes the "civilized" people of Santa Fe can be hard on her. Memory lives long there. I will not have her hearing the term "half-breed" anymore, when they think I am not listening. Her beauty sometimes attracts the wrong attention from the upper-class sons. In their estimation, she would never be good enough to marry. She does not speak of this.. but I know. She is my heart. Her mother is gone and I am dangerously old.. 86.. I realize that I look much younger.

He smiled.

-I believe she is falling in love with your Coop. Have you noticed this?

-I've noticed.

-How do you feel about that?

Eartha looked at the water rippling near her bare toes.. and then she told Pier Troya about Coop's beloved Mame. She looked over at the church tucked into the pines and then back at Pier.

-He loved her with his entire being. When she died, it almost killed him. And so I don't know how to answer your question.

Pier looked down at his hands, rubbing them.

-It is time for me to stop this work. My hands hurt and I cannot continue much longer. But Rebekah knows the craft and has much talent. She will always be able to make a living for herself, if need be. Your Coop has a good and gentle heart. Rebekah has never been in love before and so I fear for her as you do for Coop. Can he be trusted?

-With your life.

THIRTY

JUSTICE AND VENGENE

... sat beside their fire somewhere in the Rocky Mountains. They were cold, hungry and out of gun powder. It was outdated and hard to come by. Wrapped in disintegrating furs, they shared a rabbit that they had trapped and roasted. As they pulled it apart with their hands, they smacked loudly.. sucking on the bare bones.. allowing grease to run unstopped into their beards. They were aging, having wandered through the time of the mountain man fifty years before. Their breed was becoming extinct. It was over and they knew it. Civilization was ruining the west. There was no place to go.. except maybe Canada.

-That sure was some place down there. Big Spruce. Food.. close water and comforts.

Justice pulled a worn paper bundle from a leather pouch. He held the wad to his nose and inhaled deeply.

-This French soap she gave me. I could never part with it. I kinda liked her. Didn't you? Don't you think it mighta meant somethin special when she gave it to me? Those females.. sometimes they just give you hints.. then sit back and wait for the firecrackers.

-Yea, Justice. Whatever you say. But in case your memory fools you.. we did some pretty crazy shit in that town down there. She knows it and we know it. We can't go back. Let's just keep on over these Rockies.. head for Denver. And, Justice, the game can smell that damned soap, too. It's put a considerable dent in our huntin. You need to lose it.

Justice Burns stared into the fire, his eyes lighting with madness.

-I think we should go back there. I think she liked me more than you think. I saw it in her eyes.

-Really?.. and did you see how fast that Lud can fan his gun? Did you see that, you idiot? And what about those guard cabins by the bridge.. remember them? As I recall, there were a couple of damned good hands down there. Eartha's got top notch protection.

Justice ripped a last shred of rabbit and tossed the bone away, licking his fingers. He laughed.

-I got special ways with gals. She'll take to me.

-Sure, Justice.. only what I seem to remember is a couple of them ended up with broken necks.

Justice didn't laugh but sat back against his saddle, thinking about the man with the pistols.

-We'll wade down the river, Vengene. Leave a horse with our new friend here. They looked across the fire at the man that had joined them.

***

Eartha jerked awake. Something was in the cabin. She lay still, holding her breath. She had smelled an old bear in the trees before and this was the same sour, rancid odor. Was it her imagination? The wind? Another creak. She rolled on her side and tried to reach her robe. A fur covered arm pulled her forward and another hand jerked her head back by the hair as she was roughly thrown to the floor. She was trapped in the grip of an animal and it was mashing its head between her breasts. A rough stinking mouth covered hers, cutting her air off. Kicking and squealing, she fought but knew her struggle was futile. This was a giant and she didn't stand a chance. Her legs kicked wildly in the air as she was lifted off the floor. A hand jabbed between her thighs and the sharp nails cut her skin. She couldn't breathe.. but a voice screamed in her being. Survive. With all of her strength, she freed one of her hands and dug her fingers around an eye. The thing howled and smacked the side of her head. But she held on, closing her finger around the slimy ball. She squeezed, twisting her wrist, then pulled and felt the eye break loose from the socket. Justice Burns roared and fell back holding his face. Eartha scrambled toward the door on her hands and knees, but his hand snaked forward, closing around her ankle. He dragged her back as if she were a rag doll. He was looking at her in the moonlight with one eye, blood dripping into his white beard.. laughing like crazy.

-You'll pay for that. But there ain't no hurry.

Eartha screamed with all her might until his hand slapped her hard. Tiny pinpoints of light were dancing in the dark as she heard the metallic sound of a knife being pulled from a sheath.

-I'm gonna cut you up when I'm done, bitch. You ain't no different than the rest of em.

She scratched and kicked until very near the end of her life.. and then the thing was gone. Lifted off her. She gulped air and looked across the moonlit room at two figures struggling.. knocking over the lamp. A gunshot.. deafening. The smell of sulfur filled her nostrils.

Eartha scrambled backward searching for any hole to hide in. There wasn't one. A figure moved toward her.. fast and quiet. She curled into a ball on the hardwood, waiting for the sting of a knife to cross her skin.

Arms around her.. lifting her to the bed.. holding her.. rocking her.

-It's okay now, Eartha. It's okay. I'm here now. You're safe. I'm here.

She clutched him, gulping for air between silent screams. They were a cry from her soul as she tried to curl smaller into his arms.. like a terrified child. Jerking a blanket off the bed, he covered her nakedness and held her.. sobbing.. until the sun found a way to the window. As he whistled a low, soothing tune, he laid back on the bed.. pulling her with him.

Eartha's brain drifted back..

Pain was her first memory. Being slapped and shoved around. A little girl. Laughed at.. spit on. A priest that made her confess sins she didn't understand.. putting the words in her mouth just to hear her speak them. With every innocent confession that passed her lips, he would whip her, chanting.. "Thou Shalt Not". It was an endless thrill for him. "Thou Shalt Not". She could still hear voices bartering in the other room. The priest only identified them by age. I want a five-year old.. a boy.. a girl. She slept in a box at night.. hidden in his church.. where he had constant access to her. Then back to La Longue Nuit for a trade. It always took a couple of weeks for her little body to heal.. but her mind never did.

She opened her bruised eyes and slowly looked at the man holding her. It was Lud and he watched warily, wondering how she would react. She ached all over, but pushed up on an elbow. Justice Burns lay dead in a furry heap. One eye was missing. She relaxed her fist and watched as it fell to the floor.

Rising, she pulled the blanket around her, painfully limping to the door of the cabin. Vengene lay across the steps, blood oozing from his chest. Lud stepped close but did not attempt to touch her.

-Do you know where you are, Eartha?

-Home. Home at Big Spruce .. right?

Taking a deep breath, she looked at him and steadied herself against the log wall, looking out to the porch. Vengene had a hunting knife stuck in his ribs.

247

- I guess he didn't have to worry about your gun after all.

***

The next morning, Lud and Coop decided it was time to do some brush burning. They spent the day piling weeds, dragging limbs and other debris to a pile. They lit it and stood back watching until the flames had all but burned out. They had tossed it with kerosene, accelerating the flames to burn fast and hot. They stood watch throughout the afternoon, until they could turn the earth with their shovels, stamping out every last ember.. every trace of Justice and his brother, Vengene.

-Coop, let's go up river and see if we can find their camp. Their horses are probably tied somewhere.

They rode along the river until they found a cold camp but no horses. A skiff of first snow had fallen and they kicked it around, searching for a broken rein or track. Lud kneeled and stirred the spent coals with a stick. He poked at what looked like a book and scraped it out. It was covered in ash, pages partially destroyed but he could still open it to the inner pages. A bible. Lud felt a chill creep up his neck as he peeled back the charred leather cover. Written on the inside, barely discernable was the name Reverend Simon Hook. Lud jerked back as if a snake had struck at him. Coop had moved up the hill and called down..

-I found some tracks. Looks like those nags are headed down valley toward Big Spruce. Not over the mountains.

248

But then any horse with sense would. There's no tack. Those two fools wouldn't have left them saddled up here.

THIRTY - ONE

THE RIDE BACK

… to Big Spruce seemed to take an eternity, even though they pushed the horses. As they came down the trail, Lud could see one horse tied at the back of Theo's cabin. One horse.. not three. Coop worked at mending a fence just over the bridge.

-Warn Eartha that Hook is here. Tell Benno and Lil Daisy. Tell everybody. He didn't come back for a social call.

The back door of the cabin rocked open. On the floor lay Madlyn.. blood seeping from a gash on her head. Lud grew pale. This was his fault. He should have killed that bastard when he had the chance.

-He did this to get even with me. They had to go down river and we can catch up to them. Watch for Theo along the road, but we can't waste any time. Hook had to have headed down the river with her in this weather. There's no other direction to go. They can't make it far in this storm.

Freezing sleet lashed from the clouds and any hope of finding a decent track began to disappear in the muck. The minutes turned to hours and the hours eventually turned to days. They split up, questioning everyone they encountered. They went door to door in Lionshead. After two weeks of dogged searching, they returned broken hearted to Big Spruce. Hook and Mery had disappeared into thin air. At the fork of the Eagle River and Gore Creek, they could have gone in either direction.

Rebekah had sketched a portrait of Mery and now mimeographed copies were sadly distributed in town. Lud nailed ten posters on the soiled walls of the Evening Star and shoved one into the face of Kyle Pukeard, threatening violence if they were removed. The bulletins were nailed to trees and fenceposts at every crossroads. News of the reward spread quickly. With every nail that Lud pounded, he vowed to find the monster that had taken Mery. The monster that he had set free.

A fire pit had been dug in the heart of Big Spruce and became a gathering place. When it was ablaze.. people would come. They gathered to cuss or ponder their lives.. ask for help and advice.. or just socialize. They had all gathered around the pit for months after Mery was taken, trying to think of how to find her.. to hear any news. Madlyn often sat by the flames until dawn, praying that she would see her daughter walk into the light from the dark woods.

Late one night, Eartha and Lud found themselves watching dying embers pop as sparks fluttered into the light breeze.

-I don't know what else we can do, Lud. I'm out of ideas. I'd sell this place if it would bring her back. We've tried everything.. gone everywhere. The detectives have no news.. nothing. People can disappear if they are driven. I have all these years.. but still look over my shoulder. Always the hunted.

-Eartha, one day, that bastard will make a point of letting us know what he's done to her. He's a sadist and wants us to suffer for running him out. The weak and helpless will always be his target. His end is coming, I just hope I'm the one to give it to him.

Eartha watched as Lud put his head in his hands. She saw the tear fall, catching light from the fire as it dropped to the dust.

THIRTY - TWO

IT WAS HOT

… and the lettuce crop at Scot's Depot was thriving. August rains came along with healthy doses of sun. Mushrooms galore had been gathered, eaten sold or dried. The McCleods and the children were proud of the abundance and variety of produce that they reaped. The place was literally blossoming with hope, purpose and healing. Each task was carefully chosen to match the ability and age of the child. The evening meal was peppered with enthusiastic conversation, usually centered around the miracle of growing. In addition to edibles, there was an abundant selection of flowers that spilled from vases throughout the house. Town people consistently purchased produce, seeds, starter plants or additives for growing soil. Now and then, a couple would inquire about the possibility of an adoption, but Scot's Depot would not yet consider it. Not yet. However, two more babies had been dropped off on the porch since Scot's Depot had officially became a haven for little souls. If the time came, Angus and Lara would be very careful about the process. Until then, they had their dreams of someday sending each child to a good college. Additions to the house were designed and built. More bedrooms, bathtubs.. a library. They attended school at

Big Spruce under the guidance of, Miss Duncan.. a middle-aged spinster that had passed the rigid hiring process of Eartha and Co. The school year was November through April, allowing for planting, harvesting and hunting. Most, if not every child had emotional or mental challenges, but the McCleods were prepared and soothed the hurts with patience and love. Duff and his cousins were all part of the mix.

Coop had stopped by Scot's Depot to help load lettuce on the train when one of the hired men hesitantly approached him. Sam.. a decent guy that was struggling to raise a family outside of Lionshead. He had been watching Coop for some time, inwardly battling with a decision.

-How's it going, Sam? I can tell you've got something on your mind. Family ok?

-I guess I'll just get to it, Coop. That girl that disappeared out there at Big Spruce some months back. Theo's daughter.. named Mery?

Coop stopped working and sat down on the dock, peering up at Sam against the sunlight.

-I heard there's a girl up around Leadville could be her. There's a place out at the edge of town.. a pretty rough joint. Bar and restaurant on the ground floor.. rooms upstairs. They say if you're not Mexican.. don't go there. I don't know if it has a name or not, but they say it has a sign out front painted with a red rose.

By now, Sam had sat next to Coop and pulled a plug of tobacco out of his pocket, offering some.

254

-No thanks. Makes your teeth yellow and your breath stink. Except for yours, of course. What else?

-She's got a cross burned into her cheek. They say it's a brand that took up the entire right side of her face. Can you imagine some freak doing that to a woman?

***

Early the next morning, Coop jumped from a boxcar, made some inquiries and headed toward Stringtown. At least a mile isolated it from the main street of Leadville. The area was separate and forbidding. He headed for the only building that could be a possibility. A rickety deck wrapped around the second floor.. cafe on the bottom.. a piece of cardboard with "en alguiler" scrawled across it was propped against a dirty window. A wooden sign dangled at the front door but Coop could not make out the faded name. It did have a red rose painted on it.

The interior was cool, dim and filled with activity.. sounds and smells. Spices, cooking.. baking. Good smells and he was hungry. As he appeared just inside the door, silence slowly moved through the room like a ripple in a pond. The dozen or so customers looked at him without acknowledgement.. not betraying what they were thinking. He walked over to a small, shaky table and sat down. He leaned his back against the wall and waited.. and waited. No one came near him. The waitress past him many times without a glance. The bartender chewed on a straw and laughed at some joke. Undoubtedly, about the gringo that dared to be there. Slowly the chatter resumed and eventually regained its previous pitch. A few people sauntered out.. one man kicking the leg of Coop's chair as he passed. Hard. They clearly didn't want him there. They also knew that he was alone.

Coop could be stubborn, too. There was a deck of cards on a nearby table and Coop grabbed it, playing solitaire for the next hour.. not looking at anyone. On the bar was a pitcher with ice and some glasses. Coop walked over, picked up a glass and made a point of wiping it out with his shirt. Insulting. The bartender threw his towel on the bar and moved to stand in front of Coop. He was big and mean and Coop braced himself for a bruising scuffle. It wouldn't be the first time.

-What you want, Gringo?

-Breakfast if that wouldn't be too much trouble. No hurry though.

He grinned at the humorless face.

-We don't make breakfast.

-I think you do. I've been watching your customers fill their bellies for at least an hour.

-Did you notice anything else about them, Senor?

-Yep.

At that instant, Coop saw a woman pass by the kitchen door. It looked like it could be her, but he wasn't sure. She had passed so quickly. The Mexican stood watching.. confused, but intrigued, as Coop started toward the back.

-Hey? You going to cook your own breakfast?

The Mexican laughed to himself and then stopped as if he couldn't figure out what was funny. He followed Coop and roughly grabbed his arm. The woman was making fresh tortillas on a table and turned to see what was happening. Her face was horribly disfigured by a brand that had been burned into the right side of her face. The skin was puckered and purple, forming a hideous cross. Her right eye oozed with tears and was distorted by the burned flesh. But the left eye was the beautiful and bright one that belonged to Mery Tytanos. She stumbled back, putting a hand to her mouth as she recognized him. She covered her face with her hands and turned in shame. A blow from behind knocked Coop across the kitchen. He landed in an explosion of tubs and dishes, spilling sudsy water onto the floor. As he tried to regain his footing, Mery rushed forward and flung herself at the assailant.

-No! Mateo. He is a friend.

The big man pulled Mery toward him in a protective clutch, glaring at Coop. He listened to her patiently and then his eyes softened. Coop saw it. He loved her and had ceased to see her scars. Mateo squared his shoulders and looked Coop over with disapproval.

-Get yourself cleaned up. Out there is a water trough for the horses. Wash up. You're a mess. I'll get you something to eat.

Coop splashed water on his face and tried to clean the food from his clothes. He turned and Mery stood with a dry, clean towel and a hot plate of food. She shyly handed him the towel and they sat at an outdoor table used by the café workers. She sat with the right side of her face away from Coop and looked out over the valley. He shoveled food in his mouth as he admired the left side of her face. It was perfect and beautiful. One long black braid fell down her back, decorated with a mountain flower.

-I'm not going back. I know that's why you're here but I'm not going back.

She dabbed at her right eye with a cloth.

-Your folks need to know you're alive and ok.

She laughed bitterly and turned to face him.

-Do I *look ok*, Coop? What future would I have around Lionshead, or Big Spruce, for that matter? Seeing the look of pity and guilt wherever I would go? No! I stay here. I have a place here and I'm treated good. When he looks at me he doesn't see the mark that a mad man left on my face. He sees me.. the Mery that existed before Hook got his hands on me. I'm not going back.

Coop took a long drink of coffee.. knowing in his heart that she was right. But what would he tell them? They would look for her forever. Forever. She sat picking at an invisible thread on her dress.. then wordlessly went back into the kitchen.

He waited for the better part of an hour wondering what to do, when the screen door slammed behind him. Mery sat next to him with a sealed envelope in her hand.

-Please give this to my family and tell them it was given to you by a drifter.

She shakily handed him the envelope.

258

-You must never tell them where I am. I have never and will never discuss what that man did to me. It will die inside me someday and then I will find happiness here with Mateo. If you tell them, I will have to hide somewhere else. Please, hear me. I am very safe here. I have no other life.

She reached over and took his hand, squeezing it hard.. as if she felt bad for him.

-Mery, do you have any idea where he is? Hook?

She flinched at the name.

-Dead. He's dead. Mateo did that for me. It's in the letter.

***

Coop leaned against the boxcar watching the scenery stream past the open doors. He had forgotten how cold Leadville could be and found himself wishing for a warmer coat. In this country, the sun had few chances of warming the earth. He patted the envelope inside a chest pocket, resting his hand on it for a moment in sadness. Later that evening, he delivered the letter to Theo and walked across the bridge toward the barn. He found Lud grooming his horse and organizing his tack by lamplight. The two dogs, Begone and Wouton lounged in the dirt admiring his work.

-I'm going out tomorrow. Be gone for a few days. I heard about a woman up around Cheyenne. Could be her.

-It's over, Lud. He's dead. Hook is dead. It's over.

Lud dropped his brush and steadied himself against the horse. He looked across its back at Coop, his eyes darkening.. his face grim and pale. He walked around until he was close to Coop, searching his eyes for deception.

-What the hell are you talking about?

-Let's go for a walk, Lud.

They sat by the river, talking quietly. At one point, Lud slammed his fist into the sand. The door to Theo's cabin opened and he stood silhouetted in the light from within.. the letter pressed to his heart. His shoulders heaved with grief and he sank to his knees. They watched in silence, knowing there were no words to comfort him.

Lud took a deep breath and walked into the dark.

THIRTY - THREE

CHESS IS HARD

… thought Theo as he studied the board in front of him. It was his move and he wanted to make it count. The "fearless" Pyrenees, Begone III, lay flopping his tail amiably on the porch. Ma Campbell sipped on a "lemonade", obviously pleased with herself. The two had been battling over chess for years and were well matched. The hotel was quiet.. the weather warm. Madlyn was roaming through various shops.. selecting supplies to take back to Big Spruce. She labored to keep her mind busy so that it would not drift to the memory of her missing daughter. Despite the letter, she would forever search every street for Mery's face. Coop never knew what was in the letter. They never shared it. What Mery had written, ended the search, but not the grief.

-I believe I have you in a tight spot there, Theo.

He looked at Ma Campbell then silently returned his gaze to the board. His sharp black eyes darted around the pieces and then a barely perceptible smile crossed his mustached lips. He slowly moved the chosen piece and looked at her, grinning.. pushing his hat forward on his head. He'd also been watching two strangers on the other side of the street. They didn't belong somehow. One pulled a timepiece out of his pocket and twirled it around

261

by its gold chain. He unbuttoned his vest and Theo saw the derringer that was strapped on the left side of his shoulder beneath the material. City rats.. beady eyes and pointed noses.. shiny shoes. They stood debating and then walked north to the outer edge of town. Toward Pukeard's Evening Star.

-Check-mate, Ma Campbell. You're done.

She stared at the chessboard in shock and realized she was truly.. done.

-Well, I'll fix us another lemonade if you've got the guts to take me on again.

-No, ma'am, I must do some looking around. But thank you for your hospitality. You need more practice.

-Until next time.

Bowing to her, he walked down the steps, listening to the sound of his spurs hitting the wood. He relished the sound and exaggerated it as often as possible. Madlyn had bought him a fancy silver pair at Bertrand's Mercantile. He was a fine horseman but never dug them into an animal's side. They were mostly just for wearing in town. He motioned Begone into the wagon.. then jingled down the street, sniffing on a leaf of mint he had plucked from the hotel herb pot.

He rarely entered a bar.. didn't have the time or inclination.. but today he would make time. He was curious about these two strangers. He entered the cool, dark room and moved to the right until his eyes adjusted to the light. They were standing at the bar.. sipping whiskey.. looking around as if they were waiting. Theo saw their faces reflected in the dingy mirror. They noticed him without reaction, but he knew they had taken in every detail of every movement in the bar.. and town that day. Most of Pukeard's business came from transients passing through. Rarely would a citizen of Lionshead be caught dead in the place. But over the years, there had been a few.. caught dead.

Pukeard wasn't tending bar that day, but had a new-hire working. One of the men put his boot on the foot rest, exposing the handle of a slim knife beneath his pantleg. The bartender asked the classic question..

-What brings you boys to Lionshead?

-We're looking for a woman.

The bartender laughed.

-You may have found the right place. We've got a decent selection. Well, maybe not decent.. but a small selection.

He laughed at his own joke looking at them.. waiting for them to get it. They looked back at him without smiling. He felt the hair rise on his forearm and realized he should stick to his own business. He started wiping the counter moving away from them.

-We've got a picture to show you.

The man pulled out a small, faded black and white photo of a girl, dressed in flimsy clothing. It was difficult to guess her age, but she was very young. The picture was worn and dog-eared. The bartender looked at it closely and shook his head.

-Nope. Don't know her. But I ain't been here long. Just a few days. What'd she do?

-Killed and robbed a man. We've been hired by the family to find her and bring her to justice. This is an old photo so she's considerably older now. But we'll find her. No matter what it takes.. or how much time.

Theo rarely became involved in the affairs of others, but he had a bad feeling about these two. He stepped out of the shadows and ordered a shot of whiskey. They looked over at him with irritation.

-May I order a drink?

The bartender looked up and snidely responded..

-We don't serve Mexicans. You people have your own places. Now get out.

Theo looked at the two men.

-I have lived here for a long time. Maybe I would know the person in the photo.

The men looked at each other, one shrugged and slid the photo over. Theo tried not to react as he looked down at a younger version of Eartha. The face from many years past.. she had been so young. Just a kid.

-I've seen her.

-And?

-Maybe a drink will refresh my memory.

His mind was racing. How could he protect her identity from these two pit bulls? Had they shown the photo to anyone else in town? No.. or they wouldn't be asking now.

-Give him a drink. Maybe this will help your memory.

264

The smaller man tucked a five-dollar bill under the drink and looked back at him expectantly. Theo wanted to stuff the money down the man's throat but took a sip from his drink.

-Yes, I think she passed through here some years back. Down on her luck.. made a few dollars in the alley. You know what I mean. Let's see. I heard that she was headed for..

He closed his eyes pretending to remember. He pulled a pre-rolled cigarette from his pocket and lit it. The smoke drifted around his face.

-I heard she was headed for a place down in Texas somewhere. El Paso. That's it! El Paso. Let me see that picture again just to be certain.

It was handed back to him and he carefully flattened the paper on the bar, bending his head to study it. He reached for his drink again and spilled it.. the contents soaking the photo. The cigarette fell from his mouth and set the mess on fire. One of the men tried to jerk the photo from the flame, backhanding Theo at the same time. Theo stumbled back, raising his hand to his face.

-You dumb greaser!

The taller man grabbed at Theo's shirt and jutted his jaw out.

-Is it her? At least tell us that!

-Yes, I am certain. She left a long time ago and has never returned. I'm sure.

He forced himself to stumble to the door drunkenly but then strode soberly down the road to Bertrand's where he found Madlyn.

-Get in the wagon. *Now.*

Madlyn looked at him in surprise.

-Have you been drinking?

As the wagon pulled out of Lionshead, the men in the bar ordered another drink. They sat wearily at a table, looking at each other. They had been hunting that bitch for years and had only run into dead-ends.

-Shit! We should have given him a pounding for that. It'll take forever to get another copy of that damned photo, if one even exists.

The other one looked over at his accomplice and shook his head.

-There are no copies. We've been looking for her in every hell hole from here to New Orleans. Nothin. She could be dead by now. She might have been dead the day after she killed Fabian Pervice.

They looked around the pathetic bar for a moment in silence.

-What the hell.. we're still getting paid. We sort of know what she looks like.

THIRTY - FOUR

THE DUST SWIRLED

... around the pen as the horse and man danced together.. each wary of the other. Magreef had been traded to Coop for some elk hides. He was a big sorrel gelding that reflected good bloodlines.. not that it mattered now. A natural white X marked the animal's forehead.. so distinct that it appeared to have been painted. More than one previous owner had thought about putting a bullet where X marked the spot. But he was too eye-catching and could always be sold for a profit to some sucker. Coop couldn't resist a hopeless cause and this horse fit the bill. Wild, crazy and, by all accounts.. could not be trained by a civilized hand. Coop had worked with him for a month and was starting to get the picture. The horse was unpredictable and dangerous, but Coop hated to give up on him. Eartha quietly walked along the side of the barn trying not to startle the horse, but he saw her and became wild eyed.

-Sorry, Coop. I tried to be sneaky.

She bent to watch between the rails.

-You know.. Magreef is beautiful but truly crazy. What are you going to do with him?

The afternoon was mild with bits of sun between the clouds. A slight breeze delivered the scent of pines. Coop looked toward the river and watched a fish jump for a fly, flipping diamonds of water into the light.

-I guess I'll just keep working with him and maybe we'll grow old together.

-What about Rebekah? Do you ever think about growing old with her?

-Well, damn, Eartha. You're getting all misty and sentimental.

She didn't reply as Coop climbed up to sit on the fence.

-In answer to your question.. no. I don't think I'll have a life with Rebekah. Don't get me wrong. She's everything possible and I have feelings for her. But when Mame was killed something died inside me and it will never come back. I won't waste Rebekah's life. She deserves better than that.

-They're going back to Santa Fe in a couple of weeks. I guess everyone just kind of assumed..

-That's a big mistake now, isn't it? I've told her, Eartha. She knows there's no future here with me. I can't make myself love her. I thought I could but it's not going to happen.

Coop jumped to the ground, opened the gate and let Magreef run like a mad-horse back into the field. The horse kicked and snorted, twisting his body as if he were fighting an invisible rider. The sound of horse gas exploded through the air with defiance. Coop turned his back to leave when Eartha walked over, taking hold of his arm.

-I'm sorry. This is no one's business but yours. I need to tell you something and don't want a big argument.. but it looks like you're already in the fighting mood. I'll be gone for a couple of weeks.

He looked at her waiting for the rest of it, eventually tipping his hat at a comical angle.

-Okay. I'll bite. Where are you going?

-New Orleans.

He took a step back staring at her in disbelief.

-You're nuts, Eartha. What the hell would you do that for?! They'll kill you! Why would you *do* that?

-Money. Revenge. All of those things that make me "me".

She laughed, hoping to see him smile.

-Coop, I need the money and can't rest until that other bastard is dead. You heard what Theo said about those two in Lionshead. Someone will be looking as long as they get paid. Julienne Pervice is still paying the hounds.

-You need the *money*? Look around here. Things are good. Big Spruce is thriving.

-Ok, then.. just pure greed and revenge.

She looked around to make sure no one could hear.

-There's three more bags in Jasmine Robideaux's original grave in New Orleans. Do you have any idea how much?

-How much?

-Millions. The Pervices had everything they stored converted to big bills. Money handling was their business. Money and degradation. Three bags, Coop..

each at least sixty pounds. Bags of gold coins.. I can't even imagine what's tucked around that old mansion by now.

Her eyes reflected dollar signs.

-You couldn't lift that, Eartha.

-Leave that to me. I was born for this type of heist. I'm just telling you so you won't search for me in Salt Lake City or somewhere. Keep an eye on things here.. but tell Lud that I went back to Salt Lake to talk to Isabelle one more time. He'll believe that.

-How're you getting down there?

She studied him for a moment, not sure if she should tell.

-Same way I came. I'll take the rails as much as possible. But this time I'll be able to buy a ticket instead of riding the boxcars. Colorado south to Texas.. turn east at Houston. New Orleans next stop.

He missed the humor.

-Here's the beauty of it, Coop. The tracks are close to the church and the Pervice place.. the La Longue Nuit. Easy. Maybe I'll come across a horse and wagon to steal.

-Maybe it's not there anymore. Did you ever think of that?

-Oh, it's there. Some things you just know down deep in your gut. But I'm counting on you, Coop. You'll have to go into Lionshead tomorrow afternoon and get Samson at the livery. Hold it together while I'm gone and don't let Lud get suspicious.

Too late. The wheels were already turning as Lud peeked through the blinds of his cabin, watching the two. It was obvious they were cooking something up. He could smell it. He could taste it. But most of all.. he saw the way they were talking.. chummy.. secretive..

Later that evening, Lud watched Coop as he worked another horse in the pen. He rolled a cigarette and stuck it to his lip without lighting it. Taking a deep breath of mountain air, with hands in pockets, he sauntered casually down to the pen.

-How's it going Coop? Nice evening, huh?

-Are you going to light that thing, Lud?.. or just let it flop around your face.

-Eartha says it makes my breath stink and my teeth brown.

-I didn't think Eartha got that close to you. Not voluntarily.

-You probably haven't noticed, Coop.. and rightfully so.. that I'm a damned good looking man. I intend to keep my looks and my fresh breath as long as humanly possible.

He grinned as he flexed his right arm.. reached up to jerk the cigarette from his lip but it stuck.

-Shit! That hurt.

Coop spit out a laugh as he looked at paper bits glued to Lud's lip. Leaning against the fence, Lud looked at Coop intently.

-What were you and Eartha talking about? Looked serious. You guys need any advice? On anything?

-Nope. But since you're asking, she's headed for Salt Lake.. again. Gonna try one more time to get Isabelle back here. Maybe even Jubal. But do not mention it to her. Do not. It's a touchy subject.

She told me, to tell you, that she was going shopping in Denver for two or three weeks so keep this under your hat.

THIRTY - FIVE

EARTHA PULLED THE HAT

... low on her forehead. Propping her legs on the connecting seat, she discouraged anyone from joining her. Not that they would.. the train only had a handful of passengers. Eartha had rubbed some old clothes and boots with horse manure earlier, letting it dry into the material. She wore smudgy glass spectacles and looked away when someone glanced at her. Her only possessions were a gunny sack holding a few items.. jerky.. a change of underwear (or two).. a .45 with bullets.. She had hacked her hair raggedly to just above her shoulders and rubbed dirt and weeds into it. Overall, she was repulsive. Eartha was a pro at discouraging attention. The ticket had been purchased a few days earlier and the man at the window didn't question or recognize her. Four days passed and the scenery with them. From mountains to plains. The rattle of the tracks.. the sound of her mind.. the memories.. Leadville.. switch.. Salida.. switch. Grab a sausage and a drink at a stop.. switch.. Pueblo.. splash water on her sweating face and head. It was getting hotter.. pee behind a train-car.. switch.. Texas.. eat a burrito from a vendor that didn't bother to look at her face. Switch.

As the hours passed and the thrill of swatting flies diminished, she realized she had made one huge mistake. Possibly one of the biggest of her life. She couldn't pull this off. She didn't have the strength or know how. She wasn't even sure she had the guts anymore. Even though the Pervices had been fat and slow.. there was no telling who else might be around the place by now. They always had enforcers.. sadistic and heartless.. mindless men, well paid in gold and flesh. Self-doubt.. a dangerous thing.. was settling in. Her eyes felt as if they would explode if she did not release the tears and let them run down her grimy cheeks. What a stupid plan. What a fool she was to think she could make one last trip to hell.

She drifted into light sleep for the hundredth time. As she sunk against the sooty window, her leg slid off the seat and her hand relaxed a bit on the gunny sack.

She felt a presence beside her and someone tugged ever so slightly on the bag. Jerking upright, she tightened her hand around the sack, elbowing and shoving with all her might at the intruder next to her. She heard him grunt but he didn't move. She hissed.

-Get lost, jackass.

The man jerked back, blurting..

-Geez! You stink, Eartha.

The voice stunned her with familiarity. She leaned back against the window staring at the figure in the dark.

-Coop! Oh God.. *Coop*?

It was him. She threw her arms around his neck, holding him as if she would fall into the dark and never return.

-What are you doing? How'd you get here? What the hell *are* you doing?

-I've been with you the entire time. Starting in Lionshead. I've eaten the same junk and peed behind the same boxcars. Did you really think I'd let you do this alone? How much farther?

He could see her profile against the muted light of the window. A derelict looked and smelled better than Eartha. Confusion soaked her thoughts. She looked back at him.

-You have no idea what these people are. If they get me I'll go down fighting to the death, but Coop.. don't put yourself in that place. I couldn't survive if they got to you. There are a lot of hells in La Longue Nuit.

-Do you really think this is my first rodeo, Eartha?

-Have you ever been in a rodeo?

-Well.. no.

He patted the saddlebags on the seat between them, patted her on the shoulder and fell asleep for the first time in days. Watching him in the dim light, she realized there would be no turning him back. And.. oh, lord.. it was good to see him. The train would pull into New Orleans late the next night and after sleeping, they spent the hours quietly planning.. Eartha drawing maps in the air, trying to create the layout of the place for Coop. Part of the night would be spent watching the churchyard and the grave.. the one under the stained glass window of Mary and Child. The location was etched in her mind. La

Longue Nuit was less than a block away and they would watch it until dawn.

-Eartha, why don't we just get the money and get back on the train? No one would ever figure it out.. not after all these years.

-Pervice will look for me until he's dead. I killed his brother. There's others out there looking now and they won't quit until he stops paying for the hunt. There's no other way.

THIRTY - SIX

NEW ORLEANS

... 9:09 pm... just a little off schedule. The humid air clung to them as they walked the few yards to the churchyard. It was different.. rundown.. but Eartha knew the area as if she had been there yesterday. The moss clung to the oaks as the faint smell of mold drifted through the night. They crouched in the shadows.. watching. No movement.. no lights. The moon was full and illuminated their path along the north side until they stopped beneath a broken stained-glass window. The Mother and Child. Eartha's eyes drifted across broken markers.. wood and stone.. until they rested on a slight mound. It was barely perceptible. The ground was covered with soft, damp and rotting leaves.. the spicy scent drifting through her memory. Strange.. she thought.. the leaves don't crunch here.. too damp.. not like the dry, clean air of the Rockies. She dismissed the useless thought from her mind as her fingers dug into the moss and leaves. Jasmine Robideaux. Eartha looked closely at the grave and determined that it had not been disturbed. Weeds and overgrown rosebushes kept their secret.

-It's here, Coop. This is the place.

He knelt by her and felt a wave of rage and nausea rush through him. Four years old. He knew that little Jasmine

Robideaux was no longer buried there, but Eartha had told him what happened to the little girl. The bile rose in his throat as he sensed the heavy, dark, rotting evil of the place. He turned to Eartha, choking.

-You're right. If Pervice isn't dead.. he will be when we find him. How deep do you figure the money is?

-About three feet. Maybe a little more. It's been a long time.

Coop peered at Eartha in the shadowed moonlight.

-You've got a shovel.. right?

The absurdity of the moment was too much and they laughed as if they were demented. Fearing discovery, they crawled beneath the shelter of a low hanging willow until the hysteria passed. But there was nothing to disturb the dead tonight except them.

-They kept some tools in a shed out back. You go look and I'll keep watch.

As Coop disappeared around the corner of the church, Eartha's eyes moved around the unkempt graveyard. A tiny voice from a sad past whispered to her.. "How many? How many are here?"

They silently dug with their hands and a small shovel until they felt something. One of the bags. They tugged and scraped until they had released the first one from its grave. As the moon moved through a cloud, they could see that the oilcloth had held and the double buttoned wrap was intact. Eartha and Coop leaned against each other, panting as the sweat permeated their clothes. The song of the cicadas briefly lulled them into a sense of calm.

-Eartha, I do believe that sweat is making you smell a little better.

They moved the three bags into the tangles of an overgrown vine, sat in exhaustion and planned the next step. La Longue Nuit and Pervice. Eartha prayed silently. "Please let him still be alive. I want him to see my face."

It was just a block up the street.. imposing as a malignant growth. A crumbling six-foot cement wall still curled around the grounds.

-Where are the dogs? There were always dogs. What are we going to do if they have dogs?

Her voice was strangely high-pitched and Coop realized that panic was creeping through Eartha. He put his arm around her and squeezed her shoulder reassuringly.

-Okay.. here's the dog plan. You whip the big ones and I'll handle the little ones.

They crept around the block and could see the top two stories of the mansion. Intricate ironwork decorated the outdoor wraparounds but the windows were dark. Listening.. aware.. from every side.. Coop hoisted Eartha so she could peer over the wall. Quiet. Low lights from the first floor dimly lit the yard. No movement and no dogs. No small, discreet sign "La Longue Nuit" on the front street. It was 1a.m. and the train left at 3:37 headed west to Texas.

-Coop, maybe Pervice isn't here anymore. It's been a long time. No.. he's here. There would be no way to hide or clean up what they did in there. Around the side, that little cement room attached to the fence.. there's a door in the floor. A short tunnel and another door will get us on the other side. Maybe only ten feet in length. It comes out in the floor of a gazebo. The Pervices liked to call it "insurance".

The shed was covered with overgrowth. Eartha was surprised when the door gave way easily and wondered if the bastard was getting careless in his old age. The room was cluttered and dust covered. Cobwebs connected a few boxes. They moved a rug that covered a tunnel door and Coop jerked on the hinge, pulling it completely off the hardware. Lighting a match, he peered into the dark. Nothing but spider webs entwined with roots.

-Nothing has passed through here for a long time, Eartha. I sense bugs.. maybe snakes.

-I'm not going to lie to you, Coop. There are some nasty things that creep around New Orleans. But snakes? Nah. Not in Louisiana! Button your collar and sleeves tight. Tuck your pants into your boots. Wrap your bandana around your head. And if you feel something crawling on you.. just don't freak out. Don't scream. Remember.. they're more afraid of you than you are of them.

-Thanks, Eartha. Thanks for that.

They slid through the short tunnel, shoving a broom ahead to harvest the webs. When Coop pushed on the gazebo door, something metallic slid across it. Eartha's heart skipped as she listened for a bark or a voice. Coop pushed a fraction more and peeked through the crack.

The small ornate table that had covered the door now lay on its side. Less than fifty feet from the shelter was a side porch and lamplight glowed through a nearby window. Eartha squeezed up beside him, focusing on that light.

-It's the den.. library. They always left that lamp on day and night. But somebody could be in there now.

The silence of the yard shook her.. as if death had already taken claim. Crossing the space between the gazebo and house, Eartha realized how different it was from her memories. The garden had disappeared and the kennel was empty.. a gate creaked in the wind. They moved closer until the window was eye-level and Eartha could see inside. There was no activity.. no movement except the flames in the fireplace. The room was as she remembered it.. books filled the shelves.. fine art tastefully hung on the walls or placed on pedestals. A crystal decanter was filled with amber liquid and hypnotically reflected the light of the fire. Such a pleasant place.. no indication of what horrors had been played out within the walls.

Flames in the fireplace.. Eartha's attention was drawn back to the tall wingback chair that faced the hearth. Was that hair along the top edge? Long, nearly transparent white wisps of hair.. moving ever so slightly like thin worms. Or was it just more cobwebs? Her eyes dropped to the bottom of the chair and she saw the toe of a polished shoe. It jerked as a hand came to rest on the side of the chair, loosely holding a half full glass of whiskey. A ruby ring glistened in the firelight and she knew. The devil lived. Pervice was there. She stumbled back a step into Coop, covering her mouth in horror.. her eyes wide. He pulled her down and they huddled in the shadow of a broken statue.

-It's now or never. We can make the train easy with the money. Leave the old bastard here to die in his poison.

She stared at the window in a trance and started to shake.

-I'll do this, Eartha. You stay here. It'll just take a second.

He rose to a crouch and touched the gun at his side. Eartha pulled at his pantleg, afraid to be left alone for even a moment. She could barely breathe as her eyes drifted back to the wall.. back to the window.. and then the thirst for revenge and justice seared through her soul. She stood, sliding a knife from her belt. A ten-inch Bowie.. razor sharp. She had bought it at Bertrand's Mercantile and had felt its painful bite. In secrecy, she had acted out scenes of retaliation in the seclusion of the pines.. always fantasizing about this moment. It was now. Eartha rose, moving lithely toward the porch. The door wasn't even locked. My, but they were getting careless here at La Longue Nuit. She turned the handle and pushed just enough to align one eye with the interior. The door to the den was slightly open and behind it, she knew that Pervice sat sipping whiskey.. staring into the fire. Eartha slid her boots off and crept into the foyer. She was afraid to blink and her eyes stung with the strain. As she gently pushed on the door, she heard soft padded footfalls behind her.. a low, vicious growl.. one bark as Coop slammed the butt of his gun down on the massive head. A slight yelp and the brute lay motionless. The door of the den jerked open and Pervice stood in front of her, the glass of whiskey in his hand.

-Shapkit! What are you barking at now, you dumb..

His bloodshot eyes rounded as he stared at her and widened more when Eartha plunged the knife into his ample gut. He dropped the glass, clutched his belly and gaped back at Eartha.. soundless. She knelt in front of him searching his black eyes with curiosity.

-Why are you up so late, Julienne? All good children should be in their beds, but then.. you know all about that. Do you still sell them here, Julienne? Do you recognize me? Remember me? Tell the truth now. Are you here alone? Shapkit doesn't count. He's dead. Is there anyone else?

The fear and recognition grew in his eyes.. the hatred reflecting her own. He shook his head no.. but his eyes darted behind her and to the right. She knew, at that moment, that someone was upstairs. The blood pulsed between his fingers as she slid behind him.. pulling his head back against her chest.

-Look at me, you bastard. You're going to hell. And.. Julienne.. I hope this *really hurts*.

She allowed him an additional moment of terror and then pulled the blade very slowly across his throat. He didn't struggle, but only stared at her.. the light fading from his eyes as the blood gushed down his chest. She pushed back, letting his head hit hard on the marble tile.

Eartha felt nothing. Nothing. Coop stood beside her as she picked up a newspaper and rolled it.

-There's something upstairs, Coop. At the top.. to the right. Watch out.. but hurry. I'm going to light this nightmare up.

Coop ascended the stairs, gun ready and listened at the first door on the right. Nothing but a night hawk calling outside. He opened the door, bracing for a battle. No movement. By the light of the street lamp he could see someone was in the bed.. mounded beneath the blanket. The room was hot, musty and the smell of decay reached his nostrils. He pulled the covers back and saw what was left of an unforgiveable sin.

As he re-entered the den, Eartha could see that his tanned face had turned pale.

-You were right. There was something upstairs.

She grabbed the brandy bottle, took a double swig and doused everything.. drapes, chair, rugs.. Pervice. She touched the newspaper to the flames and torched the curtains. The fire spread quickly and as she passed Pervice.. she lit his wispy hair.

They sprinted from the house as the flames grew and snaked upstairs. 3:09 a.m. Powered by adrenaline, they scaled the wall and ran the short distance to the churchyard. The bags had patiently waited beneath the old willow and it took two lung-bursting trips to deliver them to the train station. They jabbed their tickets at the conductor. Looking past them, he commented: "My, my. Looks like a mighty fire back there." He had witnessed endless mayhem at this station and didn't care to question them. Eartha and Coop moved to a seat toward the back, pushing the bags on the floor. Putting one on the opposite seat, they shoved the others beneath.. collapsing next to each other. Hearts were racing. 3:37 a.m. Right on time. The flames worked their way quickly through the rotting mansion and by dawn, very little remained of La Longue Nuit.

***

In Houston, they took a buggy to a fancy hotel, booked two rooms, shopped for clothes, took baths, ordered room service and slept for two days. They were talked out by the time they boarded the train to Pueblo and sat staring at the passing scenery in silence. Eventually, Coop looked over at Eartha with a haunted look on his face.

-Do you think there was anyone else in that house?

She glanced at him then looked away.

-No. There was no one else. And if there were.. they either deserved to die.. or they're better off now.

Four nights later they arrived in Lionshead. 11:09 p.m. Eartha guarded the bags as Coop ran the short distance to Nash's Buckhole Livery. There was very little movement on the street and even less in the barn. Just Magreef, Samson and a mule. It took him a moment to locate their tack and get the horses saddled.

-I left a note and some money. Hopefully, Joe Nash will be the first to find it. I must admit, it feels good to throw a few bucks around.

-Nothing is more elusive, Coop. Right now, we need to get our story straight.. talk it through one more time. It's got to be airtight or Lud will catch on.

-I can handle Lud.

Standing near him in the dark, she hated what had to be said.

-No.. you cannot handle Lud. He's a killer and has done plenty of it. He knows ways to end a life faster than you've ever imagined. Save me the heartache.

-Thanks for the vote of confidence.

-Coop, I'm not saying that you're not capable. I've seen what you can do in the last few days and would rather have you watching my back than anyone in this world.. or the next. You're the best man I've ever known. But Lud.. he's a different breed. His blood is cold.

They rode out to Big Spruce in weary silence. Even though Coop had not replied, she knew that he had been hurt by her words.

-I'll cross the bridge alone and draw Lud's attention to the barn. I know he's been watching all these days. Coop, I swear, it doesn't seem like he ever sleeps. You stay out of site and wait until you see him come down to the barn and then wade Magreef across the river.. otherwise Lud might hear him clopping across the bridge. You know that spot where the water is shallow this time of year on the sandbar. Circle around to the back of the church and put two bags in the altar vault. I can keep his attention. Take the other one up the cemetery trail and hide it. Sometime during the next couple of days, you'll have to move it again. Don't wait too long.

-Once again.. I have one little question. Why? Why not put it *all* under the altar?

-Always have two hiding spots.

-Where do you suggest, Eartha? Under your mattress?

-No, listen.. I've thought it through. You know the cliff that circles the south side of the cemetery? Stand directly in front of Jasmine Robideaux's marker, turn right ninety-degrees and walk until you come to the three pines that grow along the rock. Behind them there'll be some dried brush wedged against the cliff. Clear it out but make sure you can replace it. There's a narrow crevice. It'll be tight but push through it.

She laughed.

-Don't worry. If you get stuck, I'll know where you are. I won't leave you there for more than a few days.

Coop stood in the moonlight.. arms crossed. She couldn't see his features and could only imagine the look on his face. She waited for a response that wasn't coming.

-Anyway.. there's a little cave there.. about four feet deep. Hide the bag in it and then cover your tracks. Get back to your place and don't light any lamps. I'll keep Lud busy. After it's all tucked away, just go about your business as usual.

He'll be watching us for days.

287

THIRTY - SEVEN

LEADING SAMSON

... across the bridge she looked toward Lud's place. Was that a match light? She pushed on the heavy door, comforted by the predictable creak. Benno and Lil Daisy had built themselves a cabin some distance back and Eartha was not worried about disturbing them. The dogs knew her in any light and offered a few greeting licks. She looked back at Lud's cabin and saw a definite light. He had heard her. Eartha shakily lit a lamp and proceeded to unsaddle Samson. She patted the horse's chest as she looked over its back toward the door. Had it opened just a fraction? She knew he was there. Eartha began to sing a little tune.. part whistle.. part hum. She felt her heartbeat accelerate as perspiration beaded on her forehead. The doors were shoved open and there stood the demon himself. Lud.

-Well, well.. Eartha! What a surprise. I thought we might have a burglar on the place. I'm so relieved to see that it's only you. Where ya been?

She smiled sweetly as she eased the bit from the horse's mouth. Lud stopped and looked at her warily, eyes narrowing a bit. Since when did Eartha smile at him?

-It's good to be home, Lud.. good to see you, too.

She knew that was overkill. As she moved around the horse, she removed her hat and fanned herself with it. Eartha took off her jacket, laid it on a bench and patted her neck with a sprinkle of water from a bucket.

-It's hot in here.

She plopped onto the seat and pulled her skirt above her boots.

-Would you mind helping me with these? They're killing me. New shoes always cause blisters.

-I'm honored.

Eartha patted the spot next to her as he tossed the boots aside.

-Come on and sit by me. Give me an update on what's been going on.

Lud leaned against the stall, a piece of straw in his teeth, coolly observing her.

-Thanks, but I'll stand. Where ya been, Eartha? What happened to your hair?

-You know where I went. Salt Lake.

-I thought you were finished with that can of worms. What happened to your hair?

She jumped up angrily and pulled her boots back on, hopping about for a moment before she landed back in a mound of straw.

-Lud, as usual you are a jackass. I'm tired as hell and I'm not going to waste my time trying to be civil with you. Where's Coop?

-He left, too, about the same time. Theo said you sent him off to look for a few more horses.

A chill crawled up her spine. She could feel the trap closing.

-No, I didn't.

She stood, moved within arms-length and boldly met his cold eyes. Backing down from Lud now would be a big mistake. Change the subject.

-My hair? What's wrong with it?

He confidently looked her over.. slowly.. knowing it would infuriate her.

-Lookin good, Eartha. Yes, ma'am, lookin good. Mormons took pretty good care of you. Except for that haircut. What the hell happened there?

She could barely resist snaking a slap at him.

-I'm not a man to be kept in the dark. But don't stop trying.

That was it. She tried to kick him but he stepped aside and she fell to the ground. Lud placed his boot on her chest, pinning her to the dirt. He had been expecting her reaction. She felt like a hotheaded fool.

-There's something going on here, little queen of Big Spruce.. and you know I'll find out. Heaven help you if you're trying to betray me.

She stood.. dusted herself off and tried to recover a little dignity. Unsuccessfully. Drops of humiliation were filling her eyes. She took a deep breath and turned from him.

But he saw it. He saw the tears and for once, felt regret. Lud turned and silently walked out.

THIRTY - EIGHT

TWO DAYS PASSED

… and there was no sign of Coop. No light in his cabin at night.. nothing. Sunday afternoon came and she stood on the bridge practicing her fly cast.. her eyes continually searching down the road. Theo was roping some old steer horns nailed to a board and waved to her. She smiled, waving back. Where was Coop? Could he really have gotten stuck in the cliff? Oh God, she had to go up there.. but Lud was watching her every move.

-Can I put a worm on your hook?

She had been lost in thought and hadn't noticed Lud beside her.

-No thanks. I'm doing just great without you. This is fly fishing, genius.. no worms.

-I'm just trying to show some interest in your hobbies, Eartha. Hey. Do you suppose he sold that crazy horse? What was the name? Magreef. That's it. Big X on the forehead.. what a temptation. It's almost like the Lord said.. shoot this horse.

-If that were the case.. you'd be covered in Xs.

Lud shrugged and turned to walk away, but stopped suddenly.. his eyes narrowing to blue slits as he looked down the river. Eartha moved closer to him, shading her eyes.. trying to see what he had focused on. A string of horses moved up the valley. At the lead was a rider on a big sorrel with a white X on its forehead.

Lud climbed down the side of the bridge and sat on his heels at the edge of the creek.. expertly laying his line across the ripples. He stuck an unlit cigarette on his lower lip, as he and Eartha sized each other up.. like boxers preparing for another round.

Coop rode up, removed his hat and looked from one to the other.. trying to read their faces. He dismounted and stepped down to the river, leaving the horses to graze along the bank. He splashed water on his face and knelt to take a long drink. Thinking all along.. "What the hell am I supposed to say?" No one spoke. He smiled at Eartha, searching her face for a clue and casually waved at Lud.

-Isn't anybody going to welcome me home? Bought those horses for you, Eartha. Had to go a ways to find a decent bunch.

He remounted Magreef and turned toward the pasture but hesitated.

-Found you a fine bay, just like you told me to.

Eartha thought she felt the bridge shift beneath her feet. She looked at Coop who knew in a heart-beat that he had really screwed up. Coop was looking at Lud.. who knew they were lying. Lud was looking at Eartha.. and she felt frozen in time.

Lud sat quietly, looking past Eartha at the hillside.. then slowly stood and lit the cigarette.

Coop took a deep breath and lightly commented..

-I thought you quit lighting cigarettes, Lud. Just wanted cold ones stuck to your lips.

THIRTY - NINE

HE KNOWS

… something is up and will not relent, Coop. We've blown it.

Coop watched as Eartha paced back and forth, sipping from a whiskey bottle. She was like a fox caught in a trap, trying to chew its' own leg off.

-Take it easy, Eartha. That's not going to do you any good. Time will pass and he'll never figure it out. Something's bound to come along that will distract him. Let it be.

-There's more, Coop. I should have told you a long time ago. Lud came here to kill me and take the money back to the Pervices. I don't know what stopped him. He could have done it anytime. He still could.. only he doesn't know Pervice is dead. There would be no reward. No purpose. Except he knows there's more money somewhere.

Coop slouched down in the chair.

-This is a never-ending story.. isn't it.

She looked at him, took another sip and plopped her head down on her arms.

-I'm sorry. I just thought he would eventually go away. I'm so sorry I didn't tell you everything.

She looked up at him with swollen, tear-soaked eyes, snot stringing from her nose to her sleeve. Coop knelt beside her and took her hand.

-We just need to bide our time, Eartha. He'll simmer down or maybe he'll just move on. I know I messed up with the horse story, but he'll dismiss it if we keep our cool. I can get rid of him, Eartha.

-Somebody would die. I know that and it most likely would be you or me.. or both of us. He won't leave after all this time without the money. We have to out-fox him.

***

Lud sat with his feet resting on a tree stump. The smoke from his cigarette drifted up toward his eyes making him squint. He was carving on a piece of French soap, humming a tune under his breath. He looked up as Coop and Eartha walked out on her porch.. laughing. Yep.. they'd been up to something.. and that something did not include Lud. Coop hopped off the porch, pushed his hat forward and strutted down the trail. He looked over and waved pleasantly as he passed the church.

-Hey, Lud. Looks like it's going to be a nice evening, huh?

Lud looked back and nodded his head without saying anything.

FORTY

STANDING AT THE BAR

… Lud gulped down a second drink. No one approached him, although he was recognized as the dubious preacher from Big Spruce. The white clerical collar at his neck had loosened and dangled haphazardly from his shirt. Eartha had gotten to him. It was time to finish this.. if he could just get his hands on the money.. he would gladly send her into eternity. After all this time, he wasn't leaving empty handed. He ordered another whiskey and carried it out to the boardwalk. It was illegal in Lionshead to drink on the street and Lud was hoping to make a point in favor of it.

Belligerently strolling down the street, Lud pushed his jacket clear of his gun.. feeling mean and craving a confrontation. Anything. A stray cat darting across the road.. a dust devil blowing a tin can.. anything to blast. A young man trotted up to him, waving a piece of paper. Maybe he would say something stupid and Lud could pistol whip him for delivering a message.

-Excuse me, sir. Are you Mr. Cadey? Lud Cadey?

Lud eyed him malevolently.

-You got a problem with that?

-Well, no.. but if you are.. and I think you might be.. I've got a telegram for you. It's marked for immediate delivery. Albert Hedeman said that you were here earlier. I guess I'm lucky to catch you.

Lud jerked the paper from the young man's hand and shoved it into his pocket without reading it.

-Depends on your definition of "lucky". You delivered it. Now get the hell out of here.

The messenger paled and turned away.

-Wait a minute, kid.

Stopping with one foot in midair, the boy fixed his vision on the street ahead. Running seemed like the best option, but he turned back to face the man, nervously eyeing the gun. Lud pulled a gold coin out of his pocket, flipped it to the messenger and sauntered back to the boardwalk.

Sitting down, he precariously balanced the chair back on two legs. The sun was setting and the quiet of the street began to cool his anger. His mind began to compose itself. He pulled the telegram from his pocket and read:

NEW ORLEANS
PERVICE DEAD
HOUSE BURNED TO GROUND
JOB TERMINATED
CONTRACT TERMINATED

The chair slammed forward onto the porch and Lud stood staring at the empty street. He whirled, kicked the bar door open and ordered another whiskey. He raised it to his lips but hesitated as he glared at the nude portrait on the wall. His mind was racing.. putting the pieces together. The owner of the Buckhole Livery, Joe Nash, congenially approached.

-How're you doing, Lud? Haven't seen your around lately.

Lud looked over at him without answering.

-Well, anyway.. could you tell Coop that he left too much money for keeping those two horses.. Magreef and Samson?

Now he had Lud's full attention.

-Yeah? Are you sure? How long did you have them?

Nash rubbed his jaw thinking maybe he shouldn't discuss Eartha's business but after all.. this man was the preacher out there.

-I guess it was about ten days. They just picked them up a few days ago. Let me tell you.. I wouldn't care to keep that crazy Magreef around much more. Bastard damned near kicked my head off. You might just pass that along to Coop.

-Oh, no worries, Nash. I'll make sure he gets the message.

Lud's mind churned murderously as he rode the six miles out to Big Spruce. They had travelled together to New Orleans and managed to get Pervice. But he knew they didn't go back just to kill the old bastard. They got the money. Lots and lots of money. The whiskey was starting to wear off as he looked around. Pulling his watch from his pocket, he strained to see the time. After two a.m. Coop and Eartha wouldn't see it coming. The moon was bright and he saw the familiar old ghost prowling in the shadow of the pines.

It hid in fear as Lud stopped and peered into the dark.

He was going to kill them both.

FORTY - ONE

LUD WHISTLED

... a tune as he crossed the bridge, knowing that Theo might hear. The first stop was the barn where he switched mounts and put a lead rope on a second. His mind was working fast as he re-saddled and led the horses up behind his cabin, tying them to a tree. He shoved a few items in his bags and then quietly crossed the bridge on foot. He tapped lightly on the door.

-Coop? You awake?

-Yeah. Lud? What are you doing?

-I been thinking about what a jerk I've been.

-That's great but it's pretty late. You been drinking?

-A little. I'll wake Eartha up then. Maybe she'll feel like talking.

-Wait. I'm coming.

When Coop gained consciousness, Lud was finishing up the ties to his hands and neck. He looked around the cabin appreciatively.

-This is nice. A few days ago, I was thinking about settling down to this kind of life. That's what ya get for thinking, huh?

He shoved a rag in Coop's mouth.

-You know I'm gonna kill you, don't you? And then, of course, Eartha. Think about that for a moment or two. Let's play a little game. Just nod your head for the following choices. One nod is yes. Two is no. Bat your eyelids if none of them work for you. Bullet? Hmm.. knife?.. hmm.. burn down cabin with you and Eartha in it? No response? Now, don't leave it up to me. There are other options.

Coop looked back at Lud with no emotion. No wild eyes, no struggle to communicate.. no pleading. Nothing. Lud wondered what it was like.. not being afraid to meet your maker. He saw it in Coop's eyes. He wasn't afraid. Lud sat back on his heels, pondering his own theory of life and death. Killing was easy after the first one or two. But he had been selective. They all had it coming.. one way or the other. Plus, the pay was great. Coop didn't have it coming. Lud cocked his gun and put it against Coop's temple.. but hesitated.. realizing at that moment.. that Coop was.. possibly.. the only truly decent person he'd ever met. He was good.. for goodness sake. He laughed to himself as he checked the strength of the ties. And then he stood and walked out the door.

But Eartha was another thing. She *did* have it coming.

***

Eartha lay gazing at the moon through the rippled glass of the window. Sleep never came easy since the night those two moth-eaten trappers had terrorized her. She sat up and considered opening the window for a breeze, but drew back. Did a shadow cross the window? Was she losing her mind? There was a brief change of moonlight as if a bird had flown by. She held her breath, hearing only her heartbeat. She was a nervous wreck and it was Lud's doing. She had to get rid of him. She jumped back into bed, pulling the quilt up to her face. There was nothing more to fear. The Pervices were dead. Just Lud. He's got to go.. of his own free will or in a pine box. It didn't matter to her. A voice spoke lowly in the dark.

-Hello, Eartha. You had to know I was coming. Right?

She squealed with fright as he crossed the room and covered her mouth with his hand.

-Now, knock it off. I know you're a little jumpy these days. If you start screaming and fighting, you'll just get somebody hurt. But then, you're good at that. You're like me, Eartha. Death just follows you around like a demented little playmate. I'm going to light the lamp now, so just stay put.

She was cornered but attempted a courageous front.

-What do you want now? And why the moonlight visit? Surely you don't think.. just because I was nice to you earlier..

Lud sat back and looked at her in astonishment.

-You're kidding, right? It never crossed my mind. I'll swear on a stack of bibles.

He looked around curiously.

-You do *have* a stack, don't you?

Eartha could smell the whiskey on his breath. Her advantage. She started to move slightly toward the edge of the bed as he snooped around her bedroom, examining items.. spraying her perfume in the air.. peeking in drawers.

-This *is* kind of cozy. Go ahead and stand up. Stretch your legs. Honestly, Eartha, I thought you'd have on something more enticing than that flannel gown. But it is a bit chilly in here. Let's be serious now.. you knew I'd figure this out.. sooner or later.

She bolted for the door, reached the handle and pulled it open only to have it slammed again by his hand. Darting under his arm, she ran to the night table, jerked open the small drawer and retrieved a knife. Thin and very sharp. She was breathing hard and felt every twitching nerve in her body.

-Lud.. don't make me hurt you. This isn't the first time I've been trapped. Just turn and get out of Big Spruce. Leave us in peace.

He laughed with genuine glee.

-Oh, I will.. when you tell me where the money is. The sooner the better.

-There's nothing left but a few bucks at the bank. Look under the mattress. There's a bag with a few hundred. Take it and get out.

She saw the hesitation in his eyes, but then he reached under the mattress.. just giving her that moment to run and jerk the door open again. Eartha ran in darkness toward the back of the church. Hail was falling hard and stung her eyes as she tried to see. She stumbled to the cemetery trail, climbing and slipping in the mud.. clutching at bushes for balance. She fell into a thorn bush and winced at the sting. Where was Lud? Had he given up?

A glow lit the night and she turned to see that the church was on fire.. the stained-glass windows detailed by flames. She lost her footing and slid back down the trail, coming to rest on Lud's boot. He knelt, snow clinging to his eyelashes. He reached behind her head and wrapped his hand in her hair. He pulled her scratched, mud-covered face close to his.

-This is your last chance, Eartha. Where's the money?

Their breath joined in the freezing air, creating an eery fog.

-In the church, you fool.

He looked stunned and confused.. turning, he stared at the rising flames.

-It's under the altar, Lud. Millions. You can still get to it.

He looked at her, momentarily fascinated with the fire reflected in her eyes. She was telling the truth. Lud dropped her head, jerking a few strands of hair from her scalp in the process. He ran, slipping down the trail until he burst into the smoke-filled church. Eartha lurched in behind him, holding her wet gown to her face.

-The angels.. they have to be turned, Lud. At the same time.

She staggered to the side of the altar and wrapped her hands around one of the forms. A burning beam fell from the ceiling and smashed through a window, showering them in sparks.

-On the count of two, Lud! Turn the other angel to face me.

***

Two bags.. black oil cloth. Lud heaved them onto a horse and mounted, turning to look at her. She stood covered in mud, her wet flannel gown clinging to her shivering legs.. strands of frozen hair stuck to her battered face. Lud pulled his rifle out of the scabbard and lifted it to his shoulder. She stood without running.. crying.. nothing. A whispered curse passed his lips. He knew that Eartha *was* afraid to meet her maker and her lack of reaction fascinated him. She was bolstered by guts.. not goodness.. just sheer guts. He lowered the rifle.

-Why'd you help me? I must admit, Eartha.. that angel contraption was pure genius. Benno figured that out, didn't he? Don't worry. I won't go after him. Just curious.. why'd you help me with it? I would never have figured it out.

With chattering teeth, she replied.

-I knew you'd kill me.

Lud looked around with disappointment.

-Well, that's true. Where *is* everybody anyway? The church is on fire!

He laughed, fired the bullet meant for Eartha into the air and rode across the bridge.

He had just about everything he came for.

FORTY – TWO

COOP AND EARTHA

… sat on the partially burnt church steps, calculating the damage. Days had past and they were both still bruised and sore. Lil Daisy sprawled on the bottom step, running her fingers through Wouton's fur, pondering the situation.

-I'm confounded. What started the fire, you suppose? Lightnin'? I didn't hear none. Did you hear any lightnin' Coop?

-Yep, Lil Daisy. I did .. and felt some, too.

-Well, I just don't know.

She stood with hands on hips, then pulled the old watch out of a pocket and gazed into the sky. Her attention was focused on a hawk that was riding the wind.

-What happens if the wind stops? Will he just drop to the ground?

As tempting as it was, they didn't respond. The stained-glass windows from Santa Fe were destroyed, glass shards glittering in the ashes. Eartha stood and offered her hand to help Coop. Both groaned at the effort of moving sore muscles. She patted him on the shoulder.

-We're lucky to be alive, Coop. He could easily have killed us. Suppose Lud is half human after all?

-Honestly? I'm tired of the legend of Lud. I believe I could have taken him. But in answer to your question..

no. I think he just decided in a blink not to do it. That fast. Besides, he got what he wanted.. the money.

-I thought for sure he'd kill us, but I guess you never really know anyone. Let's do something to get our minds straight. Want to go into town tomorrow and look around? Listen to the gossip about us at Ma Campbell's?

-No thanks. I've got to decide what to do with Magreef. If I can't train some sense into him.. I'll be trading him off. I've put plenty of time into that horse and could sell him for a decent price. He's showy and there's bound to be at least one fool out there.

***

The next morning brought a fresh feel with it. Rays of sun glittered through the pines, partnering with a warm gentle breeze. Autumn color was showing through the aspen with splashes of gold and orange. Eartha draped a few pieces of laundry across the porch railing to dry. She automatically glanced over at Lud's cabin, still half expecting to see him stroll out. A barn cat darted across the yard and leapt to a post by the horse pen. It groomed itself as Coop led Magreef out of the barn for.. possibly.. his last training session.

Eartha pulled a chair into the sun, tipping her head to feel the warmth on her face. Maybe things would come together now. Theo and Madlyn were slowly accepting the loss of their daughter.. Mery. The other one had moved into town two years earlier. Benno and Lil Daisy had found happiness with each other.. just another twist of nature. Angus and Lara McCleod were thriving at Scot's Depot.. sheltering children and releasing others.. healed.. into the world.

Tragic memories also laced her thoughts. Isabelle and Ethan.. Mame.. Axel and Jubal.. Grace and Gregory. Enough. Eartha grabbed a jacket and walked across the drive to watch Coop work with Magreef. It was a good day and she didn't want to waste it on sadness. He met her at the fence. The sun had slipped behind a cloud and a few flakes of snow drifted down. Coop looked up and laughed, pulling the collar around his neck.

-What's wrong? Another premonition?

He smiled as he reached out to touch her cheek. Tiny ice crystals sparkled in the returning sunlight.

-Eartha.. do you know what happens to devils that dance with angels?

She looked at him with curiosity but her heart skipped a beat.

-What happens to them?

-They fall frozen through the air and are warmed by the sun for just a moment. And then at the last instant before melting.. they realize.. it was worth it.

***

Coop was experienced and patient as he worked with the horse. Magreef cooperated as if he sensed it could be his last chance. Tossing the rope around the post, Coop turned to look at Eartha and grinned, appreciating the audience. He removed his sweat-stained hat and bowed. The sun lit his face and he looked as young as when she had first met him.. all those years ago. He'd fought to get her a glass of water.

A quick movement behind him caught her attention and she saw the cat swat Magreef's soft nuzzle. In a breath, the horse whirled and kicked Coop's head with all its force. Eartha stood paralyzed as she watched the red mist spray through the air, Coop sinking slowly to the ground. Magreef jerked free and galloped madly around the pen, snorting and kicking the air in a frenzy.

Eartha climbed through the railing and fell on her knees next to Coop. The sand beneath his head was already a gritty pool of red. She eased her trembling hands beneath his neck and tried to pull him closer to her heart, frantically attempting to staunch the bleeding with her jacket. His face was pale and still. She put her cheek on his and whispered..

-No, Coop. Don't. You don't have to do this now. Don't do this now..

Tears mixed with blood as she desperately cradled him to her chest. The cat sauntered over to Eartha and rubbed against her, pretending that it didn't know. Magreef, wild eyed, stood at the far end.. legs quivering, nostrils flaring. Eartha was faintly aware of Theo running across the bridge.

Two days later, Coop was buried next to his beloved Mame.

After the graveside ceremony, Eartha wrote ..

Theo, we sure didn't see this coming. There have been many things over the years that we didn't see coming, my friend, but losing Coop has finished me. I don't really give a damn about anything anymore.. not even Big Spruce. I'm gone. Don't come looking for me. It would just turn into a humiliating mess. You have helped keep this place glued together all these years and I want you to have it. Enclosed is a note to Albert Hedeman to transfer title to you and Madlyn. I hope that you will keep your life here. I know you love this place. Just tell a good story about me once in while.. if there are any. Otherwise.. make one up. Watch over Benno and Lil Daisy. There is money up at the cemetery. Stand in front of Jasmine Robideaux's grave and turn right. It's in the cliffs. You'll find it.

My best to you, Theo. You've been a loyal friend and an outstanding guard. I still laugh when I think of you strutting across the bridge with those sheep. I've taken Magreef and Samson. Eartha

She left that night with little more than she arrived with forty-five years earlier.. a few clothes, some food and a bedroll. She rode Samson across the bridge, leading Magreef behind her. Theo rose from bed, thinking he'd heard a sound at the bridge, but saw nothing as he peered out the window. It must have been the wind rattling a loose board.

Eartha rode down river, tied Samson to a tree and led Magreef deeper into the pines. She removed her rifle from the scabbard and shot the horse where X marked the spot.

FORTY - THREE

HEADING WEST

... Eartha camped three grieving nights and never looked back. Sunburned and thirsty, she stood at the edge of a cliff peering down into a ravine. A sheer drop. She studied the toe of her boot.. digging it into the dirt.. dislodging a stone that fell over the edge. It shattered like chalk upon the stones below. Picking up a larger stone, she hurled it against the wind and watched with fascination as it also turned into shards upon impact. Samson stood nearby leaning against a scraggly pinon pine. He nickered to her, feeling restless and irritated by the wind. The breeze was gusty and jerked at the ends of her long coat. Self-pity wrapped her in a familiar embrace as she sat in the dust.

-You've ruined your life. You've hurt everyone that ever loved you. And there weren't that many. You could have prevented most of the heartache. But no. You had to have money and revenge. How does it taste? Like dust? What do you have to show for it? And here's the big one.. the one you always worry about in the dark of night. *Is* there a hell waiting out there for you? This is it, Eartha. You're done. You can't go back to Big Spruce and the truth is.. you don't want to. Leave it in peace. You've been nothing but a curse to everyone that ever knew you.

Coop would probably still be alive if you didn't hire him that day in Lionshead. He'd be living in Kansas with six kids and a nice little wife. You're a curse, Eartha.. a curse.

She had worked herself into a fit of first-class self-pity.. burying her head in her arms.. sobbing. Eartha cried like an abandoned child until Samson nickered, attracting her attention. She stumbled over to rummage through the saddlebags. Where was the whiskey? She dumped everything out on the ground, grabbed some jerky and held it in her teeth as the search went on. In disbelief, she stood back and chewed on the dry meat. She hadn't even packed any. Exhausted, she leaned her forehead against Samson's, staring into his huge black pupil.

-It's a bad sign, old boy. Bad.

The wind was blowing staggering gusts as she returned unsteadily to the edge of the cliff. Grabbing the ends of the long coat, she leaned forward and spread her arms, creating a sail. The wind pushed her back and she struggled to stand steady. She leaned forward a tiny bit more.. feeling a deadly thrill. A possible answer. She imagined the sensation of flying.. recklessly defying gravity for a fraction of a breath.

The wind stopped. Eartha lurched forward, arms thrashing in the sudden calm. She reached desperately for some sage brush as the dry dirt crumbled beneath her boot and she slid over the edge. The bush held but her grip would not last long. Looking to the heavens, she pled.. just one more deal. How many times had she asked?.. just one more deal. Closing her eyes, she listened to the clatter of rocks falling far beneath. A hawk called from the abyss and she answered.. repeating her plea. The deal was made and she painfully pulled herself back to lay panting on the edge. When the ground stopped spinning, she stumbled over to Samson, threw her arms around his neck and gulped at his salty, earth-smell until her knees stopped quivering.

FORTY - FOUR

THE VALLEY

... was wide, layered with prairie grass and blue sage. Aspens lined the border with vivid gold and crimson, creating a dramatic contrast among the dark pines. The weather was warm.. a gift from autumn.. but winter would come and she'd better have a plan. For the first time in her free life, she had no strategy whatsoever. Samson shook the bridle and rudely jerked his head down for a mouthful of grass.

-Why not? Grab some grass. You've earned the right to break a few rules.

Eartha dismounted with an ache in every bone. She rested her head against the saddle and closed her eyes, feeling the breeze play with a strand of hair. It felt like the gentle touch of a hand. These days, she had more silver in her hair than auburn. The distant bugle of an elk echoed across the valley as she considered making camp near the tree line. There was bound to be water somewhere on the hillside. She pressed her cheek back against the cool leather of the saddle, closing her eyes.

At first, she thought it was far-off thunder.. distant. But there was a rhythm.. as if someone were thumping fingers steadily on a table. She turned to see a figure in the distance.. coming from the East. Along the same trail she had just travelled.. roughly a half mile away. She could make out the form as dust clouded behind him. There was something about the way he rode.. with one shoulder slightly slanted back. A chill slithered up her spine, causing her to pull her coat close. Reaching up, she slid the rifle from its scabbard and leveled it on the saddle. She pushed up on her toes to look through the scope.

Good God. She stood stone still with a bead on his chest as he came to a trot.. then slowed to a walk. Shoot, Eartha. He's here to finish the job. Why didn't she pull the trigger? Was she just going to let him kill her *now*?.. after that deal she just made up on the cliff? Is *this* how it was going to end?

Lud stopped thirty feet away and watched her.. knowing she could put a couple of rounds in his chest before he could blink. His left eye was clearly bruised and swollen.. the result of a foot she had planted on his face almost two weeks earlier.. the night he burned the church down. The purple hue created a fearful appearance as he considered her. Lud lightly heeled his horse forward a step and she ever so slightly re-adjusted her aim. The wind lifted her hat and blew it across the ground. She never glanced at it. Neither did he.

-Hello, Eartha.

He was leaning forward casually.. elbow on the saddle horn.

-I heard about Coop.

Eartha's hand trembled.. just a little.

-I shot Magreef for it.

317

Lud could see that she was battling to stay calm.

-Yea. Well.. I wish I'd have done that a long time ago. I guess we're not writing the book of life and death. But, Hey!.. That was quite a display of faith up there on the cliff. What were you trying to do? *Fly?*

She felt her brain go numb. He had seen the whole thing and was going to humiliate her.

-Where were you?

-Close enough to see that you were having a genuine episode.

-But apparently not close enough to kick me over the edge.

Eartha knew that Lud was trying to get the advantage.. throw her off balance.. shake her up so that she would make a mistake. He watched her like a predator.

-Do you mind if I reach into my shirt pocket for the makings of a cigarette?

-I thought you quit.

-I did. Just let them rest on my lower lip now. It gives me some comfort. Don't even carry matches anymore. Can't handle the temptation. Smoking will sure as hell kill me if I keep it up.

He tried to read her face.

-Sure, Lud. Why not?

Lud leisurely reached into his shirt pocket and pulled out a small white bag, along with a sheaf of papers.

-Do you mind if I use both hands?

-That would be preferable.

Eartha watched as he rolled a cigarette and carefully positioned it on his lower lip.

-You find something amusing, Eartha?

-I've got something for you, Lud. May I reach into my jacket pocket?

-Sure. Why not?

She reached into her pocket and drew something out.. hiding it in her hand.

-Watcha got there?

-I'm going to toss it over to you. Just a little something for old time's sake.

He watched her, knowing he was playing with fire. But curiosity got him.

-Okay. Toss it on over. Do your best because I don't want to get off this horse.

She tossed the item carefully and Lud whipped his hand through the air to catch it. He quickly glanced into his palm. Matches. A box of matches. Lud felt the kill-lust begin to course through his veins. He imagined his hands around her throat.. squeezing the smartass life out of her. But, he placed the matches in his pocket, laughing.

-Well now, Eartha, I've got a little something for you, too. A little larger.. a lot more expensive. This bag behind me.. now you keep an eye on my hands. I'll move slow just so there's no misunderstanding.

A crow cawed in the distance. Irritating. Lonely. Haunting.

-What's in it?

Lud looked at her and smiled.

-Hey! I meant to ask.. are you still drinking? That little habit encouraged some fairly bad behavior.. as I remember. Just a little weakness. Don't feel down about it, Eartha. Something gets us all in the end.

He smiled condescendingly.

-That's none of your business, Lud. I'm sick of this conversation and I've got places to go. Throw the bag down, if it's absolutely necessary, and get out of my sight before I squeeze this trigger.

She could feel her legs start to quiver and, sure as hell, didn't want him to notice.

-Me too, Eartha. I'm plenty tired of this little chat. Just in case you're interested, I think I'll head for Santa Fe. I've heard it's nice down there. Easy going. What a coincidence that I ran into you out here, huh? Life. You just never know. Hey.. you could ride along with me for a bit. Just like old friends.

He stopped and looked at her sincerely. Eartha thought she saw something in his look.. something fleeting.. but then.. she just had to ask.

-What "bad behavior" did my occasional drink encourage?

He turned and lifted the bag around to the side, letting it fall heavily to the ground, the unlit cigarette dangling from his lip. He lightly pushed his heels into the horse, moved a few feet forward and stopped. Leaning forward, he whispered.

-I saw you that night up at the hot springs.. in the moonlight. I heard everything you said.

He grinned as he spurred his horse to the right, knowing she would pull the trigger. Eartha heard him laugh as he laid low and galloped off. She cocked the rifle, taking two more shots. The sun was in her eyes.. the bullets raced into eternity.. and the crow stopped its racket. Samson spooked and she pulled at the reins, rubbing her hand along his neck. Hot tears formed tiny rivulets on her dusty cheek. That bastard had done it all. Hunted her.. threatened her.. humiliated her.. robbed her. Now he was riding off.. laughing. Eartha flopped down into the dust, putting her head into her hands. God what she wouldn't do for a drink right now. She could still hear Lud's mocking comments. "Bad behavior" is what he said. Eartha… bad behavior? Her laughter began as a trickle but built into a wave of hysteria. Eventually, her eyes rested on the bag and she looked up at Samson.

-I wonder what's in there.

She lay across the dirt, looking closely for any sign of danger.

-It's not moving. It's some perverted joke of his.. counting coup on Eartha.

She scooted closer and jabbed it, cocking her head to listen. Nothing but the wind. She pushed around on the canvas, feeling some give and one hard spot. She quickly unzipped the bag and stood back. After a minute or two, she stepped forward and looked in. Money.. lots of money. Half of the money that he'd taken from the church. And a bottle of Kentucky Bourbon.

Eartha jerked back. This was his last little joke. She rose, dusted off her pants and looked around the valley, expecting to see him taunting her. She shakily sat down on the bag but jumped up again, this time seeing movement at the southern borderline of trees. Eartha uncorked the bottle and took a long drink, wiping her sleeve across her mouth. She tightened the cinch, hoisted the bag up and tied it down. Just for the hell of it, she tossed the bottle into the air and placed the rifle against her shoulder, pulling the trigger. It fell to the prairie grass unbroken. She walked over and picked it up.

-Well.. that's a sign. Which way should we go, Samson? I don't have a plan and I doubt that you do. We do have money for hotels and fancy liveries. You pick it. San Francisco? Cheyenne? El Paso? Salt Lake is out.

She wrapped the reins around the saddle horn and raised her arms to the sky, feeling the last warm rays of the day. Humming a haunting, old melody, she contemplated the deal she had made on the cliff. Promises were made. How many did she have left? How many more deals could she make? She leaned forward to run her fingers through the horse's mane, feeling suddenly sentimental.

-What do you think she was like, Samson? You know. The *real* Eartha. The one buried at Big Spruce.

She sat in contemplation until her eyes were drawn to the southern edge of the valley.

Lud peered through the scrub oak, transfixed. What the hell was she doing now? Another ceremony of death? He dug a small hole in the dirt and built a tiny teepee with the matches Eartha had used to taunt him. All except one. He scraped the last one against the stone and lit the others, watching them disintegrate. He quickly added the remaining match.. just to remove the temptation. Rolling another cigarette, he stuck it on his lip.

Peering through the brush, he saw the direction they were headed. Samson was at full speed.. Eartha clung tightly to the horse's neck letting him choose the path.

The wornout hat blew from her head, allowing her hair to dance wildly in the wind. Snow began to lightly fall.

Something echoed in Lud's memory....

Do you know what happens to devils that dance with Angels?

They fall frozen through the air and are warmed by the sun for just a moment. And then at the last instant.. before melting.. they realize..

It was worth it.

ABOUT THE AUTHOR

j.a.kirby was born in a mining town.. raised in the heart
of the Colorado Rockies..
has never left.

Contact: eartha.borne@gmail.com